Praise for

THE TUMBLING TURNER SISTERS

"This novel of love, grit, and the everlasting strength of family perfectly encapsulates the social mores and pressures of the early twentieth century. The Turner sisters dare to dream big—don't miss this page-turner!"

> —Sara Gruen, #1 *New York Times* bestselling author of *Water for Elephants*

"Filled with energetic prose and colorful characters—you won't soon forget the Turner girls!"

> —Christina Baker Kline, #1 *New York Times* bestselling author of *Orphan Train*

"Juliette Fay delivers the history, mystery, and prejudice of vaudeville in a story that is ultimately about the possibility of practice making something perfect (or perfect enough, anyway), the benefits of humor and ambition, and the redemptive power of love."

> —Meg Waite Clayton, *New York Times* bestselling author of *The Race for Paris*

"Like the fabulous days of vaudeville itself, at once funny and poignant and memorable. These four sisters are endearing and entertaining, and book clubs are going to lap this one up—as will readers of historical fiction everywhere."

> —M. J. Rose, *New York Times* bestselling author of *The Secret Language of Stones*

"A great piece of historical fiction that rings true one hundred years later."

"With humor, affection, ambition, and a talent for weaving in history, Fay brings the world of 1910s vaudeville vividly to life through the travails of the tenacious Turner family."

CITY OF FLICKERING LIGHT

CITY OF FLICKERING LIGHT

◇ ◇ ◇

Juliette Fay

G

Gallery Books

New York   London   Toronto   Sydney   New Delhi

G

Gallery Books
An Imprint of Simon & Schuster, Inc.
1230 Avenue of the Americas
New York, NY 10020

First Gallery Books trade paperbackhardcover edition April 2019

GALLERY BOOKS and colophon are registered trademarks of Simon & Schuster, Inc.

For information about special discounts for bulk purchases, please contact Simon & Schuster Special Sales at 1-866-506-1949 or business@simonandschuster.com.

The Simon & Schuster Speakers Bureau can bring authors to your live event. For more information or to book an event, contact the Simon & Schuster Speakers Bureau at 1-866-248-3049 or visit our website at www.simonspeakers.com.

Interior design by Alison Cnockaert

Manufactured in the United States of America

3   5   7   9   10   8   6   4

Library of Congress Cataloging-in-Publication Data

Names: Fay, Juliette, author.
Title: City of flickering light / Juliette Fay.
Description: First Gallery Books trade paperback edition. | New York : Gallery Books, 2019.
Identifiers: LCCN 2018026340 (print) | LCCN 2018027306 (ebook) | ISBN 9781501192951 (ebook) | ISBN 9781501192937 (trade pbk. : alk. paper) | ISBN 9781501192944 (hardcover library edition : alk. paper)
Classification: LCC PS3606.A95 (ebook) | LCC PS3606.A95 C58 2019 (print) | DDC 813/.6—dc23
LC record available at https://lccn.loc.gov/2018026340

ISBN 978-1-5011-9294-4
ISBN 978-1-5011-9293-7 (pbk)
ISBN 978-1-5011-9295-1 (ebook)

The silent film era spanned from the 1890s through the 1920s. Early filmmakers were mostly clustered on the East Coast, but when the Nestor Film Company set up shop in a little California farming village called Hollywood in 1911, many soon followed.

There were two main reasons for this: Thomas Edison and light. In an effort to gain control of the growing industry and enforce his patents, Edison set up a trust of companies and hired thugs to break the cameras of smaller, nontrust studios. It was easier to evade Edison's pursuit three thousand miles away on the West Coast. As for light, Southern California enjoys almost three hundred days of sunshine annually, and it's a lot harder to make movies in the rain.

As films grew from shorts to feature length, they began to compete with vaudeville as America's favorite form of entertainment. Opulent movie theaters—or "dream palaces"—were built across the nation.

Silent movies were never actually silent. There were always

musical scores to enhance the mood, just as in contemporary films. No one referred to them as "silent" until "talkies" became all the rage. The first nationally distributed movie with synchronized sound was *The Jazz Singer* in 1927, starring Al Jolson.

An estimated 75 to 90 percent of all silent films ever made have been lost to history. When the era ended, they were considered to be of no entertainment (and thus financial) value, and many were junked by the studios. Nitrate film is highly flammable, so fires caused the destruction of many more. Fortunately, efforts by film lovers such as director Martin Scorsese have saved and preserved those we still have. As a result silent films have enjoyed a renaissance, with local festivals and televised screenings cropping up like never before.

PART 1

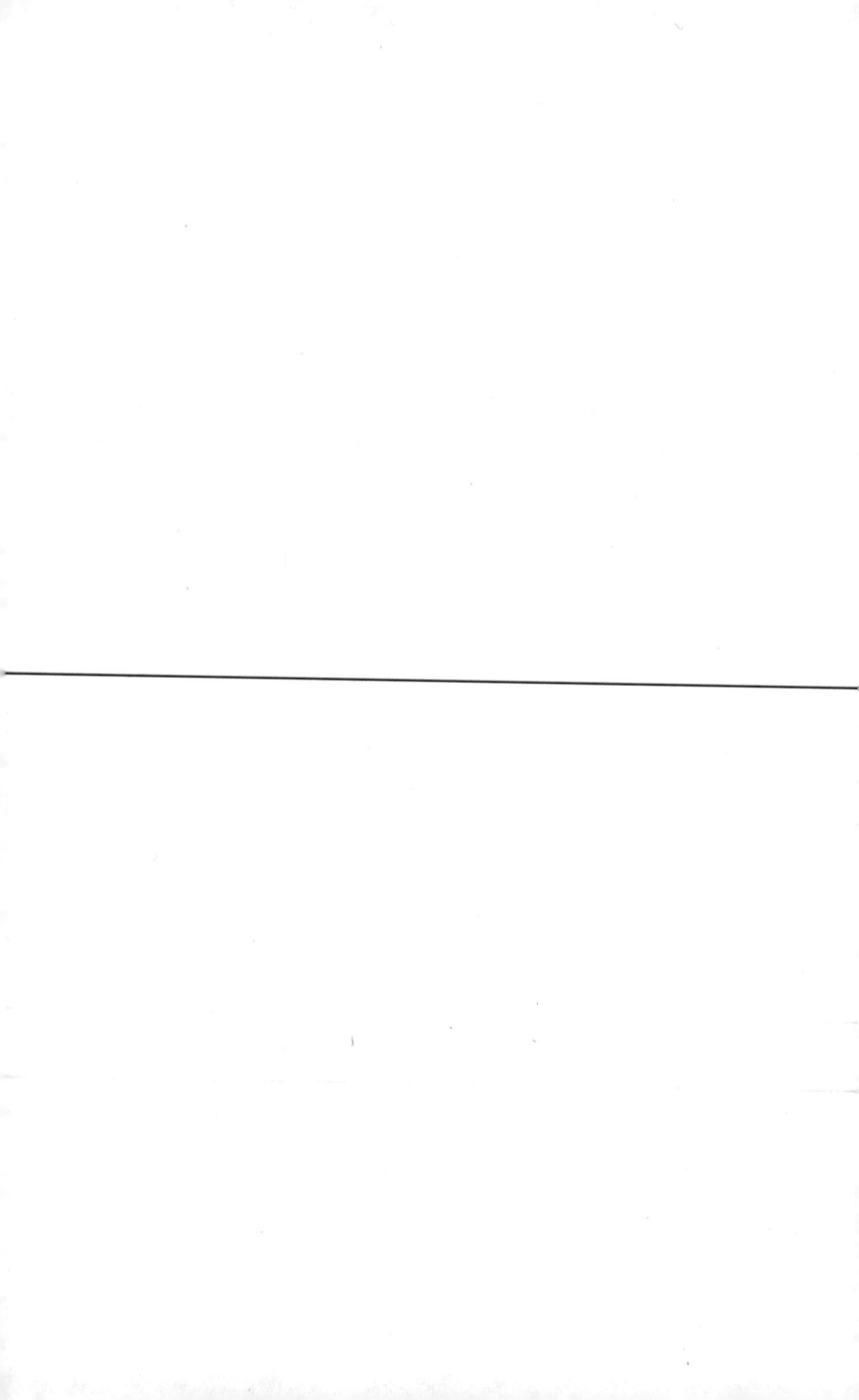

1

◇ ◇ ◇

Hollywood was built by women and Jews—those were people not
allowed in respectable professions. It was not taken seriously
as a business, so women and Jews could get into it.
Cari Beauchamp, Hollywood historian

Blood raced through Irene's veins like a brushfire, thrumming in her ears as she sat in the train car waiting for just the right moment. The window to her new life—or newest life—would open only briefly before it shut with a defeated thump.

She rubbed the spot on her hip where the awful flag costume had dug in. Mr. Chandler always ordered their costumes a size too small because "burlesque patrons like them tight." The Fourth of July had been a week ago, and the irony of seven days wearing the stars and stripes, symbol of freedom, strapped around her like a titillating little straitjacket was not lost on Irene.

Independence Day, she thought anxiously. *Better a week late than never.*

"Now?" whispered Millie, her fingers inching along the leather bench seat toward Irene's thigh, as if Irene were some sort of rabbit's foot to rub for good luck. Irene nudged them away.

Henry's eyes were on them, his gaze boring into Irene from his rear-facing seat, through the dust motes swirling between them in the merciless southwest sunlight. He cocked his head almost imperceptibly, a *what's-going-on* look.

Irene shrugged, willing her face to relax into some facsimile of composure.

Barney's massive frame suddenly filled the aisle beside them. "Ladies," he said, reptilian eyes scanning the landscape of their bodies. "And gentleman." His gaze went dull as it took in Henry, the lowest paid among them. Irene knew it was more than that; it was jealousy. Henry's good looks were made for photographs—thick dark hair and large brown eyes set off by pale unblemished skin, a study in contrasts. All the girls loved Henry, their well-mannered rascal.

None of them loved Barney, Mr. Chandler's right-hand man, as he liked to say. *Right-hand hatchet man,* they whispered privately. Irene had seen him take a girl by the hair and hit her till she dropped like a sack of laundry.

"Why're your bags under the seat?" he demanded. "Oughta be in the baggage car."

Irene sighed, feigning mild annoyance. "No room."

"We don't mind," said Millie. "Makes it easier to put our feet up." She set the heel of her t-strap pump onto the protruding case and crossed the other leg over, her dress slipping up above her knee. Her blue eyes went coy as she tugged the thin cotton fabric of her dress down a little, the lacy edge of her slip still perfectly visible. Barney's eyes took in that distant shoreline, a scurvy sailor hungry for a decent meal.

"Tickets?" said Irene.

"Now, don't go and lose them." Barney tugged them out of the pocket of his vest, spotted with whatever meal he'd last eaten. Something with gravy, it looked like. When Millie reached for hers, he pulled his hand back. "You gonna lose it?" he said. "'Course you are. Ain't got the sense God give a goat."

Irene froze. If he held Millie's ticket, what would they do? She couldn't leave Millie behind, now that she'd promised to take her. *Gone soft already*, she chided herself, and she was barely twenty-one. Uncharacteristically, she'd felt a strange need for company.

Well, you'll have company now, won't you? All the way to hell.

Millie tittered stupidly, even for Millie. "Give it to Irene to hold for me, then," she said. "She never lost a thing in her life."

Barney handed over the tickets, and Irene had to keep her fingers from gripping them too tightly. Before moving on to the next row of young girls in his herd, the huge man tossed another ticket at Henry, who had to snatch it from the air before it fell to his feet.

He was still eyeing Irene, and she gave him a sharp look. He glanced away, sufficiently cowed, and fiddled with the strap of his rucksack, which she knew held only a few personal items and a tattered notebook of jokes—mostly bad ones, if his comedy act was any indication.

There it was, the faint shushing sound Irene had been dreaming of and fretting about for weeks. The engine ground into gear, and she counted, just as she had at the last stop and the one before that, to get the timing down. Timing was everything in life. She'd learned that early on.

Thirteen . . . fourteen . . . fifteen.

As the engine strained to move countless tons of steel, the red sandstone of the Flagstaff, Arizona, train depot seemed to shudder in her view. The conductor stood at the other end of the car, scolding the porter. Irene could barely hear him over the groaning of the engine. " . . . under their seats! . . . supposed to be in baggage! . . ." He was shrunken and white haired with a mustache that trailed down off his jowls like curtain pulls. He glared up at the young black man, who shook his head—in truthful innocence, Irene knew. She herself had told him the baggage porter said the car was full, and they should stow their suitcases beneath them. The conductor poked the young man's chest now and motioned for him to get the cases.

The wheels hadn't begun to turn yet. Something was holding up the train, and if they left too soon, Mr. Chandler would send Barney after them.

The young porter wasn't moving though. She could see the anger flashing in his eyes. Things were changing. The younger Negroes who'd fought in the Great War didn't come home to be pushed around as they had been before.

Fight back, Irene silently urged the porter. *Refuse him.*

But before her thoughts could find their mark, the young man was making his way toward them. There was a screeching sound, metal on metal, and the car lurched forward.

"Now!" said Irene, and Millie began tugging at her case.

"It's stuck!" cried Millie.

"Damn thing's overstuffed," Irene muttered as her case swung wildly in her grip. "For godsake, pull harder!"

"Where are you—" started Henry.

"Quitting!" Irene hissed under her breath at Henry as the train began to roll, slowly picking up speed.

"Please!" Millie begged the porter who'd made his way to them. "We've got to get out!"

The young man shot a look over his shoulder at the conductor now barreling down the aisle toward them. He turned back and gave Millie's suitcase a hard yank. "You go on now," he said, handing it to her. "And good luck to you. All the luck in the world." He stepped back into the aisle, effectively blocking the conductor.

Irene ran in the opposite direction, case banging against her knees and the elbows of passengers as she flew by them. "Hey now!" they cried out. "Watch it!" Through the dust-speckled windows, the landscape was moving, low buildings giving way to fields and distant pines. She nearly collapsed into the door of the car, grabbing the long metal handle and tugging upward. The door flew sideways with a clank just as Millie fell into her. They staggered a moment and headed down the steps. The train was moving faster now, and Irene felt herself hesitate. If she broke her legs, then where would she be?

A sudden shove from behind and she was flying through the air. She collapsed in the hog-mown brush by the train tracks, stiff shafts of weeds poking into her knees and hands. There was a shriek, and Irene looked up in time to see Millie tumble down the railroad bed ahead of her. In another moment, a black mop of hair bobbed up out of the weeds, and Millie let out a whoop. "Ireeeeene!" she howled. "We did it!"

They watched the train recede into the landscape, and Irene felt the warm piney air fill her lungs, as if it were the first full breath she'd taken in years.

Just as the horizon had nearly swallowed the train whole, something else jumped off, a large, dark-colored blob that flopped to the ground and rolled into the brush.

Barney!

"Run!" Irene screamed. "Millie, run!"

They bolted, cases forgotten in the jeopardy of the moment. They knew what happened to girls who tried to leave before Mr. Chandler was ready to let them go. He set Barney on them with strict instructions to leave no visible marks. Mr. Chandler said bruises were a distraction to the men in the audience and encouraged the girls to comport themselves with care. The only place Barney was allowed to hit them was their heads, where hair would cover any lumps or bruises.

Irene and Millie skittered to a stand of pines, chests heaving as they gasped for breath, and hid behind a thick tree trunk. Irene peered out to see how close behind them he was but saw only the golden crowns of waist-high weeds gently swaying in the noon sunlight.

"Think he's dead?" Millie wheezed from behind her.

"Maybe just knocked out."

"Long enough for us to go back and get the bags?"

Who knew? Either way they needed those suitcases. They wouldn't get far wearing the same clothes day after day. Irene looked around. There was a dead branch on the ground, about three feet long and thick enough to do some damage.

"You get the bags," she said, hefting it as they crept forward. "I'll keep an eye out."

Millie grinned. "They sure don't teach this kind of thing in finishing school."

"I didn't go to finishing school."

"And you can thank your lucky stars for that!"

They inched through the grass and came upon Irene's suitcase first. Her uncle had bought it in some Podunk town in the middle of nowhere. That's where she and her sister had performed, mostly, though they had made it to Portland, Oregon, once and played at the Pantages. Vaudeville had its seamy side, but Irene had soon learned it was a much kinder business than burlesque.

"Mine's up a ways." Millie headed down the track, closer to where Barney had fallen.

"Let's leave it," said Irene. "We can share clothes."

"It's not just clothes," Millie said, hunching a little lower as she inched toward her case.

"What do you mean, 'not just clothes'?"

"I mean there are other things, too."

"What other things?"

"Things a girl needs, Irene."

Irene shook her head. These were the kinds of conversations they had, Irene trying to get to the point, Millie saying whatever came into her head, whether it was germane or not. Nevertheless there was something about Millie that made Irene want to line up next to her as they waited to go onstage or room with her when they arrived at a new town. She had something the other girls lacked, and it had taken a while for Irene to put her finger on it. But one day, as Millie leaned her chin on Irene's shoulder, pointed to a picture of Hawaii in the magazine Irene was reading, and said they should save up the money to go, Irene had figured it out: hope for the future.

The future can seem like a shadow, nothing but a trick of the light, when you're caught in a situation with virtually no escape. Irene often warned herself against daydreaming. Things had gone so unbearably wrong for her that hope seemed like a radical proposition. But it was like that picture of Hawaii, with its crystalline sand and turquoise waters: you told yourself to look away, but you found yourself peeking at it all the same. And then there was Millie, who seemed to have hope enough for both of them.

Chandler's Follies was a thing with no future, only the leaden now. He rigged it so you could never make any real dough. After he'd paid you, then taken back what you owed him for the hotel room and the meals, the scant costume he rented you, and the fees he charged for even the smallest sundries like shampoo or a hairbrush, you were lucky to break even.

"I take care of everything to keep you safe," he'd say as he detailed the evils of the world, which generally began and ended with prostitution. There was a perplexing elegance to him that lulled you into believing the most nonsensical things. He drank tea every morning from a silver tea set that he claimed had been brought from England by his grandfather, a younger son of a viscount. A man like that seemed to make sense simply by virtue of his noble bearing.

He might require you to strip naked every night and shake your what-have-yous in front of strangers, but he would protect you from the degradation of having your body violated. For many girls, whose prospects had dwindled to one or the other, this seemed like a fair bargain. You would give up all control of your life in order to remain safe from the ultimate sin.

It was a strange thing because little by little you came to realize there was nothing safe about Chandler. If you challenged him or stepped out of line in any way—came in late for curfew, flirted with the customers, or implied you might like to try a different line of work—an example would be made of you in front of the other girls, who were forced to watch as Barney grabbed a fistful of your hair and punched you in the head any number of times. And as you stood there in front of them with Barney's knuckles cracking against your skull, you wanted nothing more than to apologize for subjecting them to the sight of it.

"We can't chance it!" Irene hissed as Millie crept farther up the tracks.

"Trust me, it's worth the risk," Millie whispered over her shoulder.

This only served to unnerve Irene even more. What in God's name could it be? Because none of them owned a thing. Chandler made sure of that. Whatever little memento or jewelry you came with, he took "for safekeeping."

The suitcase was only a few feet away when they heard a groan like the sound of a wounded buffalo. The girls froze. Irene grabbed Millie's arm to pull her away, but Millie wrenched free and lurched forward, diving for the case. Irene raised the branch.

The figure sat up. Not Barney. Not by a long shot.

"Henry, what on earth!" Irene said and flung the branch to the dirt.

"I'm awful hungry," said Millie. "I want a sandwich."

"How much money do you have?" asked Irene.

"Eight dollars and fourteen cents."

"That can't be right—you told me you'd saved almost twelve dollars just two days ago."

"Oh, I did," said Millie. "But then I bought a few things, so now it's about eight."

"Millie, what on earth could have cost you four whole dollars?"

Millie unbuckled the straps on her suitcase and tugged out a misshapen black hat, then quickly closed up the suitcase again. "Well, I couldn't go to Hollywood and be a movie star without a new hat, now could I?" she said, reshaping the crushed felt. "It's 1921, and all my hats are from 1920. There was another item . . . but that doesn't matter now. It was just something I needed to get what I wanted."

It took every ounce of restraint Irene had not to say something distinctly unfriendly.

Henry pushed his chair back and stood up. "Okay, Millie, let's take a walk and see if we can find you something to nosh on that's cheaper than this place. Irene, you keep an eye on the bags, and we'll be back in a little while."

It was a relief to be alone, and not merely for the absence of Millie's nonsensical yammering. Irene didn't like being seen like this. Desperate. At the mercy of the strange twists of fate that had dragged her so far down in the world. Not that she had ever lived high on the hog. She'd grown up in a two-bedroom house in a little town in Ohio, with her twin sister, aunt, and uncle. They'd often struggled to make ends meet. But they'd had each other.

And she'd had ideas. Dreams really, if she allowed herself to be so fanciful as to call them that. She'd hoped to work as a reporter for a local newspaper, as she'd done for her high school gazette.

Or maybe even one of the movie magazines she loved to thumb through.

She wished she had a book or a magazine now. In burlesque reading had become a drug of sorts, a magic elixir to transport her from the self-disgust of peeling off her undergarments in public night after night and pretending to enjoy it.

A gust of wind blew Millie's hat off the table and onto the floor—the 1921 hat, which was so terribly important that the little ninny had spent four whole dollars on it, but couldn't remember to actually put it on her head. And look at it. Black felt with black silk netting for the brim, which of course was useless for keeping the sun off your nose.

"What am I going to do with her," Irene muttered as she bent over to retrieve it. It was just out of reach, and as she stretched her hand out farther to try to grasp it, a shadow fell across the floor. Irene looked up from her precarious position down by the table leg and saw him through the window.

Barney.

3

◇ ◇ ◇

The hardest years in life are those between ten and seventy.
Helen Hayes, actress

"Don't pay her any attention," Millie said, slipping her hand into Henry's as they made their way down the street. "She's just worried, and her knee hurts."

Henry glanced down at Millie's small white fingers now encased in his large tan ones, and Millie slipped them out again. She had only meant to reassure him, to put something soft between him and Irene's sharpness. Well, she had to admit that wasn't the only reason. She liked his hands—strong and well cared for. No jagged nails or bitten cuticles. Not that she minded that either. Gus, the assistant stable master back home, had so many calluses it looked like they belonged to someone on a prison chain gang. She liked his hands, too.

She liked hands, period. Or just touching, really. Once, years ago when her mother had found her curled up in only her slip with one of the housemaids like kittens in a basket, the two of them having gotten a little silly with Father's brandy, and then fallen asleep in each other's arms. "There's nothing bad in it!" she had yelled at her mother. "I just like being close!"

Mother had fired the housemaid, a lonely girl with no home to go back to, who'd been eager for the uncomplicated affection Millie was happy to provide. Millie had slipped a twenty-dollar bill into her hand and whispered, "You're lovable. Don't ever forget that."

Her mother's disgust hadn't really surprised her. Mother had never been the type to caress a cheek or pat a hand, much less wrap her in an embrace, even when Millie was terrified by a nightmare or bleeding from a bad scrape. Mother didn't touch. Millie wondered if she'd ever been held by either of her parents, even as a baby.

She'd gotten better at hiding her need for affection—but not that much better. When she and Willis Carrington were caught hugging behind the buggy shed, she thought her father might beat them both with his crop. The fact that Willis was shirtless, and Millie had wiggled her arms out of the top of her dress might have played some role in his fury.

"If we have to move away because of you, I'll lose all my customers!" he'd hissed as he'd marched her back to the house. "I'd marry you off tomorrow if you weren't fourteen!"

Millie's parents didn't seem to particularly like each other, either, though they were so much alike, she thought it a wonder they didn't recognize the cold kindred-ness of their souls and band together. Her father spent all day and most evenings at his equestrian supplies business, and her mother rarely left the house. At night they didn't sleep in the same room, much less the same bed.

Her parents never touched each other or anyone else as far as Millie could tell. Mother had had a dog she liked well enough in her own way, quietly chastising it for any small infringement while holding it on her lap. It snapped its tiny teeth at Millie when she came near, and she thought of it as a rat dressed up in a mink coat. She couldn't remember its name. Anyway, it didn't matter. That dog was dead now.

◇ ◇ ◇

As they searched for someplace to eat cheaply, Henry grumbled about Irene's temper and that she should learn to hold it a little better when she had only two friends in the world, and no prospects, and . . .

"Oh, now," Millie chided teasingly, patting his arm, "Irene's just . . . Irene. That's how she is. But she's a good person, we both know that."

"How exactly do we know that?"

"Well, we followed her to the middle of nowhere, didn't we? Are we foolish?"

Henry conceded her point with a little chuckle. "Maybe we are."

Millie laughed and took his hand again. "We just might be!"

The clerk at Cicero's Drugstore agreed to throw in a bag of day-old biscuits for the price of their minced ham sandwiches, and their spirits rose with the fullness of their bellies. As they passed the Orpheum Theatre, where they'd performed the night before, a man and a woman in stage makeup straggled out of the stage door. The man wore a long white cotton jacket and a little round mirror attached to a band around his head. It reflected light in jagged flashes as he rushed toward them down the alley. A woman in a white nurse's uniform, her oversize starched cap askew, followed him at a trot. The top buttons of her uniform were undone, and her fleshy bosoms jounced upward, as if trying to leap to freedom.

"Where we going?" asked the woman breathily as they hustled by Millie and Henry.

"Where'd you think? The train station, dumb Dora." He grabbed her by the arm to hurry her, and she tripped, barely catching herself from falling.

The stage door opened again and Millie recognized Clarence, the assistant stage manager. "Miss!" he called after the bouncing nurse. "Your purse!"

She turned, but the doctor yanked her back toward him. She twisted free and hissed, "I need that!" She took the purse and paused for only a second to smile wearily at Clarence. "Sweet of you," she murmured and then was off at a clip to catch up as he gazed after her.

"What happened?" Henry asked.

"Ah, their bit was too blue," said Clarence. "Manager gave them a warning first show, but next show it was all the same. Her with her costume open like that, arching her back to strain the buttons. The guy making ungentlemanly comments." Clarence grinned and cut his eyes toward Henry. "You know what I mean."

Henry chuckled. "Sure I do."

"Manager's fit to be tied because now we're down an act, and the bill will run short. Hard to get a disappointment act—you know, a replacement—at this late hour."

"What's the pay?" asked Millie.

"Those two were getting four hundred for the week."

Millie smiled sweetly and widened her blue eyes slightly, shining them like incandescent lights in a dim room. It was her utility expression, the one she employed until she could figure out what to do next. It never failed to buy her a few moments. "Well, we can certainly sympathize with the pickle you're in."

Clarence grinned back at her like a baby looking at his first balloon. Henry's smile was more of the *what-are-you-up-to* variety. Millie slid her hand into his and squeezed.

"I suppose my sister and I could help out for the next show till you can get a disappointment act in here. We're actresses. There's a short play we do, a really adorable skit that everyone just loves, and we'd only charge . . . fifty dollars."

4

◇ ◇ ◇

The greatest art in the world is the art of storytelling.
Cecil B. DeMille, director, producer, writer, editor

"Sweet Jesus, where've you two been?"

"What's with the getup?" asked Henry. He'd never known Irene to be particularly fussy about what she wore, but the netted hat and the blanket encasing her from the neck down were an odd combination, even for her.

"Just get in here," she hissed. "Barney's in town."

A prickle of fear ran up his neck, a memory of the beatings he'd taken before he'd grown tall enough, with shoulders wide enough, and a veneer of take-no-guff-ness that he'd practiced even more carefully than his comedy act. He'd learned to fight, kept in shape with daily push-ups and sit-ups, and could throw a good punch. But that overgrown grizzly Barney was a formidable match for any man.

When he'd first gotten hired a couple of months before, Henry had been under the mistaken impression that Chandler's troop was a step up from his previous jobs. It certainly was the least chaotic show he'd ever been a part of. No one drank too much or got into fistfights. The girls weren't running loose or sleeping with the customers. He got paid on time. The last show he'd been on was like a rolling Roman bacchanal on train wheels. He'd gotten fired from the one before that because the owner told him he was too pretty. The girls were so homely and unkempt; Henry made them look bad.

He kept trying though. He'd worked plenty of construction jobs in between gigs, mostly laying bricks like his father, but his goal had always been to make it to a real, legitimate vaudeville circuit, like his uncle Benny. The man had certainly been more of a father to him than his actual father, and Henry had wanted nothing more than to be like him, and share the noble task of inserting some happy laughter into the forced march of people's lives.

But he'd been starting to have some doubts about that. It had been years of trying and he'd never made it very far. And now, this Chandler . . . Henry was starting to see there might be a price to all the order. The girls were reasonably pretty, and as far as he knew they didn't drink too much or do drugs or run around. But as time went on, Henry had begun to suspect this was less about a sense of propriety and more about hopelessness. Some of them weren't just demur; they seemed half dead. He'd heard whispers about Barney getting rough with the girls, but Chandler had always kept him on the periphery, so he hadn't been sure.

Irene never said much, and she'd been there for almost a year. But unlike most of the other girls, he could see a spark in her. She was smart—she almost always beat him to the answer when they did the crossword puzzles together. And that Millie. She clearly hadn't read the part of the instruction manual that said she was supposed to be cowed and depressed.

Irene explained that she'd booked a hotel room for them to hide out in while they waited for the train. Then she'd cobbled together a hasty disguise using Millie's hat and a wool blanket off the back of a sofa in the lobby so she could wait for them and bring them to safety.

Irene tossed the wool blanket back onto the sofa and led them up to the room she'd rented. It had two full-size beds with slightly worn bedspreads patterned with oversize flowers. This combined with an abundance of pillows and the smell of rosewater that had obviously been sprinkled about to mask any lingering odors from previous guests, made the room seem aggressively romantic. Henry chuckled inwardly about the irony of being trapped in such a room with two lovely girls, knowing the promise of romance would not be kept.

And they were certainly lovely by anyone's standards. Millie's looks were showy; with her thick dark curls and big blue eyes she always turned heads, though most of the time she seemed not to notice. Irene's beauty was more subtle: her light brown hair fell in soft waves to her shoulders, hazel eyes framed in pale lashes. She was taller and less curvy than Millie, and her straight posture and lithe limbs gave her a kind of ethereal grace.

But Henry always said he had a strict policy about the showgirls he worked with, which amounted to: absolutely not. Best to keep complications to a minimum. While he didn't technically work with Millie and Irene anymore, that policy seemed just as wise as it always had. Maybe even more so.

"We'll stay in here until just before the train to Los Angeles is due," Irene was saying, "and hope to heaven he's not waiting at the station."

Millie sank down onto one of the two beds and slid catlike into a lounging position with one arm propping up her head. "Well, there's another option." Clarence had spoken to the theater manager and brokered a deal of thirty-five dollars for one performance of a twelve-minute skit. "The show's at eight. We'll have just enough time to make it to the train. Think of it, Irene! Thirty-five dollars for only twelve minutes of work!"

It certainly was tempting. If they were thrifty, thirty-five dollars would give them an extra few weeks of food and lodging while they looked for jobs in Hollywood.

"What skit?" asked Irene.

"Oh, I don't know," said Millie, running a finger around an enormous fabric flower. "I figured we'd come up with something."

"You mean Henry and I would come up with something."

Millie glanced up, her sapphire eyes settling on Irene with exasperated affection. "Well, yes. That's what you're good at."

Irene looked at Henry, and he nodded. "That's what we're good at, Irene. Just like Millie can sell sawdust to a lumberjack. Thirty-five bucks," he reminded her. "That's a boodle right about now."

He tugged his little notebook of jokes out of his rucksack, along with a pencil and a jackknife to sharpen it with, and turned to an empty page.

"We don't even have costumes," Irene said, but her resignation was clear. She slumped down next to him on the bed. "I suppose we could crib a story from a magazine . . ."

They racked their brains for stories they'd read or heard that could be captured in twelve minutes with a recognizable beginning, middle, and end. Then Irene came up with an idea about a runaway bride and a fortune-telling gypsy, but she snorted in frustration. "It'll never work!"

"Are you kidding? It's fantastic. It'll lay them out in the aisles!"

"We have no costumes, Henry. You can't expect an audience to buy a bride wearing a cotton day dress and black pumps." She stuck out her foot to indicate her scuffed shoes. "Or a gypsy with no crystal ball."

Millie sat up. "There's a pawn shop down the street. It had

fancy clothes on a rack along the wall; I saw them through the window. I'm going to go trade some things."

"You can't risk running into Barney," said Irene.

Millie stood and put her hat on, tugging the net down over her face. "I'll follow your lead and grab that blanket on my way out."

"You'll have to trade everything you own to get a wedding dress, Millie," said Henry. "You'll end up wearing it on the train to Los Angeles."

"Won't that get me some attention!"

As it turned out, Pick of the Pile Pawn Shop had several wedding gowns complete with veiled headpieces for Millie to choose from. She'd also found a bulbous glass vase that looked vaguely like a crystal ball when it was turned upside down and a high-necked, long-sleeved black dress for Irene to wear. Because of course Millie would be the one in the wedding gown.

"Widow's weeds," explained Millie. "The pawnbroker told me the owner married a new guy only two days after the last one passed, so the dress was barely used." She'd also found a colorful handkerchief for Irene to wrap around her head and some cheap clip-on hoop earrings.

The Gypsy and the Runaway Bride was mostly Irene's creation, though Henry contributed jokes and physical humor—notably the bride getting tangled in the train of the gown and falling flat before the gypsy's table as her entrance. The dialogue revolved around the gypsy repeatedly changing her predictions based on the woman's ongoing tale of her calamitous courtship.

Irene decided that Henry would enter at the last minute as the groom who'd been left at the altar. The gypsy takes one look at his handsome face and broad shoulders and changes her prophecy one last time: "Marry him and you'll be happy with the view for the rest of your days!"

This made Henry distinctly uncomfortable. "What kind of a swelled head do you think I have!" he said.

"Henry, it's not you. It's the character. And I'm sorry to break the bad news, but you do happen to be devastatingly handsome. Just think of that thirty-five bucks and simmer like Rudolph Valentino, okay?"

Devastatingly handsome. Henry furrowed his brows to hide the fact that he liked the sound of it. Irene had glanced at him for an extra moment as she said it, and he wondered if her matter-of-fact-ness hid a feeling or two that she didn't want him to know about. He only hoped things wouldn't become complicated. In the uncertain days ahead, they would both need a friend they could count on.

They dressed in their costumes in the hotel room, in hopes that if Barney crossed their path, he wouldn't recognize them. Millie pinned up her hair and pulled the white veil over her face, and Henry tucked his hat down over his eyes. He would walk with her to the Orpheum Theatre, and Irene would leave a few minutes later. Barney would be looking for a man and two women, and they hoped this, too, would throw him off.

The theater manager had assigned them the second spot on the bill, which would give them just enough time to get to the depot and catch the eight-forty-two to Los Angeles. They had practiced it over and over and knew their lines—but just barely. Henry would stand in the wings with his little notebook and prompt them if they needed a reminder. The skit took thirteen minutes—"lucky thirteen!" Millie had said. That was almost three dollars a minute, a princely sum by anyone's standards. They knew they would need every penny of it in Hollywood.

5

◇ ◇ ◇

We never make sport of religion, politics, race, or mothers. A mother never gets hit with a custard pie. Mothers-in-law, yes. But mothers, never.
Mack Sennett, actor, writer, director, producer

The backstage area of the Orpheum Theatre was dusty and dark like all theaters, in Irene's experience. The lobby and front of the house where the audience sat were generally neat as your granny's corset drawer, while the backstage was allowed to grow dust balls the size of bear cubs. But it was familiar and somehow reassuring to Irene. She'd spent a good deal of her adolescence traipsing from one small-time theater to the next, in places like Correctionville, Iowa, and Big Timber, Montana. Occasionally, if the theater was big enough to have dressing rooms (the Idle Hour in Correctionville had one, the Auditorium Theatre in Big Timber had four), and you were the headliner (or at least not opener or closer), you might get to relax and put your feet up between shows without risk of being mowed down by a busy stagehand. Irene and her sister had loved the luxury of having a room to themselves, where they could play cards or tell each other stories between performances without anyone shushing them backstage.

Don't get sappy, she told herself as she felt her throat tighten at the memory. Besides, the Orpheum had only two dressing rooms, and she wouldn't be there long enough even to peek at them.

Irene had limped hurriedly from the hotel to the theater, and now, swimming in black fabric, she sank down on an overturned crate and fanned herself with a copy of *Photoplay* magazine that someone had left on the floor. It had a lovely, fresh-faced Clara Bow on the cover, at whom Irene glared enviously for a moment before putting that face to service.

Henry and Millie were standing by one of the huge rope-hung cleats, going over Millie's lines. From all appearances it was not going well, Henry prompting every other sentence, and Irene wondered why they hadn't come up with some sort of dance routine instead. Millie was a wonderful dancer, though she did improvise quite a bit, which had always annoyed the other girls in the burlesque show. Irene had fewer lines, so it really was Millie's show . . .

We are going to flop, thought Irene.

She knew she shouldn't care—it honestly didn't matter if they were booed right off the stage as long as they got paid. But Irene felt a strange sense of pride in that story, and it had been a long time since she'd done anything to be proud of.

"Two minutes," whispered Clarence, and Irene felt her heart accelerate, just as it always had when she and her sister got the two-minute warning for their song-and-dance act. Her pulse never sped up for burlesque; in fact she often felt it might slow to the point of catatonia.

"Oh . . ." Millie whined. "I don't know about this . . ."

It started well, at least. The curtain rose to reveal Irene sitting behind a table, gazing intently into the overturned vase. After a beat, she lifted her eyes to the audience and intoned in a vaguely foreign accent, "I predict a snowstorm!"

This was Millie's cue, and she galloped onstage in the voluminous white gown, then turned midstride to see if anyone was following her, the train wrapping around her ankles like a lasso. Arms windmilling wildly for balance, she went sprawling with a thump onto the boards.

Irene smiled Cheshire Cat–like at the audience and said, "Right again!"

That snowstorm bit was her idea, and when the audience let out a howl of approval, it was all she could do not to grin with pride. When the guffawing crested and broke, Irene said to Millie, "You are fleeing for your life!"

Millie slowly pulled herself up onto her knees, batting comically at the veil, and said with wonder, "How ever did you know?"

Irene widened her eyes, looked left and right, then gestured to the crystal ball, as if to say *Isn't it obvious?* More gales of laughter as Irene held the pose, milking it for every last drop of applause.

"Why, I could use your help," said Millie, standing. "I believe I may almost have married the wrong man!"

Irene ran her hands around the vase, then gazed into it intently and said, "You most certainly have."

"He's charming and handsome and owns his own railroad."

"You most certainly have . . . made a mistake in running away!" Irene corrected herself.

"But he insists that his mother live with us," Millie pouted, "and she likes nothing better than to criticize every single thing I do all day long."

"You most certainly have made a mistake in running away . . . because you didn't run far enough!"

The bit went on like this, with Millie offering new information and Irene controverting herself at every turn. It was going so well until Millie found one of the jokes just a little too funny and couldn't keep a straight face. She sucked in her lips and bit down hard to keep her smile from spreading. Irene repeated her line to give Millie a moment to compose herself, but it had the opposite effect, and she broke into a giggle.

The audience began to titter, too, and this only fueled Millie's laughter.

"He always eats a raw onion before bed," whispered Henry. Millie shook her head and put her hand up to cover her mouth. Henry repeated, "He always eats a raw onion before bed!"

"He always . . ." Millie tittered. "He eats . . ."

Small islands of chuckling from the audience now built into a continent of laughter.

"Raw onions!" hissed Henry.

"Raw . . . onions . . . That's disgusting!" At this Millie completely fell apart, gasping in hilarity. The veil fell into her face, and she tugged at it till the headpiece hung limply from the back of her head. Her black hair came unpinned and tumbled out.

Irene knew there was only one thing to do: end it.

She beckoned desperately for Henry to join them onstage, and when he finally did, she stood up, threw her arms into the air, and yelled her line above the raucous laughter: "Marry him and you'll be happy with the view for the rest of your days!"

One of her hands accidentally hit the side of the handkerchief wrapped around her head, and it unraveled and fell to the ground, exposing her light brown hair.

A large man stood up in the balcony and glared directly into her eyes.

Millie could see him glancing out the window toward Railroad Avenue.

The smokestack let out an enormous huff, the wheels ground to life, and for the second time that day, Millie thought she might go completely insane waiting for a train to get moving. *I may never ride the rails again*, she thought.

"Damn!" Henry said suddenly, his gaze locking onto something out the train windows.

"What?" demanded Irene.

"He's out there," muttered Henry. "Heading toward us . . . looks winded . . ."

"Jesus!" said Irene.

"He's looking in the windows." Henry slumped down lower. "Ah, dammit to hell!"

"He saw you!" hissed Irene and popped her head up to look.

Millie sat up, too, and watched in horror as the ungainly man lunged toward the steps of the rolling train car . . .

. . . and then down he went, his large belly slapping into the dust beside the tracks.

As the train left Barney behind, Henry stood up, pointed out the window, and yelled, "*Gai kukken afen yam*, you *putz!*"

There were gasps. Millie glanced around. The train car had filled while she lay across the seat, and suddenly all faces were turned toward the three of them—the disheveled bride, the wide-eyed widow, and the man screaming in a foreign language.

"Henry, what in the world?" demanded Irene.

Henry's cheeks colored, and he looked away. "It's just something my *zayde*—my grandfather—used to say. It's not very nice. Let's leave it at that."

Millie grinned. "Tell us!"

"It means . . ." He laughed and shook his head. "It means go do something . . . unhygienic . . . in the ocean."

Irene said, "Henry!" And then she laughed. A real laugh! Millie wanted to put her hands on those smooth rounded cheeks. She wanted to feel Irene's laugh.

But she didn't. She just squeezed Irene's hand and said, "Sorry, Henry, but I'm pretty sure there's no ocean around here."

7

◇ ◇ ◇

A man usually falls in love with a woman who asks
the kinds of questions he is able to answer.
Ronald Colman, actor, producer

They had done it. Escaped with life and limb intact, now bound for Hollywood. As the train barreled through the darkened desert toward the full-color world that awaited them, Irene felt as if she were headed in the right direction for the first time in years.

For a moment, she allowed herself the luxury of daydreaming. *It'll be hard at first,* (a weak attempt to corral the fantasy toward some semblance of realism) . . . *but then it will be glorious! We'll wear beautiful clothes and meet fascinating people. We'll sleep in soft beds, and eat whenever we're hungry. I'll collect books, and Millie will collect . . . whatever it is she likes. Henry will buy a car—a convertible!—and we'll all drive around in the sunshine. People will recognize us and tell us how good, how really downright astonishing we were in our latest movies. We'll be so happy!*

Happy.

Imagine that.

◇ ◇ ◇

Millie had wiggled out of the wedding dress right there in front of the whole train car (her own dress was underneath) and then immediately fallen into a slack-mouth stupor like a child who'd spent all day at a carnival. Irene preferred to disrobe in private, and went to the train's washroom to peel off the black dress. She returned to her seat and folded it up . . . for what? The next time the strange events of her life required a fake widow's costume? But she could never have guessed that she would need one in the first place—in a day that had been one barely averted calamity after another—and so she put the dress into her suitcase, ready for its next incarnation, whatever that might be.

Fast asleep, Millie's head lolled precariously until it fell against Irene's shoulder. She generally found Millie's constant need for physical contact annoying, so she was surprised that this was strangely comforting. Between that and the warmth of the car, she should have been able to drift off.

She felt the train slowing, the wheels beneath her gliding more and grinding less.

"Seligman, last stop in Arizona . . ." intoned the conductor as he made his way down the aisle. He tapped the shoulder of a dozing gentleman. "Seligman?" The man shook his head and closed his eyes again. "Set your watches back an hour. It's ten-forty-five in California . . . Seligman . . ."

Irene thought Henry was sleeping, too, but he opened his eyes, tugged a silver pocket watch from his inside jacket pocket, flipped up the battered cover, and twisted the stem.

"I would've thought you'd have a wristwatch," murmured Irene. "They're all the rage."

Henry held out the timepiece, which was inscribed in an unfamiliar alphabet. Hebrew, she guessed. He'd never actually told her he was Jewish, but after his "ocean" outburst, he'd made that pretty clear. She'd known Jewish performers in vaudeville and could recognize the sound of the language, if not the words themselves. "My *zayde's*," he said.

"Where's your grandfather now?" she asked.

"He died when I was fifteen. But we were close. Best friend I ever had, really."

A momentary sadness came over her for the boy he once was, whose best friend had left this world when you needed friends the most: those incomprehensible years of pubescence when you could be giddy with laughter one moment and morose as a mortician the next.

"What do you make of Chandler going to all that effort to find us?" he asked, an obvious change of subject. "And for what? A combined total of about seven dollars in train tickets? Cost him at least a buck and a half to send that fat son of a gun back to get us."

"I can't really make sense of it, either. And what was he doing up in the cheap seats at the Orpheum?"

Henry chuckled. "Ah, he was just passing the time till the next eastbound train to meet up with Chandler. Not exactly the hardest working guy when the boss man isn't around. And suddenly there we were like sitting ducks."

The train groaned and lurched to life again. Millie slumped forward, and Irene caught her by the shoulders before she rolled onto the floor. She gently lowered Millie's head onto her lap, and Millie curled her legs up on the bench. "Wish we had a sleeping berth," Irene said.

Henry frowned. "We'll be lucky if we can afford breakfast when we stop in Barstow. It's a shame about that thirty-five bucks. Would've come in mighty handy. Course if I'd had some warning that we were jumping ship in the first place, I might have saved a little more . . ."

"Sorry, sorry, sorry," said Irene. "I'm truly sorry, and now that I've said it several times, I'm not saying it again. But I will say this: you're a big help, and I'm grateful you're here."

He gave her a grudging smile, and she sighed and turned to glance out the window though there wasn't a thing to see. Not so much as a lit lamp for miles in any direction.

"Can I ask you something?"

Irene didn't like the sound of that. But here they were in the middle of the night, on a train bound for a strange new place. Their fates were entwined, at least for now. "All right," she said.

"Why did you jump off that train?"

"Oh, Henry, come on now, I've apologized—"

"No, I don't mean 'without me.' I just mean . . . why?"

"Because I had to get out, and Chandler would've made it near impossible."

"I can understand wanting to leave, but why now? You'd been with him for almost a year, right?"

Why, indeed. Her life had taken so many unexpected twists and turns in the last three years, and it all seemed to . . . just happen. But it was a simple question, and he had, in the last twelve hours, earned the right to ask.

"I was in vaudeville."

"You were?" His face brightened.

"Yes, but only small-time, so please don't be the least bit impressed."

"It's better than what I was doing."

"Which was what?"

"Trying to get into vaudeville!" He laughed. "Why'd you quit?"

"The act . . . hit some trouble."

"What kind of trouble?"

Of course he had to ask. Who wouldn't? "Well, it was a sister act, and my sister . . . passed."

The look of shocked sorrow on his face—Lord, she just needed that to go away. She put her hand up, as if she could somehow slow the advance of his sympathy. Sympathy she had no right to.

"Yes, well . . ." she stammered, ". . . anyway. I just sort of drifted from one thing to the next for a couple of years, and ended up . . . where I ended up."

He nodded, and she thought—hoped—the questions were over for the night.

"So why leave today?"

She glanced down at Millie, curled like a kitten, practically purring.

"Millie?" he said. "But I thought you weren't even planning to take her with you."

Irene shook her head. "She's just so . . ."

He chuckled. "I know."

"And I couldn't stand to stick around and watch her turn into . . ." *Me*, she thought.

"One of them," he said.

"So I was just going to go."

"But you couldn't leave her."

"She can't defend herself like . . ."

"Like I can."

She looked up at him, meeting his gaze for the first time since this whole unnerving conversation started. She saw understanding there, and kindness. Far more than she deserved.

"You could lean your head against my shoulder if you want to sleep," murmured Henry. "I don't mind."

Irene wasn't the shoulder-leaning type and had every intention of declining his offer. Best not to give false impressions of distressed damsel-hood. Or open a door that should, out of necessity, remain closed. At least for the foreseeable future.

But damn that Henry if he didn't have the biggest, darkest

brown eyes, and shoulders that could hold up a building, never mind her little sandy-haired head. Irene frowned. "Well, only if it's no bother. I'm fine just as I am."

"I know you are," he said, "and it's no bother." Without waiting for her decision, he leaned his head against the seat back and closed his eyes.

"Barstow," called the conductor. "Half hour stop at the Harvey House. Get your breakfast now or wait till lunch."

Irene's eyes flickered open. Sun was streaming in the windows, and people were rustling in their seats, pulling on suit jackets or cloche hats.

"Oh, good." It was Millie's voice. "Henry, she's awake, so you can move now." Irene turned toward Millie's voice, her cheek warm from its resting place against Henry suit sleeve. "I told him you needed your sleep," said Millie. "That was a long day you had!" She patted Irene's leg. "How's the knee feeling?"

Irene extended her leg out, testing the joint. "Better," she said.

"Good! Now who's hungry?" Millie asked, grinning. "I could eat a three-ring circus full of elephants!"

"We have to be careful," said Irene. "We won't last long on the twenty bucks we've got between us."

Millie laughed. "Oh, we've got way more than that."

"You only have eight dollars," said Irene, still a bit annoyed about the hat. "I've got twelve and change. Henry, how much do you have?"

"Only about ten."

"I've been keeping the best secret," said Millie, leaning out to squeeze both of their arms, exposing more of her cleavage than was considered entirely polite. "I was going to tell you after the show, but then everything went haywire with Barney, and after all that running I was so tired. You can barely move in a wedding dress! I bet they're specially designed so it's hard to run off if you change your mind."

"Millie," said Henry. "What secret?"

She tapped her knees back and forth rapidly like a drumroll, then threw her hands in the air and said, "Ta da! I stole the silver tea set! I bought some silver polish and told Chandler I'd clean it—see it wasn't just the hat I spent money on, Irene. I told him I gave it to Barney to pack. Then I sold it at the pawnshop in Flagstaff for seventy-five dollars! The guy offered me forty, but I just started putting it back into my suitcase till he said 'Now hol' on there!'" She squeezed their arms again and let out a squeal of joy. "Let's get steaks!"

Irene didn't know whether to laugh or throw her hands around Millie's neck. She looked at Henry, who had clearly come down on the side of strangulation. "*That's why Barney was after us!* Millie, you . . ." he sputtered, "you nearly got us killed!"

Millie's face fell. "Well, I can't help that."

"You can't help stealing his most prized possession so he sends his goon to track us down like dogs?" He shook his head and muttered, "This kind of *meshuggah* I cannot take."

"I'm certainly not your sugar if you're going to talk to me like that!" Millie crossed her arms.

"I didn't call you 'my sugar'!" hissed Henry. "I called you crazy!"

"What's so crazy about seventy-five bucks, I'd like to know!"

"Millie," said Irene. "You put us in danger with that stunt. We were all terrified!"

"*I* wasn't terrified," said Millie petulantly. "I mean, I was worried. I wasn't happy. But I knew it would work out."

"How in holy hell did you know that?" steamed Henry.

"I don't know," said Millie. "I just had confidence."

"That is *far* more self-confidence than any person should have . . ."

Irene could hear the words Henry had chosen to bite back: *especially you.*

"Not *self*-confidence," said Millie quietly. "Confidence in the two of you."

Henry cut his eyes at Irene. He had no snappy comeback to that.

"Millie," she said, "Where's the money? Because it's a lot, and you have to keep it somewhere safe."

"It's in the lining of my suitcase, but I'm giving it to you first chance I get."

"You want me to hold it for you?"

"Not for me, silly. For us. It belongs to all of us."

Henry shook his head. "Millie, I'm not thrilled with the way it happened, but you cooked up the scheme and carried it off. That's your money fair and square."

Millie's face went wide with surprise then cinched down into fury. "That is *not* how this works! I got the tea set, but you got me off that train, Irene, and you two wrote that play, and Henry, you carried everything when we were running for our lives. I couldn't have done any of that without you. It's *our money.*"

8

◇ ◇ ◇

A tramp, a gentleman, a poet, a dreamer, a lonely
fellow, always hopeful of romance and adventure.
Charlie Chaplin, actor, writer, director, producer,
on his most famous character, the Little Tramp

s she stared out the train window after breakfast, Millie
could hear Irene and Henry talking in low voices about
where the three of them might find lodging, and where
they would look for work, what kind of money they might need,
and what kind of wages they could expect. She found it slightly ir-
ritating. She didn't want to think about Hollywood as a place she'd
have to plod along, thinking about boring things like where to live.
She'd read the magazines; Hollywood was a place where nobody
worried about anything!

To distract herself from their tedious talk, she watched as the
desert slowly rolled up its skirts to reveal secret hills and forests,
and imagined that she was the first person on earth to lay eyes on
such a hidden, unpeopled quarter.

But of course she wasn't. Who had laid the train track, for
goodness' sake? Millie understood reality, of course. She'd had
plenty of that at Miss Twickenham's Finishing School for Young
Ladies, which had seemed less likely to "finish" her than to finish
her off.

Miss Twickenham—a matronly woman who spoke with an English accent to parents but slid into the speech and behavior of a slaughterhouse foreman when the floors weren't scrubbed to her satisfaction—seemed more interested in getting the greatest possible amount of work out of the girls than in teaching them social etiquette. There had been plenty of opportunity, and motive of course, to build a rich fantasy life—daydreams and half-made plans that swirled in Millie's head as she pulled turnips from the gritty soil or stood facing the wall, shoeless on the cold tiles, for the least little infraction. At least then she could be alone with her thoughts; daydreaming was harder while getting lashed with a switch across her bottom for major crimes like whispering to a neighbor during lessons on the absurd variety of ways to fold a napkin. It was a napkin, for goodness' sake. Its only purpose was to lie hidden across your lap and keep the soup off your skirt when you sat at the table. And after the lashings, she couldn't sit down anyway.

The train climbed up into a mountain pass, with wondrously tall peaks. Was Hollywood in the mountains? She'd thought it was near the ocean, and that was half the reason she'd wanted to come! She'd spent a summer in Beverly on the North Shore of Massachusetts once and thought it was paradise on earth. But Father rarely came, as he was tending to his horse supplies business. Mother didn't like the sand in the house, nor the smell of fish, nor the wind—the blissful breezes that blew up from the shore and tickled Millie's skin and made everything seem so new. And possible.

They'd never gone back.

They'd spent every subsequent summer in their heavily draperied home in Springfield, Massachusetts, where any breeze that made its way inside was reduced to a shriveled puff.

The train was slipping down out of the mountains now—the San Bernardinos to her left and the San Gabriels to her right, as

it turned out. She'd asked the conductor and was slightly disappointed to learn they had names, confirming once and for all that
hers were not the first eyes to gaze upon them. But of course, she
knew that. It was just fun to imagine.

The train stopped in a little town called San Bernardino, then
continued westward through what seemed like endless acres of
orange groves. She'd gotten an orange in her Christmas stocking
every year as a treat until she was fifteen and things starting going
awry at home. It was the last orange she'd seen. The next year she'd
gotten coal. And the day after New Year's she'd be packed off to
Miss Twickenham's.

Old Twick, Millie thought. *Wouldn't she fall into a dead faint to
see me now.*

Surrounded by oranges.

◇ ◇ ◇

"La Grande Station!" called out the conductor with unprece-
dented urgency. "La Grande! City of Los Angeles! End of the line!"

The entire population of the train smoothed the tangles from
their hair and the wrinkles from their clothes as the train groaned
its way into the heart of the city, a sort of slow collapse after hurl-
ing itself across the continent for so many days.

Bags and suitcases were collected and coats thrown over arms
in the summer heat, as passengers shuffled toward the train doors.
They stepped down to a depot yard clogged with people—some
arriving, some departing, and many searching the sea of faces for
the ones they awaited and claimed with embraces.

So much hugging! thought Millie enviously and moved a step
closer to Irene till their shoulders touched. "Don't lose me," she
whispered, and Irene took her hand as they wended their way to
the street.

"Head to the cabstand!" Henry raised his voice to be heard above the clatter of shoes on pavement and voices calling out. Irene scanned the chaos of long touring cars, two-seater coupes, and every size in between, and gripped Millie's hand a little tighter.

The taxi stand along Santa Fe Avenue was a seemingly endless line of vehicles in various states of dented-ness. An older man in a tweed cap leaned against the fender of the first in line. As the three of them approached, a strange little smile flickered across his face so quickly Millie wondered if she'd really seen it at all.

"Where to, ladies?"

"And gentleman," corrected Millie.

The cabbie gave a noncommittal grunt at Henry, and the three of them climbed into the back of the cab, which smelled of stale cigars, body odor, and orange. In fact there was an orange peel sticking out from under the front seat.

"Where to?"

"Hollywood," said Irene. "Can you recommend any boarding-houses in the area?"

"I suppose so," he said. And there was that flicker of a smile, almost like a tic, as the old car rattled its way up Santa Fe Avenue. "You'll want to stay at Mrs. Ringamory's place. Good food, reasonable prices. She knows a lot about the business, too. Actresses, right?"

"Yes," said Millie at the same time Irene said, "We'll see."

"Figured as much," said the cabbie. "The girls all call her Mama Ringa."

Millie liked the sound of that. A cozy place with good food and a woman so warm and helpful the girls call her mama. "And what about Henry?" she asked. "Is there a place for him?"

"The YMCA up on Schrader. 'Bout six blocks from Ringa's. I'll drop him there first."

"Oh, we don't want to go just yet," said Irene. This was clearly something she and Henry had worked out. "Please just let us out in the center of town. We want to walk around a little."

As they drove, Millie looked out the window at the palm trees and the tiny houses interspersed with what seemed to be lesser-known castles, with their enormous doors and carefully manicured lawns. California. It was what she and Irene (mostly Irene) had been planning for weeks, and they'd made it happen. The getting here part, anyway.

"This is it," the driver said after a while, with no effort to hide his boredom. "Hollywood."

"Look at that!" said Henry. "Olympic Studios. I've seen that name on plenty of flickers." The two-story, white clapboard building took up half the block and looked more like an oversize home than a business. The second floor had a long veranda punctuated by a series of about twenty thick white pillars, with enormous iron-framed lanterns hanging in between.

The driver pulled over.

"Are we getting out here?" asked Irene.

"As good a place as any if you want to see it. Hollywood Boulevard is a couple of blocks north. They both run east west. Sunset goes all the way out to the Pacific."

"Ocean?" said Millie, thinking of that glorious summer in Beverly. "Can we walk?"

"Sure," he said with that sly smile. "Only take you half a day. It's twelve miles, easy."

He scribbled an address on a piece of paper, tore it off, and hung his arm over the back of the seat to hand it to Irene. "You'll want to end up here before it gets dark. Tell her I told you."

"And who are you?"

"She'll know."

He said the fare was a dollar and seventy-five cents. Henry and Irene exchange looks. "You sure?" said Henry.

The man eyed Henry like he was deciding how well done he'd like to cook him. "Yeah," he said. "I'm sure. And no charge for the tip on where to stay. I threw that in for free."

When the cabdriver pulled away, they stood in the afternoon sun on a sidewalk in the middle of Hollywood, California. It looked and felt and even smelled different from anywhere Millie had ever been before. Bright and lemony, and so darned hopeful!

This is just right, she thought. *Just what I was looking for without even knowing.*

They strolled west on Sunset Boulevard, maneuvering down the busy sidewalk, taking in the palm trees and the cars speeding along, everything from rattling old flivvers to long, brightly colored phaetons. A woman rode by in a little coupe, top down, copper colored, and shiny as a new penny. She wore bright red lipstick and a sheer yellow scarf tied loosely over her head and crossed at the neck so the ends luffed behind like dainty flags.

"Actress?" Millie asked the others.

"Or heiress," snickered Henry.

I was an heiress once, she thought. But her parents had made clear that they had cut her from their will after things had gone decidedly downhill from Miss Twickenham's Finishing School for Young Ladies. Or School for Slaves, as Millie liked to call it.

But here she was with Irene and Henry, two wonderful people whom she loved. Yes, she did, she just loved them. Her father owned a shiny car, and she'd ridden in it plenty of times. It had never made her as happy as being here with these two friends.

◇ ◇ ◇

At Sunset and Gower, there were more studios—CBC and Christie were two of the names they saw—but the buildings were much smaller and more slapdash-looking than Olympic, as if they'd been built in a morning after a long night of drinking.

"We could start our job search here," said Henry.

"Or we could start at Olympic, and see if we end up here," said Irene.

He smiled. "I like your thinking."

"Well, Olympic is no Warner Brothers or Famous Players-Lasky. I'm not trying to start at the top. I'm just trying not to start at the bottom."

A police officer stood on his wooden box in the middle of the intersection directing traffic. As they waited for his signal that it was safe to cross, a long black touring car, extra tires mounted on the sides, hurtled down Gower toward them, then screeched through a turn onto Sunset followed immediately by a police car. A man hung out a window of the touring car with a gun, thrusting it over and over at the police car, and blue-uniformed men dangled from the windows of the police car, aiming back at him.

Henry immediately corralled Millie and Irene into his arms and pressed them up against the wall of a studio. After a moment, they heard laughter and dared to come out of their huddle to see what was happening.

A boy of about twelve was pointing at them. "They thought it was real!" he sang out. "You dopes, it ain't real! You hear any gunshots?"

Millie peeked beyond Henry's arm to see the police officer who'd been directing traffic shake his head in annoyance. Then he wagged his finger in the direction of the opposite corner, where a handful of men stood around a contraption atop three long wooden legs.

"There's the camera, right there!" the boy told them. "It ain't nothin' but a flicker!"

◇ ◇ ◇

As they meandered up Sunset, Henry carried Millie's suitcase, his rucksack slung over his shoulder. About once a block he offered to take Irene's battered case, but she kept insisting she could carry it, which annoyed Millie because it intruded on her fantasies about all she was seeing around her: the shoe and clothing stores filled with styles she'd never even seen yet, and restaurants serving delicious food, interspersed with lemon trees and houses.

"Just give it to him!" she said finally, startling Henry and Irene both. "You've got that knee, and he won't stop asking till he has it." Irene glared, but she gave him the suitcase.

They passed a restaurant, its front windows open, white linen tablecloths swaying in the light breeze, the aroma of fresh bread wafting toward them. Millie looked at Irene.

"We'd better find this Mama Ringamory's in time for dinner."

"But can't we have a little something now? We have the money."

"Until we find work, we have to be careful, Millie. That cab ride alone cost us almost as much as a meal for the three of us at this place would."

On the next block sat a long two-story stucco building with gracefully scrolling wrought iron letters: THE HOLLYWOOD ATHLETIC CLUB. Just then they saw a short, slim man with a shock of wavy black hair heading down Sunset toward them. Irene stopped suddenly and stared. "Chaplin," she breathed. "That's Charlie Chaplin."

"It can't be," said Henry.

"Let's talk to him!" said Millie. But Irene grabbed her arm, and they stood gawking. The man suddenly turned his feet out and walked the last few steps to the door of the club in the penguin-like gait of his beloved Little Tramp character, then touched the brim of his homburg, winked, and whisked into the building.

Irene clamped her hands over her mouth. "Chaplin!" she squeaked through her fingers. "I've seen every one of his pictures at least twice. He's brilliant!"

They laughed and squeezed one another's arms, and Henry said, "Our first day in Hollywood, and we see a star—not twenty feet away!"

"Even better," said Millie, "he saw us!"

"It's good luck," said Irene. "I just know it."

That luck seemed less certain after they asked directions to the address the cabbie had given them and turned up a side street. Suddenly the heady brightness of downtown Hollywood began to change. Behind the stores and restaurants that lined the boulevard, people lingered in alleys: a man in a threadbare suit jacket smoking a cigarette leaned idly up against the back of the building as if he had grown there like moss; a cluster of women with skirts shorter than they should have been eyed Henry as they passed.

A few blocks later, they were in front of a house—at least they assumed there was a house, somewhere down the dark walkway crowded with overgrown hedges on either side. A branch took Millie's black hat right off her head as they followed it. The house itself was tall and narrow with a sort of turret on one side. A few of the wooden shingles on the porch walls around the front door hung askew, as if the door had been slammed so often it had caused them to come loose. There were large ring hooks in the ceiling from which a porch swing might have hung, but that was gone now.

"You sure about this?" murmured Henry.

"I'm sure it's no worse than some of the places we stayed with

Chandler," said Irene, but the way her eyes flicked from peeling paint to the bare bulb above the door belied her confidence. "It'll do for now."

She rang the bell, and the door was soon answered by a girl with tomato-red hair cut short and plastered to the sides of her head with pomade. She looked Irene up and down, turned, and yelled toward the back of the house, "Mama! More girls!" Then she walked away.

A large woman, tall and lumpy like a camel with saddlebags, lumbered toward them. "What have we here! If you're looking for a warm bed and good food, you've come to the right place!" When her broad frame reached the doorway and she spied Henry, however, her face fell. "You somebody's boyfriend?" she said flatly.

"No—" said Henry.

"Not at all!" insisted Irene. "Just a friend. He walked us here to—"

"No men allowed," the woman said sternly. "Not even on the porch. Say your goodbyes now, girls, or our business here is done."

Irene stood uncharacteristically dumbfounded by the woman's blunt dismissal, so Millie jumped in. "Henry, you can find the YMCA, right? The cabbie said it wasn't far. Why don't we come by after breakfast tomorrow morning"—she was making this up as she went—"and we'll make a plan. We'll all find out what we can, and then meet up to share the news."

Henry and Irene seemed startled by this sudden outburst of sense from Millie, but they nodded in agreement. "Nine o'clock, then," said Millie with a definitive little clap of her hands. Then she lunged at Henry and hugged him as if he were heading off to battle instead of the YMCA. He hugged her back, and it felt lovely.

Irene held out her hand for Henry to shake. He took it, then suddenly leaned forward and gave her a quick peck on the cheek. "I'm glad I jumped off that train," he murmured.

Irene's face went a little rosy. "I am, too," she said.

◇ ◇ ◇

Mama Ringamory ushered them into the house, which was dark even though the sun had yet to fully set. The front room was likely a parlor at one time, but now it was crowded with a long wooden table, scarred and slicked with grease in several places and flanked by benches on either side. Through a doorway that had lost one board of its doorjamb was a kitchen with blackened pots hanging from a metal ring over the stove. There was a smell of bitter vegetables wafting toward them. Cabbage, Millie guessed, or turnips. Mama asked their names, where they were from, and what line of work they'd been in until now.

"Vaudeville," said Irene quickly.

"Dancers?" Mama said. "We get a lot of dancers here."

"Actresses," corrected Irene. "We have a skit we do about a runaway bride and a gypsy. Brings down the house every time."

Well, at least that one time it did, thought Millie, *but that was because I got the giggles.*

Mama shrugged, as if in the end it didn't matter one whit to her if they were dancers, actresses, or ditch diggers. "Price is nine dollars a week, includes dinner and breakfast, but no lunch. And you'll have to do some chores. This isn't a hotel, you understand. Also, you'll share a room with two other girls, two to a bed. Payment in advance, and no refunds if you decide to leave before the week's out." At this she held out her hand.

Irene took the bills from her little string bag and paid out the eighteen dollars. "Oh, by the way, it was a cabbie who told us about you. He said you'd know who he is?"

"That'll be Al." Mama's eyes went half-lidded with annoyance. "His way of letting me know he wants his cut." She hooked a thumb toward the stairs. "Third floor. Room on the right."

Dinner was late. And bad—mostly cabbage. Mama said she cooked it with a ham bone, but Millie figured that pig must have been made out of wishful thinking. Not quite the savory home cooking that she'd been hoping for, but she was so tired, she almost didn't care.

The other girls at the table weren't terribly friendly; they seemed more concerned about getting their fair share of the salty, overcooked meal and swallowing as fast as possible. Most of them headed out for the night right from the dinner table. "To a dance party," Mama Ringa told Millie and Irene as they carried the other girls' dishes to the kitchen. But those sullen faces didn't look like they were heading to any kind of party Millie had ever been to.

Their small room on the third floor felt even smaller by virtue of a sloped ceiling and only a single gabled window to let in any air or light. The wallpaper was so yellowed and faded it was hard to discern a pattern. In the corner nearest her head, a piece of it had peeled back to reveal the previous paper, blue-flowered vines on a lemon-yellow background. She wished she could peel it all, and be surrounded by those happier colors.

That night she lay back-to-back with Irene, listening to the soft snores of the two girls in the next bed. Despite the disconcerting creaks of the strange old house, Millie felt herself slip into a state of satiny-soft calm. Irene was near, Chandler's Follies was far, and it seemed that whatever the next day would bring, they would manage somehow.

Irene suddenly rolled over to face Millie and whispered into the dark, "Are you awake?"

"Uh-huh," said Millie, turning toward her.

"When we jumped off that train yesterday, you said something about how they didn't teach you that kind of thing in finishing school . . . that was a joke, right?"

"Well, it was supposed to be funny, if that's what you're asking."

"What I'm asking is, how do you know what they teach in finishing school?"

"Because I went to one, silly!"

"I thought finishing school was for rich girls."

"I suppose it is. My father was always complaining about how expensive it was. Which was the real joke of it, because it was more like a workhouse than a fancy girls' school."

"So . . . your family is wealthy?"

"Oh, yes. I mean, we're no Vanderbilts. But we have a big house, and my father was the first person in our neighborhood to have a car."

"How on earth did you end up in burlesque, for godsake?"

Millie felt the ripple of shame that always accompanied thoughts of her parents' abandonment. It had been her fault, of course. She could never seem to be the kind of girl they had demanded, with diminishing hope, that she should miraculously turn into. Even a burlesque stage had felt strangely less confusing and airless than home.

She didn't like to talk about it. But it was Irene asking. Irene, with her comforting bossiness and her dogged loyalty—even though Millie knew she was not the kind of person who inspired loyalty. At least she never had been before.

"I let the dog out."

There it was. Her secret was out now, too, and it was more of a relief than she'd expected. She let the dog out, and as bad as she'd felt at the time, it was funny how it didn't sound quite so terrible when she said it aloud to Irene.

"You . . . what?"

The whole story came tumbling out of her.

"My mother's dog. It was this tiny little thing that sat on her lap all day long. One day she was taking a bath, and I thought it might like some fresh air, since it was always cooped up. But then it wouldn't come back, even though I called and called and looked all over. It never liked me, that dog. I don't know why. Always growling and snapping whenever I got near Mother.

"Anyway, a fox got it. Or maybe a coyote. I felt terrible, and my mother went straight to bed and canceled the big holiday party for all of Father's customers and wouldn't even come out for Christmas. So I got coal in my stocking, and they sent me off to that awful school as soon as it opened the day after New Year's. I mean, as *soon* as it opened. The chauffeur dropped me off at seven in the morning, and I waited on the porch in the freezing cold till nine."

"But that doesn't explain how you ended up in burlesque."

"Oh, well, I went to that school until June, and then they packed me off to my father's blind old aunt. I led her around and read books to her all summer. I was so good! Better than I'd been in years! I didn't kiss any boys, or kill any dogs, or leave the house without my corset on, or anything! But they still said I had to go back to that awful school—it was better for everyone, they said—and I couldn't face another day there, so I ran off."

"Didn't they search for you?"

"Oh, they didn't have to search. I told them where I was going."

"Where did you go?"

"I went and worked on a farm near the blind old aunt. I

thought it would be so lovely because they had horses. Growing up I spent every free moment at my father's stables, and I can do anything—muck out stalls, brush and curry them, or even just talk to them when they feel out of sorts. The farmer didn't want a girl doing 'man's work,' but he let me work in his vegetable field weeding and such. It was hard, but no harder than the school, and at least I was making a little money. Besides, I was sure my father would come and get me eventually."

"How old were you?"

"Sixteen."

"You were sixteen years old, working as a farmhand, and he didn't come get you?"

"Wouldn't even send train fare. Said I'd already disgraced them more than enough, and running off to work on a farm, with dirt and pigs and farm boys, was the last straw. Then the winter came and the vegetables were all picked and the farmer didn't need me anymore, and you know how it is—not much work a girl can do without a teaching certificate or a nursing license. I didn't even have a high school diploma. I waitressed for a while, but I could barely keep ahead of my rent in the boardinghouse I stayed at and I was always broker than broke. So when Chandler came through with the show, I joined up."

"Oh, Millie." Irene sighed. "You were so young! How could they let you go like that?"

"You have to understand," said Millie patiently. "They're not like me. I used to imagine I was adopted, and I always hoped they'd sit me down one day and tell me, and I'd hide my relief and pretend to be sad they weren't my real parents. But they never did. I still think I'm adopted, though. Because I don't think my little apple could possibly fall that far from their tree."

9

◇ ◇ ◇

Like my dear old friend Marie Dressler, my
ugly mug has been my fortune.
Wallace Beery, actor, director

Henry woke up early—too early—to the sounds of the men in the dormitory around him snoring and snuffling, one clearly having a dream about "Bertha . . . oh, honey . . ."

He should have been able to sleep like a well-fed baby in a cradle. The men's dormitory in the newly built Hollywood YMCA was clean and airy, the walls a soft white, as were the thin sheets and cotton blankets on the cots laid out in tight but tidy rows across the large room. A gray wool blanket lay folded at the foot of every bed for cooler nights. The mattress was just thick enough to protect from the feel of the metal webbing that crisscrossed the low frame, but unfortunately it did nothing to muffle the creaks and squeaks of forty men rolling over all night long. Henry had slept in far worse places, of course, but never in one so populated. The sheer number of humans alone made the place sound like an overbooked tuberculosis ward. For a dollar a night it was a bargain, but barely.

The California light, almost biblical in the descriptions he'd heard, was softly whispering in around the curtains. *Zayde's* watch, which he'd kept tucked under his pillow away from wandering hands, said it was five-forty-five. He rose and tugged on his pants, the one pair he now owned since he'd left his suitcase back on that train in Flagstaff. God only knew where it was now.

He needed fresh clothes. And coffee, as hot and black and free flowing as possible. So he buttoned up his criminally wrinkled shirt and walked downstairs, out to Schrader Avenue and down the block to Sunset. No stores would be open, but he could sleuth out a decent haberdashery or even a secondhand shop. His *zayde*, a talented and opinionated tailor, would've been appalled at the idea of his buying someone else's ill-fitted clothing. But *zayde* had taken his leave of this world, and Henry was on his own now, as he had been since the age of fifteen. As much as he missed the old man, there was still a very tiny, petulant teenage part of him that had taken his *zayde*'s death personally, as if it had been a choice instead of a natural consequence of living to such an old age. And so Henry would buy the used clothes, which would serve the dual purpose of keeping himself minimally appropriate-looking and sticking it to the old man.

He had walked for several blocks, past a barbershop, a milliner, and a small movie theater called the Iris, and headed into a little diner with BETTY'S BOUNTY painted on the window. The shop was deep and narrow, with shallow booths lining one wall only feet from the stools, which stuck out from the long scratched wooden countertop on the opposite side. The kitchen was in back, and Henry could hear the gentle clanging and scraping of metal on metal—spatula on griddle, he figured—the occasional gruff murmur, and the higher pitched, "Get the potatoes on before the rush," or "*Vey ist mir*, Zeke, that's gonna burn."

Early though it was, they'd already had customers that morning, as evidenced by the lipstick-stained coffee cup and a plate sticky with yoke on the counter. Next to it lay a disheveled copy of the *Hollywood Citizen*. Henry slid onto a stool and tugged the paper down the counter toward him. He was just beginning to leaf through when a woman approached from the opposite side of the counter. Her gray hair was wrapped tightly in a colorful handkerchief, and she wore a spotless white apron tucked neatly around her ample middle.

"Coffee?"

"Yes, please. And toast."

"Fried egg is just a nickel more." She indicated a sign titled SPECIALTIES behind her. It would only be a total of fifteen cents. Henry gave her a nod and a smile of thanks. She turned to go but stopped and glanced back at him. "You in the flickers?"

"Not yet," he said, grinning. "But that's the plan."

"With a face like that," she said, "you'll do all right. You want my advice?"

"Absolutely."

"Just get in—the studio, I mean. Just take anything to get in the door. Then let that face do the work for you."

Henry colored at this, and she chuckled. "Aw, bashful, too? Even better! Just don't lose that when you make it big. Women love bashful. It's confusing, you know? Big star . . . bashful? Doesn't make sense, so they eat it right up."

"I should be paying you for all this advice," Henry joked.

"No need," she said airily as she turned to deliver his order to the kitchen. "But tipping for good service isn't frowned upon."

Henry glanced through the newspaper as he ate the food that soon arrived. Dunn's Menswear was having its first Dollar Day next week, which would apparently "go down in the history of this community as the greatest bargain event ever attempted up to this time by any of its merchants!" Henry doubted that but hoped he might be able to find some inexpensive yet not too poorly constructed clothing to augment his pitiful wardrobe.

In the Business News section, there was an article titled "Women Reformers Call for Censorship!" It described the growing concern about poor role models in films like Keystone Kops and Gloria Swanson's *Why Change Your Wife?*, the plot of which involved a woman dressing more provocatively to recapture her husband from a conniving second wife. "Such films promote the disrespect of police officers and immoral behavior of young girls, and are simply an invitation to indecency!" stated one disgruntled woman from Coffeeville, Kansas.

At the end of the section there were job listings, but no call for extras, which Henry had assumed were always needed. The waitress came back with his bill, and he said as much to her.

"Extras—*feh*," she scoffed. "Any fool can do it—they've got hundreds of 'em. Now, if DeMille's shooting, sometimes they need more, 'cause he likes those big numbers. But they generally don't have to advertise. People get off the train and head right to the studios." She glanced down at the paper. "Okay, here now," she said, tapping her bony finger at an ad. "Can you hammer a nail? Because Olympic is looking for carpenters to build sets."

Of course he could, or any number of other grunt-level construction jobs, as he'd done between comedy gigs for the last six years. But a different ad caught his eye, one that would get his toe, possibly a whole foot, farther in the door and closer to the action. He smiled up at her. "*Zei gezunt*," he said and put a quarter on the counter.

"Be well, yourself!" She grinned and tucked the quarter into her apron pocket.

◇ ◇ ◇

It took twenty minutes to walk down Sunset to Bronson and find the entrance of Olympic Studios—longer than he'd anticipated.

It was eight o'clock now and he hoped he could accomplish what he'd come here to do and get back to meet Irene and Millie by nine as promised. A look inside the arched gate of the employees' entrance on Bronson almost made Henry turn around on the spot anyway. Some unforeseen calamity seemed to be unfolding as people rushed from one window-less building to the next, with calls and screams erupting from one that looked like a barn. As if this were an everyday affair, scores of people of every age, gender, and dress sat on benches along the buildings, reading newspapers or just closing their eyes in the sun. There were women in old-fashioned shirtwaists with their hair done up in buns sitting next to scantily clad, heavily made-up flappers, girls in little frilly dresses and boys in knickers, about twenty cowboys, and even a guy in the goggles and leather jacket of an aviator.

A man in a rumpled suit walked between the benches, glancing up and down, and people began to put down their reading material and sit up straight. "You," he said, pointing to one of the matronly women, "and you, too," he said indicating a man in overalls and a battered straw hat.

"How 'bout me?" said one of the cowboys.

"Nah, no westerns today."

A woman strode by, petite with large eyes and curly brown hair, in her thirties, Henry guessed. She wore a blue serge dress with a dropped waist and long sleeves she pushed up to her elbows. She clasped a file of papers in one hand, a pencil curled in her fingers against it.

"Pardon me," Henry murmured.

Without breaking stride, she glanced up as if she'd heard some small unusual sound but couldn't place it. "Pardon me," Henry said with more force. The woman slowed a moment to make eye contact but kept walking.

In two long strides, Henry caught up and walked with her.

"Where can I find the tailor's shop? I understand there's an opening . . ."

A wry smile. "You're a tailor?" Her voice was round and warm.

"Yes, well . . ." Henry stammered. "There's an ad in the paper here—" He held it out for her, as if she could possibly read the small type as she walked at such a clip.

"There's no tailor shop, but I'll take you to costume."

"Why, thanks! I'm Henry Weiss, by the way."

"Eva Crown."

"Are you a secretary?"

That wry smile again, but this time a few degrees cooler. "Some like to think so." She approached an oversize wooden door and waited for him to open it for her. The sudden darkness in the building after the bright sunlight left him blinking for a moment, but Eva Crown seemed to have no trouble as she led the way down the hall. "Keep going past the set to the far side. When you come to a small man who acts about a foot and a half taller than he actually is, you're at costume. Good luck, Henry Weiss."

She turned quickly and double-stepped up the stairs.

Henry followed the hallway down to an open area and had to shade his eyes from the intensity of the arc lights. They hung above the action taking place in what appeared to be a bedroom.

"Scream, dear," a tall man in a well-cut suit was saying as he stood facing the bedroom. "I mean really scream."

A girl with brown hair in ringlet curls sat up from a reclined position on the bed. "Obie," she whined. "The audience won't know if I'm really doing it or not. Besides, I'm tired of screaming. My head hurts!"

A heavyset man standing behind the large black camera box murmured, "Well, if she hadn't been tossing 'em back all hours . . ." The director shot him a bitter look, then smiled back at the actress.

"Bess, dear, the camera can tell if you're pretending. And if the camera can tell, the audience can tell." The girl flopped back down onto the bed with a huff of annoyance.

"Roll the damn film," he muttered to the cameraman. "And . . . action!" he called cheerfully.

A large man with a protruding belly and copious black eye makeup stormed into the room and slammed the door behind him. He glared at the girl, face lit with a sinister smile, hands at the ready to grab her. The girl sat up, gasped at the sight of him, and promptly let out an ear-splitting scream.

Henry glanced over at the director in time to see him exhale with relief and murmur to the cameraman, "You got that?"

"Yup," he replied, without taking his eye from the lens.

"Thank God. Otherwise I might have to kill you."

"Not today, Mr. Oberhouser. But there's always tomorrow."

Henry made his way through the back of the room toward a door on the far side with the words COSTUME CLOSET scrawled across it. He knocked, but no one answered. He knocked again, and the door flew open.

A man, no more than five feet tall, stood there with large shears in one hand. His eyes traveled from Henry's slicked black hair slowly down his wrinkled shirt and tie to his dusty pants and rested on his scuffed shoes. The short man shook his head and sighed. "No wonder they sent you. *Look* at you, for godsake."

Shame hit Henry like a punch in the chest. His *zayde* would've been just as disgusted.

"Take it all off, and I'll press it," the short man said, waving Henry in and closing the door. "But if you came here looking for something else to wear, you're out of luck. I keep telling them, I only dress the girls. The men wear their own clothes unless it's historical."

"Oh, no," said Henry, shaking his head, "I'm not . . . I'm here for the job." He indicated the newspaper now crumpled in his hand.

The other man looked at him blankly for a moment, then pointed to the door. "Out."

"No, wait—"

"Wait? For what?" He balled his small fist and leaned it on his hip. "For you to take yourself seriously? When you came in here for a job, looking like *that*?"

"I know, I know!" pleaded Henry. "I look terrible. I left my case on the train, and I've been wearing this for two days. I can barely stand myself!"

"You look like you got *thrown* off that train," the small man scoffed.

"Actually," said Henry. "I jumped."

"Jealous husband?"

Henry shook his head. "Worse."

An eyebrow arched in question.

Albert Leroux had been Edward Oberhouser's tailor, and a year ago had been hired—"conscripted" he insisted to Henry—to produce costumes for the director's films. Soon he was doing all the costuming for Olympic Studios, "without a shred of help! I went to Obie—that's what we call him, those who really know him—and I said, 'I cannot. *I can not.*'"

"How could you possibly do all that yourself?" Henry sympathized.

"Exactly! It's like you in that horrible burlesque show—absolutely untenable." Albert stood, holding Henry's pants high in the air, brushing the dust out of them. Hanging like that, they seemed to be the same length as Albert's entire body. Henry sat in nothing but his summer union suit. Sleeveless, the thin striped fabric ran only to his thighs.

In his lap was a lady's dress, pale satin with mere piping for shoulder straps and so little fabric it wasn't much bigger than a pillowcase. Albert had given him a needle and the perfect matching thread and told him to fix the popped seam at the hip. "She had no business wearing it so small," Albert muttered. "I told her I'd take it out for her, but she insisted it would fit. That split proves who was right on *that* score."

Henry had spent many days in his *zayde*'s shop doing the "child's play," as the old man liked to joke: the popped buttons, the split seams, the ripped hems. Henry couldn't create an entire suit from mere fabric and thread as his *zayde* could, but he could mend a seam with his eyes closed.

"Very nice, very smooth," said Albert, running a finger across the right side of the fabric when Henry was done. He hung the dress on a hanger and hooked that onto the pole that ran from one end of the small room to the other. "Nineteen dollars a week," he said. "And you start right now."

Nineteen wasn't bad. Henry knew he could do worse. But sewing wasn't the only thing he'd learned from his multitalented grandfather. "Twenty-six," he said. "And a lunch break."

"Well, la-di-da," said Albert. "Shall I pour you some tea, Your Majesty?"

Henry sat very still and didn't blink. He let a little smile play across his mouth, as his grandfather always did when he went to buy fabric in the garment district. That unblinking smile said, *I'm a nice guy, but I'm prepared to haggle you into a stupor.*

Albert crossed his arms and glared. "Twenty-one and you spend your first week's salary on decent clothing."

"Twenty-three," said Henry. "And I start right now, spend my first week's salary on clothes . . . and I get a lunch break."

"Oh for godsake, what's the obsession with lunch!"

"I like lunch. And I like you, Albert. You seem like a smart guy and a good tailor, and I'd like to work for you. For twenty-three dollars a week. And a lunch break."

Henry found his way to the hiring office on the opposite side of the lot and got the paperwork completed, then returned to do the diminutive man's bidding for several hours. When it was almost noon, he asked for his hard-won lunch break and hustled out across the lot, hoping he had enough time to make it to Mama Ringa's and back.

10

◇ ◇ ◇

You're too little and too fat, but I might give you a chance.
D. W. Griffith, director, writer, producer, to a then unknown Mary Pickford

He's got a head like a cantaloupe and he can't act.
D. W. Griffith, referring to Douglas Fairbanks.
Griffith, Pickford, Fairbanks, and Chaplin, four of the most successful
people in the industry, formed United Artists in 1919.

"Henry!" called Millie suddenly as they walked sore-footed up Hollywood Boulevard. When they'd gone to the YMCA to meet him, no one had seen him all morning. Wandering around looking for him, they'd ended up at the other end of Sunset, at Chaplin Studios on La Brea.

After searching the Chaplin lot for some time, they had finally been pointed in the direction of the little window where the extras were supposed to register, but the man there shooed them away. "We're full up for girls," he'd said.

"But couldn't we just put our names on the list?" Irene had asked.

"Listen, sister, have you ever been to a Charlie Chaplin movie?"

"Yes, of course!"

"Well then you know that it's mostly fellas, with one or two dames thrown in. We just don't need ya."

The night before, as they were washing dishes, Mama Ringa

I've got this." Millie slid her hands over the lace bodice of the wedding dress she wore.

The woman actually laughed. "Well if we have any pictures with bronco-busting brides, you'll be the first girl we call!"

Irene's responses were shorter, unfortunately. "I'm twenty-one, five-foot-five, a hundred twenty-two pounds, thirty-four bust, twenty-nine waist, and I can't do any of those things except dance. I do have widow's weeds . . ." and she gave a little half-hearted smile. The registrar responded with a sympathetic look and set her gaze on the next girl in line. Irene noted, however, that she had made no additional notes.

At least she knows we're not liars, she thought.

The rumple-suited assistant director stopped short when he saw Millie in the wedding gown, the veil arranged artfully in her hair, as she sat next to Irene on one of the benches. "You come straight from the ceremony?" he asked.

"Don't be silly," said Millie, widening her eyes at him until she could think of the next thing to say. "I'm heading there after I work for you."

His stony face broke into a quick grin.

"And who's this? Your poor old widowed mother?"

"My dear friend whose husband died in a . . ." She looked at Irene. "How did he die?"

"It was a . . . a train wreck." Irene looked sorrowfully up at the assistant director. "He was the engineer, and the brakes went, and he had to stay on the train and try and keep it from derailing in the middle of a crowded depot. And he did, but it derailed anyway a mile outside of town." She had read a story like this in the newspaper a couple of months back.

"Jesus, sorry kid," said the man and continued walking down the bench of extras.

"So much for the milk of human kindness," muttered Irene.

"At least it wasn't true," said Millie. "It's not, right?"

"Don't you think if I had a dead train engineer husband, you'd know about it?"

Millie considered this for a moment. "No, I don't think I necessarily would. You're not the type to tell your secrets, Irene."

Irene shifted on the bench, feeling the heat of the sun as if it were a physical weight on her head and chest. "I don't really have any," she said.

"I guess they're not secrets then," said Millie. "I guess they're just things you don't tell anyone."

Irene had to admit there was some truth to that. She'd spent three years avoiding her past, only to find it was like trying to outrun your shadow. No matter how far or fast you ran, there it was, attached to you.

Not unlike Millie, Irene mused, though Millie was no shadow. More like one of those little birds that rides along happily on the back of a rhinoceros. *Which makes me the rhino.*

Irene sighed. "What would you like to know?"

Millie blinked at her a moment, her face placid, but Irene got the strange sense that Millie was carefully sifting her thoughts. "Well, everything I guess," she said finally.

So much for sifting. Irene laughed. "Blue."

"Blue? What's blue?"

"My favorite color."

"Jeepers, who cares about that?" said Millie. "Tell me about your family."

Irene knew Millie would pester her until she said something. "Well, I lived with my aunt and uncle."

"What about your parents?"

"My mother died in childbirth. Two at a time was too much for her. And I suppose our father was overwhelmed at having two little babies to care for, so he gave us to his sister. He didn't even name us. She did. She always used to say, 'I gave you both names that start with *I* because I want you to be individuals.' But there was no 'I,' really. It was always 'we.'"

"A twin!" Millie clapped her hands together.

"Identical, in fact."

"What's her name?"

"Ivy."

"Ivy and Irene. Is she just like you?"

Irene chuckled. "Not at all. My uncle used to say, 'Ivy's got the talent; Irene's got the grit.'"

"Talent for what?"

"Singing, dancing. Making people smile. Just general happiness, I guess."

"She's a performer."

"We both were. My uncle took us on the road. On the vaudeville circuit. We were Ivy and Irene, The Sweet Sister Songbirds."

The Sweet Sister Songbirds. Irene had thought she would never be able to say those words aloud again. But sitting here with Millie, who listened patiently and didn't seem to have a judgmental bone in her body . . . it wasn't as soul bruising as she'd thought it would be.

"I've never heard you sing."

"Because I'm not very good at it. I always had to sing the melody because I never could figure out how to harmonize. That was Ivy's job. She was a better dancer, too. So I danced and sang my best, and no one ever knew she was the one making the whole thing work because we looked exactly alike. I got half the credit, but I should only have gotten a quarter—if any, really."

"Why was it your uncle who took you?"

"Our aunt had a good, steady job as a secretary, and she thought we'd be safer with a man to look out for us."

It was more information than she'd given out about herself in years, and she had the feeling that she was rattling on like some shut-in desperate for company. She'd said enough, she decided. But there was Millie, gazing at her placidly, neither shocked nor pitying.

"And now Ivy's—?"

Irene looked away. What was Ivy now? An angel? A cloud? Just another set of bones buried in the dirt?

"We had the Spanish flu. And God chose her."

A current of sorrow passed over Millie's face. "Oh, no," she whispered.

Irene would've given anything to erase the memory of that hotel room where they'd faced death side by side. The Montvale in Spokane. They'd been playing The Empress Theatre when Irene had collapsed onstage. Ivy had taken ill soon thereafter.

"My name was the last word she said. I've often thought of that. How a person's last words can sort of . . . I don't know . . . sum it all up. Like 'The End' when you finish a story. I summed it all up for her. But I'm still here, and I don't really know what my summary will be. It should have been her. But now it can't be, because I've lived three whole years without her. My story went on."

"I'm glad of that."

"I guess I'd be gladder if I knew what I was here for. I always thought I was here to be Ivy's Irene. But that job's over."

"You're my Irene, now."

It was a sweet thing for Millie to say, and Irene smiled indulgently. She wished she believed it, but it was hard for her to fathom that she would truly belong to anyone ever again. She hoped she would someday. And maybe that was the difference. Before she'd jumped off that train, she hadn't even wanted to.

"Why didn't you go home?" asked Millie.

"I just couldn't."

Millie nodded. "Because it was too full of Ivy."

"I knew if I saw our home and our town and all the places we went together, I was sure I would've just . . ."

"Started crying and never stopped."

"It sounds silly, but I couldn't—"

"It's not silly. You were sad, Irene. Just too sad."

"My aunt never forgave me for not going home for the funeral, but my uncle understood. He knew the *I* in our names never meant individual." Irene sighed. "So he let me join up with a chorus line, but when the show disbanded . . . I didn't really have the talent to get much better than back row. And then I ran out of money . . ."

"And then Chandler found you. He has a knack for getting a girl at her low point."

"Does he ever."

Millie snuggled closer on the bench and whispered in Irene's ear, "Thank you for telling me all this. It means the world to me."

They sat there the rest of the afternoon with the fake cowboys and fake Indians, fake society girls and fake farmers. At least they thought they were fakes. Some of them seemed quite realistic. A tan-skinned man in a wide-brimmed black hat sat on a bench across the walkway. In his lap lay something folded up, made from soft leather. On top was something black—was that hair?—and a colorful strip of fabric. By the very fact of his not wearing the costume, he seemed more authentic than the man a couple of benches down who wore fringed pants and stripes of paint on his face that were streaked with sweat.

By mid-afternoon, with the heat of the day baking through

her dark clothes, Irene was thirsty and tired. Millie had pulled the veil over her face to shade herself from the sun's rays, and every once in while a soft little snore whispered from behind it. Irene was about to pat her arm and suggest it was time to go when the assistant director made another round.

He stopped in front of the man with the black hat. "You a real Indian?" he asked.

"Yeah, I'm real."

"What's your name?"

"Stars Lying Down."

"Not Running Bear or Dancing Elk or something?"

The man scrutinized the assistant director for a moment. "What are you looking for?" he said. "Because I just need work."

"Doesn't matter a whit to me. We just don't want some guy holding up the shot because the face paint ain't right."

"I won't hold up the shot."

"You got any other names? What do your friends call you?"

"Depends on the friends."

The assistant director chuckled and shook his head. "Yeah, me, too."

"Dan," said the man. "Dan Russell."

This seemed to reassure the assistant director immeasurably. "That your costume?"

"I don't wear it on the bench. There's not much to it, and I don't like to alarm the ladies."

He stood and tucked the leather bundle under his arm. He was a little shorter than Henry, slightly shy of six feet, Irene gauged, and his shoulders weren't as broad. But there was something quietly powerful about the subtle yet efficient way he stretched his spine to get the kinks out from sitting so long. As he strode down the walkway toward her, he held his shoulders back, and she couldn't help but watch the elegance of his gait.

The crew had hungrily eaten every morsel, and Louise had only been disappointed that the plate of egg salad sandwiches had been practically licked clean by the time she saw it. "Egg salad's my favorite, and these had all the crusts cut off. Like the bread wasn't soft enough already, you had to get rid of anything that wouldn't melt in your mouth like cotton candy."

As it turned out it had been a lucky thing the others had been so greedy. Sitting on a sunny table all afternoon, the sandwiches had gone bad. "They're all puking their guts up right about now," she said with a cruel little smile. "Serves 'em right."

The pay was four dollars for the evening and that was all Irene and Millie needed to hear. "Do you need men, too?" asked Millie.

"The owner's so desperate for bodies," said Louise, "at this point I think he'd take any stray dog that could stand on its hind legs and hold a tray of drinks."

Two hours later, just as the truck pulled up to the curb, Henry jogged up the street. He dabbed at his forehead with a handkerchief. "I got your note," he panted. "Where's the party?"

Louise eyed him appreciably. "They never say whose house," she said, "so we can't gab about it to crashers. But don't worry, buster, it'll be worth your while."

Practically licking her chops, thought Irene, her dislike of the redhead suddenly blooming like algae.

They piled into the truck, which was already loaded with five young women and two men whom they could barely see in the scant light from two small windows in the doors. The airless truck cabin, fitted with benches along the walls, rattled along, uniforms swinging back and forth on a pole that spanned the width of the truck. Louise smiled slyly at Henry. "You'll need the tallest set," she said. "Wouldn't want you to be uncomfortable in any important areas."

To his credit, Henry gave her a withering look, and said simply, "Thanks for the tip."

The truck turned up a winding road and finally came to a hard stop. A moment later, the back doors flew open. "Out, out, quickly please," instructed a thin man with an even thinner mustache.

"The manager," whispered Louise. "We call him Kaiser behind his back."

Another truck had pulled up and emptied out, and they were about twenty waiters and waitresses in all. The Kaiser, back straight as a ship's mast, waited for absolute silence.

"The women will dress in one truck, the men in another," he instructed as his assistant handed out uniforms. "You will each be given a tray from which you will serve beverages. When the tray is empty, you will retrieve any discarded glasses from your immediate area and return them to the kitchen where you will be given more full glasses. Some of you will be stationary, some will be roving. I will decide who does what, so do not ask for a particular assignment. I know several of you are with us only temporarily, and so I will impress upon you the most important rule of the evening. *You may not speak to the guests.* If you are spoken to, you may answer only with the fewest words necessary for a courteous response. You will not gawk, you may not even seem to *notice* the guests. You are statuary, moving only to provide service. Anyone interacting with or even looking particularly closely at guests will be immediately escorted from the premises and left to return home on foot."

The uniforms were made of scratchy black material—ill-fitting black suits for the men, calf-length dresses for the women, with white aprons and ruffled caps they bobby-pinned server's hope, and the prospects were impossibly dim. These people barely noticed her. She was a ham sandwich; they were squid.

Millie was assigned to rove among the guests, murmuring one word and one word only: "Champagne?" This allowed her to take in one opulent room after another: the banquet hall with that huge chandelier; the music room where a ten-piece band played sparkling renditions of "Second Hand Rose" and "Saint Louis Blues," as guests twirled across the parquet floor; the grand parlor with its potted palms, gilt-framed paintings, and silk upholstered furniture in mauves and grays. Her family socialized with the Springfield, Massachusetts, elite, but she'd never in her life seen anything as unabashedly ostentatious as this. "New money," she could hear her mother say with disdain. *And she'd have been right,* thought Millie. It was spit-in-your-eye wealth.

As the evening wore on, the guests grew thirstier and their behavior responded accordingly. Out on the vast stone patio overlooking the pool, two couples smoking and howling with laughter beckoned her over.

"Come on now, ladies," one of the fellows cackled, "give us those shoes."

This sent one of the women into convulsive laughter that looked almost painful, while the other shook a limp finger at him and slurred, "Now tha's not entirely 'propriate."

"'Propriate, my ass, Dolores! Gimme the damn shoe!" commanded the other gentleman and held out his hand.

"Billy, Billy, Billy." She shook her head, wobbling back and forth like it might come loose altogether. "You are no gentleman. *You* are a *shoe-sniffer.*"

Billy simply picked her up and threw her over his shoulder like a duffle of dirty laundry, pulled off one of her pink satin kitten-heel pumps, held it out to Millie, and said, "Pour."

The other fellow erupted into gales of laughter, gasping "Shoe! Shoe!" at his date. She staggered around trying to lift her foot to her hand without falling over till he caught her by the waist. She handed up a shiny red patent leather pump, and both men watched with glee as Millie dutifully emptied two champagne glasses into the shoes, effectively ruining them.

They downed the booze in gulps, one man pouring a good bit of it down the front of his no-longer-crisp tuxedo shirt. Then they heaved the shoes into the pool while one woman clapped and staggered around on one heeled foot and one bare; the other seemed to have gone to sleep over her date's shoulder. He turned to look at Millie, and said, "You're still here?"

Henry, stationed out by the kidney-shaped pool, watched the shoes sail into the water and bob around like colorful little fishing buoys. The pool house had apparently been designated a vow-free zone; he'd seen the same portly gentleman with the same thick gold band on his ring finger go in and out with three different young women so far, each emerging with ruffled hair and smeared lipstick, adjusting a strap or tugging down a slip.

"Thank you, Mr. Wilmington," the last one murmured. "I can expect to hear from your office tomorrow?" He dismissed her with a perfunctory smile and a pat on the bottom.

Afterward he stood a few feet away from Henry, lit a cigarette, gazed out across the pool to the cacophony of light and sound pulsing from the mansion, and shook his head. "Can't stop." Then he chuckled. "But why should I?"

◇ ◇ ◇

By three in the morning, most of the guests had either left or been discreetly removed by the house staff to the warren of bedrooms on the second floor. By four, all the glassware had been collected, and Kaiser was orchestrating the retreat of the kitchen staff.

Irene straightened her aching back and approached him to ask if they might be placed on a list for when he needed extra servers. "After a night like tonight? I saw more chatter with guests than I've ever seen in my entire career! And don't think I didn't notice some of you pocketing rolls and little sandwiches to take home."

"But my friends and I . . . we didn't—"

"I don't know who it was. You all look the same. But none of you will be in my employ again, you can be certain of that."

When the truck emptied them out at Ringa's, the light was just starting to simmer below the horizon, the birds in the jacarandas warming up for the morning's syncopated jazz performance.

"I'm not sure whether to get an hour of sleep or go find coffee somewhere and head straight to work," said Henry. He bid them goodbye and headed off into the sunrise.

Irene and Millie tiptoed up the stairs. Louise had pocketed her four bucks and headed out with one of the other waiters who'd been demonstrably more taken by her attentions than Henry. The girl who shared her bed was missing, too, leaving Irene and Millie alone in the room.

"At least we made eight dollars," said Millie, curling herself against Irene.

"I'm not sure if it was worth it. Even if I got offered a lead role tomorrow, I'd probably fall asleep midscene."

"Did you see all those other girls?" Millie yawned. "So pretty."

"And so many of them."

The starlets with their sparkling outfits, the other waitresses glowing like Clara Bow even in the ugly uniforms. Irene had known the competition would be stiff, but considering all the other parties likely going on across the town that night, with more starlets and more gorgeous serving girls angling for any toehold in the business, she wondered if it might be insurmountable.

Especially for a ham sandwich like her.

12

◇ ◇ ◇

*I'd rather jump from a moving train or ride a motorcycle fifty
miles an hour or take a ride in an airplane than eat.*

Jean Acker, actress

After only an hour's sleep, Irene and Millie were back on
the benches, struggling to keep their heads from bobbing
like rag dolls every time a casting director walked by. They
didn't wear their costumes, only sat with them folded on their
laps. Irene had decided to follow the lead of Stars Lying Down,
who seemed to know far better than them what might improve
the chances of being chosen.

"I kind of liked wearing it," said Millie.

"You just liked all the heads that turned, wondering why a
bride's strolling down Sunset on a Wednesday morning."

"Of course I did," said Millie. "Why else would I do it?"

"Well, I think we're better off in everyday dresses. They may
not shoot a movie with a bride or a widow for months, and then
where would we be?"

Several assistant directors strode among them, but the only
interest they received was when Millie stood to stretch, arching
her back, and whispering a little too loudly about how sore her
bottom was. They sat in the sun, hungry and thirsty, but afraid to

leave their spots for fear that someone might come along, looking for girls just like them—a brunette with a caustic streak and a wide-eyed, raven-haired, relentlessly cheerful beauty—and they wouldn't be there.

This went on for almost a month. They registered at other studios, of course, and checked in regularly, but when they walked home with Henry in the afternoons they all agreed their best shot was at Olympic where Henry had his ear to the ground for inside information. It was August now, and the temperature hadn't dipped below eighty during the day in a week. Henry came by with cups of water for them during his lunch break, but Albert kept him busy, and he couldn't always get away. He was upbeat and encouraging, but Irene could tell he didn't care much for the work he was doing and would've been far happier sharing the bench with them all day—except of course that he was the only one of the three of them earning a paycheck.

"He misses us," said Millie one day, after Henry had dropped off a dill pickle and rolls.

"I'd rather be working—at anything—than sitting here hour after hour," Irene said halfheartedly, laying down yesterday's edition of the *Hollywood Citizen* she'd found in a trash bin.

That was the day everything changed.

It was three o'clock, and by then bench-sitters tended to file out, knowing it was unlikely there would be a sudden unanticipated need for extras that late in the day. But Millie had nodded off, Irene had lost track of time reading an article about the pool at Hollywood High School now being opened to girls, and the crowd had thinned out considerably.

One of the assistant directors strolled over, the one with the wrinkled suit they'd learned was named Wally. "You girls waiting for a trolley?" he teased.

Millie stirred and smiled up at him, her face soft with sleep, eyes catlike. She reached her arms up to stretch and leaned to one side, revealing the top of a rounded breast. Wally made no effort not to stare. Irene folded her paper and nudged Millie's side so she collapsed giggling.

"Well, now, uh," Wally mumbled. "I was thinking that maybe Carter and me could take you girls for a bite to eat, talk about some possibilities here at the studio."

"Oh, that'd be wonderful," said Millie.

"Who's Carter?" asked Irene.

"My cameraman," said Wally, with a little puff of his chest.

As an assistant, Wally wasn't likely to have his own cameraman; that was the province of directors. Irene didn't like the looks of this and said, "I think we'd better—"

"We'd love to," said Millie. "Where to?"

Wally looked as surprised and pleased as if he'd just found a dollar bill on the ground. "Carter and me'll come up with something topnotch!" He winked and scurried off.

"Why do you always have to be so suspicious?" said Millie.

"Did you see his face? And 'my cameraman'! He doesn't have a cameraman any more than he's got wings on his back. It's just a line, Millie. The only thing he wants is a date."

"Who cares if it's a line! The only thing *I* want is a steak and a baked potato the size of a football. I'm sick of that lousy slop Ringa serves—and so are you."

Millie was right about that. Mama Ringa had girls jammed to the rafters, and the food was terrible, what little of it there was. They'd searched around but they hadn't found anything as cheap, and the places that had seemed a little nicer were even farther away from the studios. Henry had offered to help—he'd all but insisted—but Irene wanted to wait and see if they could get jobs before the tea set money ran out. "It's just temporary," she kept telling him. For the sake of their stomachs she certainly hoped so. Girls like them, desperate for a decent meal and a night out, were just what guys like Wally banked on.

"Are you coming with me, or am I going alone?" said Millie.

You're going alone, Irene thought, but before it left her mouth, into her mind popped a flickering image of Millie at sixteen, abandoned by her parents, reluctantly leaving back-breaking farm work, heading off to god-knows-where, and ending up in Chandler's Follies. And of her own sweet-faced sister.

They're not the same, she told herself. But it didn't seem to matter.

13

◇ ◇ ◇

It was brutal. I called it mud, blood, and flood.
*Dolores Costello, actress, on filming Noah's Ark, during which
countless extras were taken away by ambulance*

"Can I borrow a dress?" Millie asked Agnes, one of the four other girls who now shared their crowded third-floor room. Mama Ringa had said there would only be two other girls, then promptly squeezed in one more bed and two more girls.

Agnes, tall with a big chin, dressed only in a slip and clearly no underwear, looked Millie up and down from her perch on the windowsill. "What for."

It was not a question. It was an answer that was the beginning of "no." Millie knew the likelihood of Agnes being generous was slim, but she persisted. Millie often got her way in unlikely situations. Except of course when she didn't.

"I have a date tonight, and I've been wearing the same three dresses over and over again, and he's seen me in all of them. In burlesque we always shared dresses."

"Oh, *burlesque*," Agnes drawled, wedging herself even more tightly into the window, the only one in the attic room, greedy for every hint of a breeze that might sidle by. "Aren't we highfalutin."

"What's highfalutin about burlesque, for Pete's sake? It's stripping, Agnes."

"Yeah, and that's all it is." Agnes hung one of her legs out the window, and for a brief moment Millie wondered if she might jump.

"You'd better pull that leg back in. If Ringa sees you showing your wares like that, you'll be out on the curb."

"Ringa," Agnes sneered. "Acts all proper. Where you think I get the money to pay her?"

"I thought you were working at that dance hall her brother owns."

"Dancing." Her eyes went flat and dull. "That's the front room. There's lots more rooms in back."

Millie wandered closer and leaned against the window jam, facing Agnes. "Can you quit? Or tell him you'll dance but nothing else?"

"Sure, I can. Except you only make a nickel a dance—can't live on that. So when Ringa throws me out for shortin' her on the rent, I can just go ride the rails with the rest of the hobos. Then I'll be cold, dirty, and giving it up for free."

"You tried the studios?"

"Jesus, of course I did!" Agnes exploded. "You think I came here all the way from Boise to lie down for a buck and a half?"

"No, I didn't mean—"

"You're not getting one of my goddamned whore dresses, so shove off!"

"Every girl in the house was in line down there," Irene said when she returned from the bathroom. "I was five seconds away from making Lake Irene." She grinned at Millie, but Millie didn't grin back.

"I'll hold it until we get to the ..." She glanced at Agnes. "Until we get there."

The two men were waiting outside, Wally with his foot leaning jauntily—if a bit awkwardly—against the running board. "Well, aren't you two pretty!" he called out before they'd even come down the steps from the house.

There was some confusion about where everyone was to sit. Millie thought she and Irene would sit in back, but Wally said to Irene, "You sit up front and enjoy the view. Millie'll sit in back with me!"

They rode out to the beach, to the Rendezvous Ballroom on Crystal Pier. Irene and Carter were having normal date conversation: Where are you from? How long have you been in Hollywood? Where did you learn to be a cameraman? Carter, with his round face and thin lips, was shy. Irene drew him out, but Millie could hear the strategy behind Irene's questions. On exactly what rung of the studio ladder did Carter stand, and could he be of any help to them?

It was the opposite for Millie. Wally drove the conversation all over the place. In fact, she was beginning to suspect that he'd had a few before picking them up. He wanted to know strange things about her, like did she like to swim and had she ever eaten oysters and how many boyfriends had she had. He didn't really want to talk about his work at the studio, "didn't want to brag," he said, and she hoped there was something to brag about.

The Rendezvous had seen better days, and there was nothing terribly sparkling about Crystal Pier. But the food was so far superior to Ringa's that Millie was happy to eat and eat and laugh at Wally's ridiculous jokes and eat some more. She tried not to think about Agnes, half out the window, nor about whether the same fate might await her if studio work didn't materialize soon. But as Wally danced her forcefully around the room, past the enormous windows looking out over the sea, she couldn't help but be grateful that she was anywhere but back at Ringa's, contemplating what might happen when the silver tea set money ran out.

"It's getting too stuffy in here!" She laughed breathlessly as they collapsed at the table. "Let's go walk on the beach and cool our feet in the water."

"That sounds nice," said Irene, glancing at Carter. He was an absolutely terrible dancer, and Millie knew Irene was happy to try something he might excel at. Like walking.

A look passed between Carter and Wally then. *A man look,* thought Millie, and she was glad of it. Let them get a little hopeful. A hopeful man would promise things.

So she was not surprised that after they'd taken their shoes off and tickled their toes in the foamy water's edge and she'd giggled girlishly about how good it felt, Wally suggested she might walk in one direction with him while Carter and Irene walked in the other. Fine with her. It would give her more room to flirt, slide her soft fingers up his arm, and say vaguely naughty things that would incite a certain amount of witlessness (or in Wally's case *more* witlessness) and she might then be able to extract some promise of work.

"Let's all stay together," said Irene, eyeing Millie meaningfully. "It's more fun that way."

Wally eyed her just as meaningfully and said, "Your friend's got some strange ideas about fun, don't you think?"

"We'll all meet back here in an hour," said Millie and hooked her arm in his. She avoided Irene's gaze as they turned and headed off down the beach.

The flirting and finger sliding were going quite well, she thought, and she took control of the conversation for the first time all evening. "Now, Wally," she cooed. "I won't be able to stay around Hollywood and have fun nights like this with you much longer if I don't get some work. I can't pay the rent with my good looks, now can I?"

"Oh, I don't know about that," said Wally, grinning stupidly. "Your looks seem like cash in the bank to me!"

"Aren't you sweet." She snuggled a little closer and let her breast graze his arm. "Well, that tells me you might pick me the next time you need a girl extra. Me and Irene, of course."

"I just might," he said. "Or maybe . . ."

"Maybe what?"

"Well, maybe there might be something better than being an extra," he said. The flush in his cheeks told the temperature of his desire. "We should maybe sit and talk about it."

"We could do that right now," she said. "Right here on the beach."

"Aw, now the beach is no place to have a serious conversation like that." He looked around, head swiveling eagerly. "Let's sit like respectable people, up on that veranda over there."

Millie frowned. "But that's someone's house. We can't just go sit on their veranda."

"Place is dark. No one's home. It's all ours!" He gripped her hand and tugged her away from the shore and up the steps to the house. The porch was furnished with a cluster of white wicker furniture from which all of the cushions had been removed.

"Must've gone up to the mountains for the cooler air," he said, tugging her down onto a divan. The latticed wicker dug into her backside, and she let out a little "ouch!"

"Is that lovely bottom of yours a little tender?" he murmured. "My lap is nice and soft."

"I'd like to hear more about the work you can get me at the studio," she said as he tugged her onto his thighs. She could immediately feel his arousal.

"Plenty of time for that," he moaned. "Right now there's more important things . . ." He slid a hand up under her dress so fast she didn't have time to bat it away.

"Hey, you can't—"

He grabbed her hard through her panties. "I just did."

"Wally, no! Stop that!" She tried to elbow herself away from him, but with his other arm he cinched her in tight to his body. Then he flipped her onto her back, held her wrists tight with one hand, and pried her knees open with the other.

"Please!" she begged, straining every muscle to resist him. "*Please no!*"

"That's right," he hissed in her ear. "I like a girl who makes it more of a challenge."

14

◇ ◇ ◇

"I had twenty-eight costumes in *The Queen of Sheba*, and if I'd
worn them all at once I couldn't have kept warm."
Betty Blythe, actress

Henry knew it was hot outside. Didn't he bring cups of water
and apples to Irene and Millie every day? It was August, for
the love of Mike. Of course it was hot.

Still he sulked about sitting in the claustrophobic, if cooler,
Costume Closet, as Albert called it. With Albert. Who was annoying as often as he was entertaining. His stories of the early
days, when the studios were just rented barns and they made a
two-reeler in a day, could be fascinating. But Albert was peevish
and persnickety, as likely to complain as to take a breath.

Henry's grandfather never complained. He either fixed the
problem, or he got even with the person who'd caused the problem. If Henry complained about his father (and there had been
much to complain about), his *zayde* would generally respond
with, "Oy, the kvetching!" effectively ending the conversation.

"And did I tell you Obie's pestering me to go on location? In
the desert! It's some sort of Arab scenario. And where am I supposed to sleep? On the sand like a lizard?"

Oy, the kvetching.

There was a polite knock on the door.

"Oh, for goodness' sake, what now?" said Albert.

The door opened, and light splintered in around the edges of a very tall person.

"Obie!" cried Albert. "We were just talking about you."

Edward Oberhouser smiled. "I suspected as much." His gaze shifted to Henry. "I'm not sure we've met."

Henry stood and extended his hand, taking in every detail: the famed director, both artistically and commercially successful. Henry matched him in height, but not in stature, and searched for something not completely foolish to say.

"I'm a great admirer! Of your work, I mean. Your pictures, that is. Films."

Albert arched an eyebrow.

"And I yours," said Oberhouser. "Nary a split seam in sight."

"Obie," Albert scoffed. "Don't make fun of the boy."

"I'm actually quite sincere, Albert. A torn costume holds up the shot, and I've noticed a great improvement in that area recently."

"I was overwhelmed!" Albert blustered. "Forced to do things too quickly!"

"Exactly why it was so wise of you to hire an assistant."

"Well . . . yes . . . I suppose it was."

"And I know you're not keen to go on location."

"I will if you really need me. I mean, *really* need me."

"I was just wondering if maybe . . . I'm terribly sorry . . . your name again, please?"

"Henry. Henry Weiss, sir."

"I wonder if Henry might be interested in location work. That way you can do the critical costume design and preparation, which is, of course, so important. And Henry can fix the split seams." He turned back to Henry. "Do you think you might be available to join the crew and me in the Mojave?"

"Well . . . yes."

"It's all right," she said. "I hate to admit it—I hate even to think about it—but I had to do a bit of that myself after my vaudeville days were over."

"Some of the nicest girls I know were in burlesque."

Though her smiles had been generally of the sassy variety, this one was pure gratitude. "We do the best we can with the cards we're dealt."

Henry didn't think he'd always played his hand as well as he could have, so he certainly knew he was in no position to judge.

Soon they were pulling into Barstow. Everyone began to rise and gather their things.

"I thought we were going to the Mojave Desert," Henry said to Gert.

"Oh, well, it's out there somewhere. This director always goes for realism, but you have to have a place to put up the cast and crew. The cost goes way up on location, so Barstow's good enough."

"How'd you find that out?"

"I make friends, Henry. Just like you."

The costumes for *The Queen of Sheba* could barely stand up to the term.

Flimsy hankies is more like it, thought Henry as he reviewed the racks in his room in the Barstow Harvey House, which doubled as the Costume Closet. He wasn't there long. One of Edward Oberhouser's assistants came along to say he was to be on set at all times. "And bring your sewing basket," the fellow said with a smirk.

Henry brought his costume supplies box (which he wrote in

conspicuously large letters across the front), and got on the truck with the rest of the crew, bouncing along a bad road out of town a mile or two. It was desert, all right, with the mercury register-ing 105 degrees. Henry was given a chair not far from the di-rector and scenario writer, Eva Crown, who seemed to bob their heads together and confer after almost every take. He already had mending to do—one of the drapes of fabric from King Solomon's robe had pulled away from the shoulder—but he couldn't take his eyes off the scene unfolding before him.

The queen and her retinue were traveling to Israel for her audience with the king. Three very realistic-looking chariots, or-nately decorated with primitive figures of warriors, were loaded with gifts of incense, gold, and jewels, and female extras posing as handmaids. Henry knew from his Hebrew studies as a child that the queen should arrive on a camel, but apparently finding, renting, and hauling camels to Barstow had been vetoed by the producer. Besides, chariots with teams of horses were so much more exciting.

Betty Blythe rode in a chariot driven by a handsome extra, bare-chested and wearing a leather skirt. She herself was wear-ing a cloak, but the director wanted it to come loose and ex-pose her scanty costume underneath as the wind blew against them.

"Fine by me," said Betty Blythe. "It's hell on a griddle out here."

As the chariot headed through the dunes and rocky outcrop-pings toward the camera, Betty let the cloak slip from her shoul-ders. Her costume was a sort of filmy net vest that came only to her navel, and revealed her nipples almost as clearly as if she were stark naked. Betty was amply endowed, and as those lovely orbs approached, the barest whisper of a sigh went up from the male extras hanging around behind the camera in their palace guard costumes.

Eva Crown shook her head. The cameraman, a short burly man named Wilson Grimes, the same one Henry had seen that first day at the studio, groaned.

"What are you two griping about?" said Oberhouser. "It was perfect."

"Apparently you weren't watching her driver," said Eva.

Wilson called out to the young man. "You got a cold?"

"I'm fine!"

"You sure?"

"Ab-so—" And then his chest began convulsing. He kept his mouth clamped shut, but he was clearly coughing. Betty leaned away from him, face pinched in distaste.

"He hacked like that all through the take," said Eva.

"Dammit," muttered Oberhouser. "All right, let's get someone else in there."

"All the men are dressed in their palace costumes," said Eva. "It'll take time to get someone switched out and switched back. We need to get the palace scene in by nightfall, or it'll mean another day of on-location production costs."

"Henry could do it!" a voice called out from the scrum of queen's handmaidens, and Henry recognized Gert Turner's voice.

"Who in the hell is Henry?" said Wilson.

Henry rose hesitantly from his chair. "I believe she means me."

Oberhouser, Eva, and Wilson stared at him a moment.

Then Oberhouser smiled. "Hello, Henry."

Henry and the coughing extra went behind the equipment truck. Henry stripped and put on the leather skirt, and the other guy covered his nakedness with King Solomon's robes. Then a makeup person was called in to slather Henry with brown grease paint and outline his eyes with black liner.

"Have you ever driven a chariot, Henry?" asked Oberhouser wryly.

"I grew up in New York City, sir," said Henry. "The only thing I've ever driven is a hard bargain."

The director nodded appreciatively. "You're about to make an addition to your résumé."

It was both harder and easier than it looked. With the whole cast and crew waiting, the horse trainer gave Henry a speedy and anxiety-producing lesson on how to use the reins, what to say to get the horse to go or stop, and most concerning of all, what to do if the horse got spooked and took off, which mostly amounted to letting the animal run himself out. Oberhouser, on the other hand, was far more concerned with Betty Blythe's safety and general happiness, and instructed Henry to control the animal at all costs.

Fear crackling through him like a faulty electrical cord, Henry got into the two-wheeled chariot and immediately unbalanced it. He barely caught himself before he tumbled out, leather skirt flinging itself around his thighs. The girl extras let out a little cheer at this, which did nothing to assuage his anxiety.

He got himself situated, reins in hand, legs spread wide for stability. Then Betty Blythe stepped in and tripped over his foot. She went down like a sack of scantily clad flour into the front of the chariot, and Henry had a terrible time hanging on to the reins and trying to help her.

"I'm so sorry, Miss Blythe . . . terribly sorry . . . are you all right? . . . Should I—?"

"No, you shouldn't," she said, grabbing onto the side of the chariot and pulling herself up. "You keep to your side of this bucket, and I'll keep to mine, okay, Tarzan?"

The easy part began once he'd cracked the reins and yelled

"Yah!" as loudly as he'd been instructed. The horse took off at a stately trot, and all Henry had to do was keep himself upright. He hoped Miss Blythe could do the same, but if she couldn't . . . well, that was her problem.

The horse trotted by the camera, and Henry hauled back on the reins as he'd been told. In his eagerness to bring the whole episode to an end, however, he may have tugged a little too forcefully because the horse suddenly reared up on his hind legs and dropped down to a hard stop. Henry and Miss Blythe both went crashing into the front of the chariot, and the leading lady would've flipped completely out of it if Henry hadn't gotten a hand on the back of the flimsy vest and held fast.

She turned around quickly, twisting herself out of his grasp. "For godsake," she hissed, "what were you raised by, grizzlies? Quit pawing me!"

She flounced out of the chariot and over to the director, who was conferring with Wilson, the cameraman. Henry followed a few paces behind, mortified, exhausted, and just glad the whole thing was over.

"Did you get it?" Betty asked Oberhouser.

"I'm so sorry, darling, but the horse was too slow."

"Too slow? We were about to break our necks out there!" She shot her thumb at Henry. "If he hadn't grabbed me, I'd be lying in about sixty pieces in the sand."

Oberhouser gave Henry a little nod of gratitude and said, "I know it felt like that, but I can only say it looked like you were trotting off to a picnic, not speeding toward an appointment with the King of Israel."

Miss Blythe let out a string of curses (some combinations of which were new to Henry) ending with, "And if I break my dimpled ass, your picture is in the shitter!"

"I'm sorry, dear, but the shot requires—"

"Uh, actually, Obie?" said Wilson. "The horse doesn't have to go much faster." They all turned to the cameraman. "If he does it at a slightly quicker clip, but I turn the crank slower—maybe ten frames a second—when it plays at the standard sixteen, it'll look like the horse is galloping when it's only cantering."

The horse and chariot were brought back to the start, and Henry and Miss Blythe climbed reluctantly back in. She turned to him just before Oberhouser called for action and snarled, "Hold on to your nuts, Tarzan, because this is the last take I'm doing."

She grabbed his hand that was wrapped around the reins, lifted it high and brought it down fast, making the reins slap hard onto the horse's back. "Haw!" she hollered, and they were suddenly flying across the desert, Betty with her shoulders back, chest out, *smiling* for godsake, as the robe slipped down and revealed all that God and random luck had given her.

Henry was furious. Just for spite, he let the horse run himself out before reining him in. Betty ordered, "Get this rig back. There's a drink with my name on it."

The horse circled back on his own, his eye on the trainer holding out an apple. When he came to a stop, Betty got out and headed directly for her car, a champagne-colored Pierce-Arrow that gleamed like amber, the driver with a cocktail shaker in hand.

"Henry!" called Oberhouser, and Henry made his way over to the director, knees still a little shaky from the hellacious ride.

"I'll go and change now," he said. "I'm sure I need to put a stitch or two into her costume where I grabbed it."

"Never mind that," said Oberhouser. "You were quite impressive. That ferocious look you gave made a great improvement to the scene."

Henry chuckled. "That was no look."

Oberhouser took a step closer. "She's insufferable," he murmured. "They all are."

"How do you stand it?"

"I was a high school dramatics teacher before I became a film director. Same job, *much* better pay."

◇ ◇ ◇

Henry was told to stay in costume. They shot a scene with the queen disembarking from the chariot and heading toward King Solomon's palace—which wasn't actually there, of course. They'd shoot that angle when they got back to the lot, where a palace exterior had been built. But Oberhouser wanted realism, and the wind had kicked up. Sand swirled dramatically, and he couldn't resist an opportunity to show the fortitude of the great Queen of Sheba as she battled her way toward her destination. Betty had fortitude in spades, as it turned out, fortified as she was by several rounds from her driver's cocktail shaker.

The scenario called for her to march toward the palace guards, head high, which she was able to accomplish for a couple of steps until she tripped over a stone (or possibly her costume, or possibly nothing at all), and began to crumple to the ground. Henry had been told to follow her while holding his ferociously protective look and was able to catch her under the armpits before she hit the dirt.

She looked up at him with a boozy smile. "Tryin'a touch my tits?"

Henry smiled back tightly and said, "Trying to keep your costume clean." (The title cards would later say "THANK YOU, LOYAL SERVANT!" and "I REVERE YOU, MY QUEEN!")

Oberhouser and Eva Crown were happy. It was over in one take.

◇ ◇ ◇

That evening, after slathering himself in cold cream to get the greasepaint off his face and torso and taking the longest shower of his life to get the cold cream off, Henry went down to the Harvey House dining room for dinner. He scanned the hall crowded with cast and crew and remembered the last time he was here, a month ago now, with Irene and Millie. He missed them, his only two friends in the world at the moment, and wished they were there so he could regale them with the story of his brief stint as Betty Blythe's chariot driver and stumble catcher.

There was an open seat at Oberhouser's table, and Henry felt a brief jolt of excitement at the possibility of sharing a meal with the great director. But his courage failed him when he saw that the others at the table were Eva Crown, Wilson Grimes, and Fritz Leiber, the leading man. Henry knew he was far down the food chain from the likes of them.

There were a few open spots, and he noticed several of the girl extras glancing his way. *Nothing like being bare-chested with the leading lady to spark interest,* he thought. But then he caught site of Gert Turner. She simply tipped her head toward the seat next to her, as if she didn't care if he took it but was pretty sure he probably would.

And, of course, he did. They were friends now, after all.

15

◇ ◇ ◇

When I went to work in a studio, I took my pride and made a nice
little ball of it and threw it right out the window.
Dorothy Arzner, writer, editor, director

Irene watched Millie hook her arm with that idiot, Wally, her
shoes dangling from her fingertips, all giggles and fake innocence, and made a mental note to give her a good talking to
when they got back to Ringa's. For a girl who'd been on her own
for the last three years, since the tender age of sixteen, she could
be such a dunce.

Wordlessly, Carter watched them go, too.

"Your friend's an idiot," said Irene.

"We're not really friends," said Carter. "And your pal isn't exactly Madame Curie."

Point taken, thought Irene.

She stared out at the black water, light flickering off it like a
thousand skipped rocks. The Pacific Ocean. She'd seen it before
from the train window when they'd traveled down the coast from
Seattle once, but she'd never touched it. And now here she was,
ankle deep.

"Ummm . . ." said Carter, an obvious and awkward search for
something, anything, to talk about. "How do you like Hollywood?"

So far it's awful, she wanted to say. But that wasn't really date conversation, was it? And yet, how could she respond without lying completely?

"To be honest, it would be a lot more enjoyable if I had a job. We'll be out of money soon." She had just handed Ringa another eighteen dollars for their fifth week of rent. The tea set money was gone, and Henry was paying for them now. He kept saying he was certain something would turn up, but it was all starting to feel pretty dire.

Carter nodded and squinted in thought. "I can probably get you a little work as an extra."

"Really?" Irene felt her body surge with real hope for the first time in weeks. "Because we'll take anything you've got."

He frowned. "Except the next picture I'm working on is *Lewis and Clark*, and either you're Sacagawea or you're out of luck. They've already got Betty Blythe lined up for the role, so it'll be at least a month or two before anything new comes up."

A MONTH OR TWO? she wanted to scream. Why had he even bothered to mention it?

Her feet were cold, and she began to wonder if maybe there was a burlesque house around that she could look into. Just for the short term, she told herself. Just till something better came along. Of course, there was always that dance hall Ringa's brother owned, but Irene suspected there was more to it than that. The girls who worked there came back looking dead-eyed—and occasionally unaccountably bruised.

"Can you type?" Carter said suddenly.

"Type?"

"Yeah, you know." He wiggled his fingers out in front of him.

Her aunt was a secretary and owned her own typewriter, an outrageous luxury. She used it for practice, claiming that girls who could type over a hundred words per minute got all the jobs. She had often let Irene and Ivy practice and given them simple drills to do.

"I can type," said Irene.

"Maybe there's a spot in the scenario department. Most of the writers do their work in longhand at home. Then they send them in to have them typed up properly."

"How much does it pay?"

"Not much, probably, but it'll be a raise from what you're getting now."

"Which is nothing."

"Exactly."

They stood there in the water, and Irene asked every question she could think of about the scenario department, the writers, how the scenarios got from one place to the next, who was in charge, and the like. Soon the waves were only lapping at their toes.

Then she saw Millie.

Irene had the strange sensation of having been punched in the stomach, all the air out of her, none coming in. She began to walk toward Millie, and the things she hadn't quite noticed but had somehow sensed now came into sharper focus. Hair disheveled. Dress askew. And where were her shoes?

Millie was saying something, her lips moving but not much sound coming out. At a few paces away, the word became clear. "Irene," she whimpered. "Irene."

Irene grabbed her by the shoulders, and Millie leaned into her. "What happened?"

"Just get me home."

Irene looked at Carter. He looked away.

"Carter," said Irene firmly.

"Where is he?" Carter asked Millie.

"He was in no hurry. He already got what he wanted." To Irene she said, "Do we have cab fare?"

Irene drilled Carter with a look. "No, we do not."

Carter shook his head and muttered something to himself, but Irene could make it out. *Dumb bastard.* She wondered if he meant Wally or himself for agreeing to go along on this miserable evening to begin with.

"Come on," he said and started up the beach.

The ride back to Ringa's was silent. Irene sat in back with Millie, who curled herself against Irene as if the car were Antarctica and Irene was the only warm blanket for miles. When they got there, Millie began to make her way slowly up the walkway.

Irene went around to the driver's-side window. "Thanks," she said.

Carter shrugged. "Least I could do, I guess."

"I'll be in tomorrow first thing. You'll take me to the scenario department, right?"

He nodded, gazing back at her, and she could tell he wanted to kiss her. After everything he'd just seen. Millie all a mess. His friend, who wasn't really a friend, left behind. The whole night gone to hell, and he still wanted to kiss her.

But she needed that job—any job—and she knew he was the one who might be able to help her get it. And so she leaned in.

He pulled back, which surprised her.

"I don't kiss girls who don't want to kiss me back." He put the car in gear. "We're not all Wally." Irene stepped back onto the curb, and he pulled away.

Millie was sitting on the front step. "I can't go in just yet. I need a minute."

"Was it . . . was it your first time?"

"No. But I never . . . I mean . . . no one ever, you know . . . hurt me like that."

"Sometimes they get a little . . . in a hurry." Irene's experience was limited to the occasional boy she'd flirted with and kissed during her time on the road with her sister. But shows only lasted a week before they moved on to the next town and the next new bill of performers, so none of it had ever gotten too serious. She'd been petted and pawed and done a little exploring of the male form herself, but that was as far as she'd gone.

"This wasn't just in a hurry, Irene." Millie's chin quivered and a tear rolled down her face. "He . . . he pinned me down."

An image of sweet little Millie struggling under the weight of that stupid oaf came to Irene, and she thought she might be sick. She wanted it to go away, to un-see it. She wanted the whole night to go away and wished Millie had never accepted the invitation to dinner to begin with. Hadn't Irene warned her? Hadn't she said this was just the kind of thing that could happen? She'd always heard it was the girl's fault, that she must have been a "bad girl" and was asking for it in some way.

But Irene knew Millie. And going off with Wally might not have been the brightest idea, but there was nothing about her that was "bad." Irene herself had once sat on a hay bale in an empty barn and let a boy put his hands under her blouse. But when his fingers had roamed southward, and she'd whispered, "Okay, that's enough," he'd stopped. He hadn't pinned her down and torn her dress and forced his manhood into places it wasn't welcome.

He'd stopped.

Wally hadn't. And that wasn't anyone's fault but his own.

◇　◇　◇

The next morning Millie didn't get up. "I ache all over," she said.

"Are you sick?"

Millie didn't answer for a moment. "No, Irene," she said slowly, as if Irene were from another country and might have trouble translating the words. "I'm sore."

That punched-in-the-stomach feeling hit Irene again, and she didn't know whether to lie back down on the bed and put her arms around Millie or pick up the wash basin and throw it against the wall. *That bastard.*

The other girls in the room buzzed around like gnats, sidling between the three beds that left only knee-width aisles to get to the door. She wanted to scream at them all to go—*scram, for chrissake*—so she could talk to Millie.

"I'm going to the studio and I'm getting a job," she said. "No, *two* jobs, one for each of us. And then we're getting out of here."

Millie gazed up at her, and tears formed in her eyes. "I'm so sorry," she whispered.

"For what?"

"For letting this happen. For making you mad."

Irene sat back down on the bed and took Millie's hand. "I'm not mad."

"Yes, you are."

"I'm mad at him for doing this to you!"

"I'm sorry you have to be mad about anything. Or upset. Or, you know, kind of sick-feeling."

How does she always know? thought Irene.

"This was not your fault, Millie."

"You don't think so?"

"I know it for a fact. He had no right—no right at all." She could feel her fury coming to a boil again and had to will herself to stay calm. "And there's something else I know: we're in this together." She squeezed Millie's hand. "You get hurt; I feel sick. That's how it is with friends."

Millie began to cry in earnest now. "You won't leave me?" she whispered.

Irene cupped Millie's cheek and gently brushed at the hot tears with her thumb. "I won't leave you."

◇ ◇ ◇

As Irene strode down Sunset Boulevard, she told herself she had a task to complete, with no room for weakness. She tried not to think—about anything—but certainly not about Millie, so beaten down she couldn't get out of bed. Or about her own sister, in another bed, unable to rise for a very different reason. It had been three years now, but Ivy's face, even paler than Millie's, was carved into Irene's memory like a scar. And it had been all her fault.

◇ ◇ ◇

At the studio gate, Irene squared herself to face the tasks at hand. She found Carter relatively quickly.

"She okay?" he asked.

"No," Irene said. "But she will be. And we both need jobs."

He took her to a two-story building with a plain wooden sign that said SCENARIO DEPARTMENT, up the stairs, down the hall, to a room tightly packed with eight tiny desks the size of sewing machine tables. In fact, they were *actual* sewing machine tables, which Irene realized when she looked down and saw the foot treadles. On top were stacks of paper and identical Corona No. 3 typewriters in various states of wear.

"Why isn't anyone here?" asked Irene.

"It's only seven-forty-five," said Carter.

"I'm used to getting here early to claim a seat on the benches."

"It's a little more civilized up here. But not much. Miss Clemente runs the place, and she . . . well, she should be in anytime now."

"Where are you going?"

"Back to work—I can't stand around here all day."

"What happened to you getting me a job! Should I tell her you sent me, at least?"

"Aw, she probably doesn't even know who I am." Carter frowned. "Tell her . . . tell her Eva Crown sent you. She makes more work in here than anyone." He began to inch away, then turned and walked quickly for the door.

"Carter!" But he was already halfway down the stairs. Irene looked around. The walls were bare, the plaster chipped, and there was only one window. *I'll bet they fight to sit by it.*

It occurred to her that there might be some sort of speed test, and she hadn't put her fingers anywhere near a typewriter in years. She sat down at the sewing table by the window, rolled some paper in, and closed her eyes. She typed a song she and her sister used to sing, about a little girl praying for her father in the Great War.

> *O kindly tell my daddy that he must take care.*
> *That's a baby's prayer at twilight for her daddy, "over there."*

Suddenly Irene could hear her sister singing the harmony, high and sweet, and her fingers froze on the keys. It had been a long time since she'd heard that voice so clearly. She clenched her eyes shut, wanting it to go on, but then a door opened and the fragile memory disappeared into the air like a breath.

"May I help you?"

Irene opened her eyes. Standing before her was an older woman in a brown dress that hung off her thin frame like it was meant for someone two sizes larger. She had short brown hair, small brown eyes, and skin that appeared to have suffered a ravaging case of chicken pox. Irene hopped up quickly. The strap of her

16

◇ ◇ ◇

Benzedrine and marijuana are as accessible as gumdrops.
Frances Marion, writer, actress, director, producer

Millie tried not to think about it, but her thoughts seemed to fly back to the previous night no matter what she did. Eventually she gave up, and the images flooded her. Wally wrestling her onto her back, wrenching her arms above her head, the wooden spines of the wicker furniture digging into her hips and shoulders, every muscle in her body straining to resist him.

Why? she kept wondering. *Why would he force me? How could that possibly feel good to him?*

The loveliest part of wanting to touch someone was them wanting to be touched, the happiness you brought them. Wally hadn't cared about her happiness. He hadn't even cared about her terror and pain. Millie understood there was evil in the world, that people could be cruel. People had been cruel to her—Miss Twickenham and her switch, Chandler and his threats, and even her own parents. But she'd never known anyone who'd clearly and shamelessly enjoyed it.

Things had sometimes gone badly for her—*Oh, let's face it,* she thought, *they've almost always gone badly.* But until last night she'd never doubted that her luck would turn, that the world was a good place, and happy times awaited. Now, in the face of such evil, the worst not only seemed possible . . . it seemed probable.

The hours passed, and she missed Irene so much. Irene would make her think about something else. Irene would be the brick wall around her when she went down to dinner at that long table Ringa had, with all the girls eyeing each other and trying to get more than their share.

The light was fading, and Millie told herself to hang on. Hang on till Irene came. There was an ache in her stomach, and she couldn't tell if it was hunger or just more of the pain that seemed to throb right through her bones. She had lain there all day waiting, hadn't had a morsel.

The doorknob turned, and Millie sat up. She didn't want Irene to think she'd lain like a weakling in that same curled-up position all day long. Which she had. But she didn't want Irene to know, because Irene wouldn't have, and she wanted to be more like Irene. She promised herself she would be. She would flirt less and complain less and not be so . . . so . . . like herself.

"Day off?" sneered Agnes.

Not Irene.

Disappointment dropped on Millie like a baby grand, and she suddenly had the wild thought that jumping out that window—Agnes's window—might not be so bad. She shifted in the bed and winched at the pain in her hip.

Agnes eyed her. "What's wrong with you?"

Irene's sharp mind would have come up with a retort right quick, but Millie's brain was exhausted from trying to fight off Wally over and over again all day long. "Nothing."

Agnes leaned against the dresser. "How was your date?" She hit the last word as if it were a childish notion, like a unicorn.

What would Irene say?

costumes on the only chair in the room, depositing them into a crumpled heap on the floor beside the bed.

"I was going to suggest we get a cup of coffee in the dining room. Why don't I meet you down there?"

"Oh, yes, that would be much . . . more . . . that would be better."

Because for one thing I could be properly attired, instead of looking like the morning after a hell of a night.

As soon as Oberhouser closed the door behind him, Henry was exchanging his shirt for a fresh one, rooting around in his case for his nicest tie and cleanest socks, applying an extra dollop of pomade to his black hair, and generally fussing like a girl about to go on a blind date.

Get ahold of yourself, man! He cinched his tie just a little tighter, squared his shoulders, and smiled into the mirror. It was all wrong. He looked like a phony, like some greased-up pretty boy with no substance. But then inspiration came to him: *zayde. All-business.*

He stopped smiling, let his shoulders go loose. Whatever the director wanted, Henry vowed he would not say yes immediately. He would play just a little bit hard to get, which was as close an approximation to actually *being* hard to get as he could manage under the circumstances.

In the smaller dining room, Oberhouser sat on the far side of the horseshoe-shaped counter, legs crossed casually, coffee cup in hand, deep in thought. As Henry crossed the room toward him, he had a moment to study the man. Slightly receding hairline, but no gray at the temples of his sandy brown hair. Likely in his mid-thirties, about a decade ahead of Henry. Intelligent hazel eyes, aquiline nose—the face of a man who was happy with himself, but without the air of conceit Henry was beginning to notice on so many at the studio. True, it was an accomplishment even to be employed by a reasonably respected company—Olympic was no Poverty Row operation, as so many of them were. Nor did it have the industry power of a Famous Players-Lasky. But Oberhouser had so far been given the freedom to do as he liked, and his films were both commercially successful and artistically admired. He had more right than most to be pleased with what he'd achieved.

He broke from his ruminations as Henry approached, gave a smile and a nod to the chair next to him, and raised a finger to hail the Harvey girl. Henry wondered if he'd ever made an inelegant gesture in his life.

The Harvey girl poured his coffee, and Henry decided to take it without cream for a change. Black coffee was so much more . . . tough. Businesslike. *Zayde*-like.

He took a sip, burned the tip of his tongue, and nearly dropped the cup. Oberhouser politely pretended not to notice, but Henry saw the slightest crinkle around those hazel eyes.

"So, Henry. I have a proposition for you, one which will likely make Albert steaming mad, but it can't be helped. I'd like you to continue as an extra for the rest of the picture. Actually, as the queen's head guard, you'd be a bit more than an extra, but as a player with no name, an extra is what you're called. However, there'll be more than the usual five dollars a day in it for you. Twice as much, in fact. How does that sound?"

"Well, it sounds very nice," said Henry, trying so hard not to laugh and slap his thigh in excitement that a little sweat broke out on his back. "But I have to ask . . . I mean, it would be foolhardy of me not to think of . . . After the filming is over—what then?"

Oberhouser nodded. "Albert clearly needs you, and if he loses you for a month, he's going to want to hire someone else."

Henry's good spirits deflated. "It's just that, well, I'm new here, and I need the work. I have to consider the long term." That last line was very *zayde*-like. At least there was that.

Oberhouser uncrossed his legs and leaned a little closer. Henry could smell the sharp, clean scent of his aftershave. "Eva's very keen on you. She's particular about who brings her stories to life, and we both felt you added a sort of gravity to the scenes you did for us yesterday." He looked around and then chuckled to himself. "I really shouldn't say anything at this point, and of course there are no guarantees, but as long as everything goes well during *Sheba*, we'd like to screen test you for a bigger role in our next picture."

18

There's a little bit of vampire instinct in every woman.
Theda Bara, actress, writer, famous "vamp"

At lunchtime, Irene double-stepped down the stairs and out across the studio yard. She had only twenty minutes, after all, to accomplish a great deal. First she had to track down Wally.

He wasn't hard to find, smoking a badly rolled cigarette and leaning up against the edge of a set made to look like a saloon. There were several other men there, too, a couple of them made up as cowboys, and one Indian with black hair to his shoulders and a colorful piece of cloth tied as a headband. It was the man from the benches, the one who hadn't worn his costume to avoid offending anyone. He'd certainly been right about it being rather brief, revealing sinewy thighs and calves, his bare chest lean and muscular. He'd had short hair when she'd first seen him, so this was apparently a wig.

Dan Russell. She was surprised his name came back to her so easily, considering they'd never spoken a word to each other.

Wally was nattering away, and none of them seemed all that interested. Irene had a thought that she could walk up and punch him in that gargoyle's smile of his, and no one would lift a finger to stop her.

"Wally."

His head jerked up at the grit in her voice, and he threw his cigarette down as if he'd been caught with contraband.

He eyed her warily. "Yeah?"

"Can I speak to you a moment?"

He shrugged and made no move toward her. But the others moved away, wandering off as if they'd suddenly remembered they had far better things to do. Dan Russell gave her the briefest look, his dark eyes serious, before heading off.

"What do you want?"

I want you to die a prolonged and painful death. "I want you to recommend Millie for a job at the studio somewhere. Get someone to hire her as an extra."

He spread his stance a little wider and said, "And why would I do that?"

"Because you told her you would."

"I never said that, and besides, why would I help her? She left me hanging for cab fare on the edge of the goddamned ocean. You all did. I don't even know why I'm talking to you."

Cab fare. Every demon Irene had (and she had a few) rose up inside her, screeching behind her eyes and steaming behind her fists.

"You know why." Her voice sounded blackened.

"All I know is I'm out a buck twenty-five. I'll tell you what. You pay me back, and I'll think about it." He puffed out his chest like a vulture warding off other animals from its prey. "And that's a damn good deal, I don't mind saying. Lots of girls would pay a buck and a quarter to get hired. A lot more than that, too."

With that he stuck out his hand palm up.

Irene's eyes went wild with astonished rage. Suddenly all she could think of was causing him pain. A punch in the face wouldn't be a tenth of the agony he'd caused Millie, but it was a start. Her fist cocked back and she couldn't wait to see it land on that smug grin.

"You wanna hit me?" he snarled. "Go ahead. I'll have you thrown off the lot so fast and so far, you'll land right back on that beach. Then I'll smear your name to every studio in town."

She hesitated. She'd lose her job and that nineteen-dollar pay-check.

In the moment it took her to consider, he turned and stalked away from her. She had wanted so badly, *so badly*, to hit him, or grab him by the back of his crookedly cut hair, yank him to the ground, and kick his ribs till every last one of them broke.

But she didn't. She couldn't risk the consequences. And now he would never pay for what he'd done. He'd gotten off scot-free, because how could she ever exact any revenge at all? Lord knows she couldn't tell anyone—it wasn't something people spoke of. And if they did, it would be to cluck their tongues about how stupid Millie had been.

She watched him walk away, and she hoped somewhere deep down, he felt bad. Maybe he didn't have nightmares about it, as Millie certainly did—Irene had heard her crying out in her sleep. But nevertheless she hoped his actions haunted him.

He walked up to the men he'd been smoking with before and began to talk; she could see his head moving and his hands gesturing.

He's bragging.

She had to be wrong—how could anyone brag about being that cruel? About overpowering someone so much smaller and forcing her to do something that normal men would never make a woman do against her will.

Then he hooked a thumb toward her, and she knew her instinct had been right. He was telling them how this dumb dame thought she could get something out of him because he'd had his way with her ditzy friend.

In unison, the men glanced over at her, and the rage that filled her made her heart crash inside her chest like a train wreck and her vision blur. But she could see one thing. She saw Dan Russell walk away.

◇ ◇ ◇

"Powder room," said Miss Clemente at exactly three o'clock. Every girl raised her hand, so Irene did, too. One by one they were excused to freshen up.

Irene had spent the last two and a half hours addled by fury and typing a mistake into every fourth word. When it was her turn to go, she passed right by the powder room and hurried to Costume, hoping desperately that Henry hadn't been called out to some distant set for repairs.

Fortunately he was there. Unfortunately he was being summarily fired by Albert Leroux.

"I gave you a chance when you came in here all rumpled like a vagabond! I trained you and let you have your precious *lunch break*, and this is my thanks?"

"Albert, you've been wonderful to me—"

"So wonderful you treat me like some worn-out shirt you toss in the rag heap! You come here straight from the station—from Obie's personal train car, I imagine—and the first thing from your lips is that you're leaving me for greener pastures!"

"You have to understand—"

"No, I most certainly do *not* have to understand. I *don't* and I *won't*!"

Irene waited, but the conversation was going nowhere, and she wasn't going to jeopardize her hours-old job so some strange little man could vent his spleen on Henry. And why was he suddenly quitting, anyway? She knocked and peeked her head in the door. "Pardon me."

"Irene!"

"And who's this?" demanded Albert.

"A friend," Henry answered quickly. "Is everything all right?" His back to Albert, he gave her a meaningful glare, cutting his eyes back toward the irate little tailor.

"Well, no, it actually isn't." At least she was being truthful.

He took her elbow and guided her out of the room, saying "What's the trouble?" loud enough for Albert to hear. When they were down the hall, he let her go and grinned.

"You saved my bacon! I thought he'd never stop."

"Look, I only have a few minutes, so I just wanted to let you know I'm working in the scenario typing pool, and that's why you won't find me out on the benches."

"That's wonderful! How'd you land that? Millie will miss you something terrible. Is she out there now?"

Irene hesitated. She would have given her right arm to unburden herself and tell Henry the whole sordid story. But there were no words for a woman to tell a man such a thing; there were barely words to tell another woman. "She's back at Ringa's. She wasn't feeling herself."

"Well I hope she's better by dinnertime, because I'm taking us all out. I got a job as an extra, and they might want to screen test me!"

"Henry, that's wonderful! I can see why Albert was losing his marbles."

"Albert's always losing his marbles. Say, can Millie sew? Maybe she could take my job."

"I don't think that was the type of thing she learned to do in her family." Irene patted his arm. "I'm really so happy for you."

Henry's smile was a tad sheepish, as if he'd just gotten praise from a teacher. "And I'm happy for you, too. How'd you land the typing pool?"

"Someone I met. I sort of pried it out of him."

"Of course you did," said Henry. "Smart girl!"

Not that smart, she thought. *Not smart enough to make that bastard pay. Yet.*

When Irene made it back to Ringa's at six o'clock, Millie was dozing. Irene didn't like this. Millie needed to pull herself together, not indulge in late afternoon naps. Besides, Henry would be waiting for them.

"I'm tired," said Millie. "And I'm not hungry anymore."

"Where did you get food? Ringa only started laying out dinner a few minutes ago."

"I didn't. I was hungry for a while, and then I just wasn't." She pulled the blanket up to her chin. "Besides, I don't want to see Henry."

Not hungry. The back of Irene's neck prickled.

"Why not?" she said, attempting an offhanded tone. "You adore Henry. It'll be good for you to get out of here and be a little bit happy."

Millie just stared at her, an empty look that worried Irene even more.

She tried another tack. "What have you been doing all day?"

"Agnes came back—"

"Agnes. She's trouble."

"No, she was nice, and—"

"Agnes was nice," Irene scoffed.

"She actually was for once, and—"

"Millie, please get up. I really think you need a decent meal and to get out of this bed."

"I don't want to see Henry."

"For goodness' sake, why not?

"Because he'll know."

Irene sat down on the bed. "He won't know."

"He might. I'm not myself."

"I already told him you stayed home because you weren't feeling right."

"And how," muttered Millie.

Irene took Millie's hand, and Millie clung to it. "Please come. Henry's got some good news and he'll be so disappointed if you're not there."

Millie let go of her hand. "Tell him I'm sorry. And maybe tomorrow."

◇ ◇ ◇

The Musso & Frank Grill, with its mahogany paneled walls and leather banquette booths, was too swank for Irene's outfit. She told herself she'd get a new dress with her first paycheck. Or maybe she'd get Millie the dress. That would cheer her up. Then she remembered her paycheck would only cover their rent with a dollar to spare. The luxury of splitting a sandwich at lunch would have to do for a celebration.

"Miss?" said the maître d, clearly unimpressed.

"I'm meeting someone here."

"The bar is in the other room."

The bar. Of course. Because she didn't look like she could afford drinks *and* food. Or that she could date a man who might be willing to spring for both.

She stepped into the side room and immediately heard her

so it's not high living or anything, but it's clean and safe, and the rent is only ten dollars and fifty cents a week. You should apply."

Irene had heard about it when they'd looked around for other living arrangements. It was a dollar and a half more than they were paying now, and multiplied by the two of them, three dollars a week would make them go broke even faster, so she'd decided against pursuing it. But she had a job now, and she was starting to get a very bad feeling about Ringa's—even worse than when she'd walked in the door. Maybe safety was worth continuing to borrow a little more from Henry. "I'll try and stop by this weekend and see if they could take us," she said.

Gert leveled a look at her. "Or tomorrow morning. The house director's up early."

19

◇ ◇ ◇

*I'm a very strong person. I don't know if you know
that or not, but take a look at my chin.*
Gloria Swanson, actress, producer

Millie wasn't awake when Irene came in that night, nor when she left the next morning. But she'd been awake for a long time in between, her thoughts roaming wildly through the solitary darkness, with Irene asleep beside her.

She tried to call up what had made her happy, what she'd dreamed about before she'd come to this terrible town. Back in school the girls had all wanted to get married, pining for someone handsome, rich (always handsome and rich), and hopefully kind, to rescue them from the shame, poverty, and boredom of spinsterhood. But that wasn't Millie's goal, not remotely.

She'd dreamed about riding her horse Calliope at breakneck speed, wind buffeting her face and limbs, thighs hugging tight to the animal's sleek coat, feeling the impossibly powerful muscles clenching beneath her. She'd thought about exploring the sensual pleasures offered by the stable boy in the hayloft afterward, the horsey smell of him, the way his calloused hands could be so gentle. But never about walking down the aisle with him. Or anyone else.

And if you weren't the marrying type, what exactly were you?

A "new woman," educated and unmarried, with enough money to comfortably make your way in the world with no man in sight? That didn't seem to fit, either. For all her wealthy upbringing, Millie wasn't terribly well educated, unless you counted all the different kinds of forks there were and what they were used for, depending on the meal, season, and how upper crust your guests might be. Nor did she (or Irene) have nearly enough money to qualify. Besides, she didn't want to live a life devoid of men. She liked men. Or some of them, anyway.

Wally on top of her flashed into her mind, as it did about every other minute it seemed, and she fought against it as she always did. But this time she tried something different. She replaced it. She thought of all the times she'd canoodled—or more—with various nice men she'd come across. She thought of the stable boy; his smell, his hands.

And when that stopped working, she thought about heroin. Because that felt good, too.

Very, very good.

◊ ◊ ◊

"You're a grubber, you know that?" said Agnes.

"Just one more time. I promise I won't ask again."

"Even if I felt like sharing—which I don't—I only have one, and that's for me."

"But I'm in pain."

"You're not in that much pain, not a day and a half later. Take an aspirin and shove off."

Millie didn't know how much a vial of heroin cost, but it was more than she had, which was nothing. Irene kept all their money in her purse, which never left her side. She didn't trust leaving it at Ringa's. Irene was smart like that.

Agnes had a bruise on her thigh. Millie saw it briefly when Agnes took off her dress and her slip rode up her legs for a moment. It was made up of four darker spots the size of quarters. Or big fingers.

Millie had a similar constellation on her own leg, so she knew there was a corresponding single thumb-size mark on Agnes's inner thigh. Agnes sat down on her bed with a thump and rooted in her purse for the little tin box.

Millie got up and tugged on a dress as fast as she could. She needed to get away from Agnes and the tin box and the glaring reminder of her own injuries.

◇ ◇ ◇

She hurried along Hollywood Boulevard with a strange sense of being chased—by what she wasn't exactly sure. Agnes and her bruises? Eventually she stopped to catch her breath outside a restaurant, and the smell of something rich and meaty curled around her. Food. It had been a long time since she'd eaten anything substantial.

There was a trick she'd learned in Chandler's Follies, when the half sandwich and cup of broth he'd let them have didn't fill her stomach even to the halfway mark. She'd pretend she was going to the powder room and go out behind the diner instead. In the trash cans, she often found the remnants of a meal that some lucky son of a gun had been too full to finish.

Millie snuck down the side street and around to the alley in back. Sure enough she found a half of a Reuben sandwich with only a bite or two taken out of it. She ate as if she had been shipwrecked for days, which in a strange way she had been. Shipwrecked on an island of pain and shame.

She polished off the Reuben and picked carefully through the trash to find a meatball, then a wad of some sort of noodle dish. She didn't recognize the flavors and didn't care. There was even a whole piece of chocolate cake!

As she licked the icing from her lips, wishing there was something to drink, she noticed a door opening down the alley. A young man in a uniform with big brass buttons and epaulets—a bellhop? No, a theater usher. He'd come out for a cigarette break.

Millie brushed the cake crumbs from her fingers and walked over. He watched her approach, cigarette frozen in his fingers. She realized he'd been holding his breath when he suddenly exhaled a stream of smoke and then coughed until his eyes watered, all the while keeping her in his sights. She had that effect sometimes. She was used to it.

"Hi there, fella," she said brightly as she approached.

"Hello, miss." He was no more than sixteen, she guessed.

"I've got a little problem, and I'm wondering if you might be able to help a girl out."

His eyebrows went up and he nodded.

"I bought a ticket for the show, but the wind blew it right out of my hand!" There was no accounting for the fact that the air hung so heavy and motionless it must have been hard for birds to stay aloft. The boy nodded again, the flush in his cheeks growing bright as radishes.

"Would it be all right if I just entered through this door, here? That way there won't be any fuss about the ticket, and it will put everything to rights."

He stepped aside and held the door open for her.

"So sweet of you," she murmured as she passed him. "Would you like to show me to my seat?" Of course he would; he had his little flashlight out in no time.

She snuggled down into a soft leather seat of what turned out to be the Iris Theatre. The newsreel was already rolling, a gaggle of older women in long skirts and high-neck blouses crowding around a minister. The title cards said he was railing about the debauched morals of the film industry, and Millie thought it was a pretty funny thing to show in a movie house, right before a movie.

Soon enough, the real entertainment began. *The Great Moment* was about a young girl whose rich American father wanted to marry her off before she became too much like her gypsy mother. The girl was played by Gloria Swanson, who was as sultry as ever in her spangly, scant gypsy costume. With her black hair and pale blue eyes, people had sometimes commented that Millie was a ringer for the starlet.

Gloria Swanson. She was probably only a few years older than Millie. And look at her now. Rich and glamorous and starring in just the kinds of movies the old minister and his biddies had been complaining about. An article in *Photoplay* magazine hinted at a rebellious lifestyle and possible assignations with her leading men.

We've got that in common, too, thought Millie. Hadn't her parents complained constantly about her rebelliousness? And there had certainly been an assignation or two.

But the similarities stopped there. Gloria was in full control of her life, with the money and power to do as she pleased. Millie's best meal in weeks had been from a garbage can.

As she sat in that theater with a full belly, watching her near twin on the screen, Millie's spirits plummeted with the thought that she might never have a better day than this.

20

◇ ◇ ◇

Give me any two pages of the Bible and I'll give you a picture.

Cecil B. DeMille, Oscar-winning director, producer, editor

Henry bumped along in the truck with the rest of the extras up through the Cahuenga Pass, smirking privately to himself. Hollywood prided itself in being so urbane—the latest fashions, fanciest cars, wildest parties—as if it were just a half step behind New York City. And yet here they were, just a mile or so from Hollywood Boulevard, and they might as well have been on some minor mountain in the unpopulated wilds of Wyoming.

They were headed to the Back Ranch, as it was called by the studio. The downtown Hollywood lot was used mostly for indoor scenes or small capacity exteriors, and of course it held Olympic's headquarters, the Scenario Department, and the like. The Back Ranch held everything else.

The land had only recently been acquired by Olympic and was in a far more rustic state than its city counterpart. It was also vastly larger. The high brick walls in the process of being built around it were filled in by huge lengths of canvas in some places. There was a main building that acted as a business office outpost of the city lot. Nearby stood a huge open-air shelter, the roof held up by rough-cut posts, and wooden picnic tables where the extras sat in the shade awaiting their scenes.

Henry walked slowly, keeping an eye out for Gert Turner, and soon found himself at the far side of the shelter. From there he could survey a good portion of the lot. There was a stand of pines next to a lovely (if strangely symmetrical) pond. Nearby was the facade of a quaint little village that could be used for anything from medieval times, to a Swiss hamlet, to revolutionary Boston. It was propped up from behind by angled boards, and several of the extras lollygagged and smoked in the shade it threw. There was a city block with storefronts and a variety of vehicles: Model Ts and roadsters and delivery trucks. Farther out there was an arena that Henry thought might be for horse or car races. At the far end was a hill with trees and outcroppings, perfect for any number of western scenarios. Beyond that, who knew? Henry hoped at some point he'd get a chance to explore.

Right in front of him was a long stage of maybe a hundred feet, cut up into five three-sided compartments, a different scene in each. Along the top lay lengths of muslin to diffuse the unrelenting California sun as it lit the scenes below. Several of the sets were in use at the moment, and he could see a woman dressed in rags rocking a baby; a fancy parlor where the smartly dressed leading man and lady were engaged in some sort of quarrel; a bootleggers' backroom card game; and a doctor's office where the young patient kept accidentally kicking the poor physician.

Soon the call came to head out to the palace set, and as he climbed onto what was basically a hay cart with ten other extras, Henry found Gert.

"Where's your makeup?" she asked. On her lap sat a little metal box with a latch on it.

Henry's stomach sank. "Am I supposed to have my own? The makeup girl pasted me up in Barstow."

"They probably knew the tailor didn't come with his own greasepaint." She chuckled. "Though in Hollywood, there'd be stranger things than a man with makeup." She patted his arm. "Don't worry, I'll share."

"Why are you so nice to me?" he teased.

"Your uncle gave me great advice." She affected a gruff tone. "It's like war! A soldier helps another soldier; a vaudevillian helps another vaudevillian! Don't make *tsuris*—this life is hard enough!'"

Henry laughed. "Don't make problems. Words to live by."

"I try. I don't always *succeed*. But I try."

They were let out near a remarkable structure. Henry had never seen an actual Israeli king's palace, of course, but if he had, he was sure it would look just like this. Massive stone columns (upon closer look they were cement plastered over plywood) framed an enormous wooden door that was pincushioned with large brass studs.

Gert helped Henry spread the brown greasepaint all over his face, chest, and back as they watched Edward Oberhouser, Eva Crown, and Wilson Grimes argue about the angles and heights of the cameras, snatches of their conversations audible above the buzz of the crew and cast.

"When we laid this all out last week, you said—"

"Yes, but there's a bit of a haze today, so we can't shoot it from here if we want to—"

"But if we don't see his face, it will be as if he were just another extra."

Henry murmured to Gert, "Why don't they just get started and see how it turns out?"

"Oh, they will. You'll be sick and tired of how often they do it.

But they have to waste time now getting it mostly right so they don't waste everyone's time for days getting it mostly wrong—and waste lots of money into the bargain."

There were tables and a makeshift canopy for shade, and one of the extras had brought a deck of cards. Several others had brought books, and one enterprising young lady had brought her knitting. There were separate tents for Betty Blythe and Fritz Leiber, into which they quickly disappeared, and Henry wondered just how rustic the accommodations actually were when he heard a Victrola being cranked.

> *Every morning, every evening, ain't we got fun?*
> *Not much money, oh, but honey, ain't we got fun?*
> *The rent's unpaid, dear, and we haven't a bus*
> *But smiles were made, dear, for people like us*

Not much money, thought Henry, gazing at those two well-equipped tents. *Boy, is that playing in the wrong place.*

A couple of the extras got up and turkey-trotted around in the dusty encampment, and everyone laughed. Henry was more interested in the ongoing discussion-verging-on-argument continuing by the camera. He casually strolled a little closer. Eva Crown argued for shots that supported the storyline, while Wilson Grimes insisted they couldn't get it from this or that angle. Edward Oberhouser listened carefully to each, playing King Solomon far better than Fritz Leiber in Henry's estimation, as he conceded points to each in approximately equal measure.

After an hour or more of discussion and repositioning of cameras from here to there and back again, the extras were called. Makeup and costumes had to be checked by the continuity clerk to make sure they all looked exactly as they had in Barstow. When every last hair was in place, both literally and cinematically, Betty

Blythe and Fritz Leiber were roused from their tents, only to find that Betty had one less string of pearls around her long pale neck, and there was a scramble to find them.

At long last everyone was ready. The queen and her entourage—Henry, the other two chariot drivers, and Gert as one of eight handmaidens—were to process up to the door and await King Solomon. When the great door opened, all would bow down to His Highness, except for the queen, who would deliver an appropriately deferential-yet-regal curtsy.

There was a problem with the curtsy, however. At first it wasn't deferential enough, with Betty merely tapping the toe of one foot behind the other. Then a bit too submissive, as she bowed low to the great king, breasts swinging tantalizingly into midair.

"That works," said Wilson, stifling a grin.

Eva Crown threw the scenario pages into the dirt and said, "Oh, for godsake, Edward!"

They started all over again.

Eventually they got that shot and moved to the next: King Solomon would welcome the Queen of Sheba and escort her into his palace.

"Ready! Camera! Action! Go!" called out Oberhouser. Then to Fritz Leiber, "You extend your arms to her . . . Cut!" Henry could feel, more than hear, a collective sigh of frustration from the extras nearest him.

"Now, Fritz, you aren't asking for a hug, old fellow," called Oberhouser. "You are offering a magnanimous gesture of welcome. More regal, less chummy, all right?"

He cued the cameras again. "Extending your arms . . . that's it, that's nice . . . now motion to the door, inviting her to enter . . . good, good . . . and you say something like . . . 'I, Solomon, King of Israel, welcome you to my palace, where I shall entertain you!"

Fritz Leiber began this speech with great dignity, intoning, "I,

Solomon, King of Israel, welcome you to my palace . . . where I shall impregnate you!"

A loud, snorting laugh burst out of Henry so quickly, he hardly knew where it came from, eliciting snickers from the other two chariot drivers. This set off a cascade of giggles among the handmaidens, and soon the whole cast and most of the crew was doubled over in fits of laughter. Wilson Grimes furrowed his brow and fiddled with his camera, but his shoulders were clearly shaking. Even Miss Crown had a hand to her mouth to cover a smile.

Edward Oberhouser crossed his arms and waited for silence. When the last titter had dwindled, he addressed Henry. "Mr. Weiss, I intend for this film to come in on time and on budget, a difficult task if we have to waste precious minutes and film on unproductive takes."

Henry's cheeks burned with embarrassment. "I apologize, Mr. Oberhouser. It won't happen again." And it didn't, but the episode left Henry feeling bitter. Yes, he'd been the first to laugh, but everyone else except for the director could barely contain their amusement, too. Leiber's line—and even more so, his delivery—had been legitimately funny, especially since impregnating the Queen of Sheba is exactly what King Solomon ultimately did. And how much time and film had really been wasted anyway—a minute? A foot?

His thoughts simmered over the next hour, threatening to come to a boil once or twice, as the rest of the scenes were shot over and over, and the sun finally hit a point near the horizon that Wilson Grimes insisted that "if we shoot one more take, it'll look like an animated coal bin."

As the crew began to pack up the movable props and equipment and the cast prepared to leave, Oberhouser motioned Henry over. He put a hand on Henry's shoulder and leaned in. "Thanks for taking it on the chin back there," he murmured. "A director has to assert his authority where and when the opportunity presents itself, and I can't exactly dress down the leading man, now can I? The fellow's making more money than Hearst on this little flicker, and I'm not allowed to antagonize him." He chuckled. "I think not having his precious feelings hurt may actually be written into his contract."

Henry felt relief wash through him. "Thanks for letting me know. I felt terrible."

"You seemed more angry than ashamed. I thought you might bite someone!" the director said wryly. "Which, by the way, was exactly the look I wanted for the queen's head guard."

21

◇ ◇ ◇

If it isn't for the writing, we've got nothing. Writers are the most important people in Hollywood. And we must never let them know it.
Irving Thalberg, producer, writer, director

When Irene got back to Ringa's after work, Millie wasn't there, and Irene felt a pinprick of panic. "Where's Millie?" she demanded of the girls in their room as they got ready to go down to what passed for dinner. "Who's seen her?"

"Not me."

"I just got here."

"Who's Millie?"

Agnes, slumped against a headboard gazing out the window, didn't answer.

"Agnes, where's Millie?"

Agnes turned slowly toward Irene's voice. "Who?"

"For godsake, Agnes! Millie! You know her!"

Agnes recoiled. "Don't yell."

Irene huffed an aggravated sigh and tried to calm the bucking bronco in her chest. "Then answer me."

"She left. Long time ago, I think."

Irene stared at Agnes. The girl only seemed to be breathing a couple of times a minute, as if her body had lost the ability to automatically inhale and she had to remind herself to do it. There was a little tin next to her, and as Irene eyed her, Agnes slid it under her thigh.

Dope fiend, thought Irene. She'd seen it once or twice before in burlesque, though Chandler tended to throw out any girl he suspected of being on the stuff. Newspaper articles always made addicts sound sinister and dangerous. But Agnes just looked terribly broken.

We have to get out of here.

Just then Millie walked in, looking pale.

"Where've you been!"

"I went to the movies."

"The movies? How'd you get in? You don't have any money."

Millie shrugged. "Snuck in." Her gaze slid around the room, at all the girls looking at her, and came to rest on Agnes, and she smiled. As if she knew. *As if she were jealous.* Irene felt a chill hit her bones.

"Bring your coat downstairs with you. After dinner, we're going out."

The house at 6129 Carlos Avenue was imposing from the street, and Irene wondered if she had misheard Gert Turner about the ten-fifty a week. How could a room at this minor mansion cost so little? Wide marble steps led up to a deep front porch, with a similar-size balcony on the second floor. Four enormous carved pillars stood sentry across the house's facade, and the roof overhangs were decorated with rows of delicately scrolled brackets.

"It looks a little like my house," murmured Millie. "Or, I mean, my parents' house."

"It looks a little like my house, too," said Irene. "If you take off the top two floors, the porch, the pillars, and all the doodads. Then make it about a quarter of the size and wait for the paint to start peeling."

They rang the doorbell and were soon greeted by a woman who introduced herself as Marion Hunter, the director of the Studio Club. She appeared to be somewhere in her early thirties, with brown hair twisted into a braided bun at the nape of her neck. Irene thought this was strangely unfashionable for a place that had been set up to serve girls in the film industry, but Miss Hunter's face seemed kind, and this was far more important than her hairstyle.

"How can I help?" she asked as she escorted them into the front parlor. It was simply decorated for such a large room in an otherwise ornate house: a scattering of settees and chairs, the occasional table or standing lamp. Two young women were practicing making dramatic faces at each other in the oval mirror at the far end of the room. They glanced over at Miss Hunter and quietly left.

"We use this room for lessons, rehearsals, and little performances," Miss Hunter explained, "so we keep it sparsely furnished. More space for big entrances." She smiled, and Irene could imagine that young actresses might tend to err on the side of grand gestures. "Of course when we need a larger stage, our patronesses Miss Pickford or Mrs. DeMille can usually find something for us."

Mary Pickford, the world's greatest movie star, and Mrs. Cecil B. DeMille, wife of one of the most celebrated (and well-paid) directors. Irene suspected they had no trouble at all "finding" whatever they wanted, whenever they wanted it. With patronesses like that, the relatively low cost of Studio Club lodging suddenly made sense.

After a few more moments of small talk, with Irene's anxiety building all the while as to whether the club would save or reject them, she got down to brass tacks.

Miss Hunter hesitated. "We do have a vacancy. Very recent, in fact. Just an hour ago."

"Oh, that's such good news," said Irene, trying not to sigh audibly.

"Why did she leave?" asked Millie.

"She, um . . . well, she had a medical condition and had to return home."

Pregnant, thought Irene.

"I hope she gets better soon," said Millie.

Miss Hunter smiled. "That's very kind of you. I'm sure she will."

In about nine months, thought Irene.

"I wish I had better news," Miss Hunter went on, "but unfortunately I can't accommodate you both. There's only one bed available."

"Oh, well," said Millie, at the same time Irene said, "We'll take it."

Miss Hunter glanced from one girl to the other.

"We'll take the spot," Irene said with finality.

"Oh." Millie glanced away and laced her fingers tightly together. "Okay."

Irene opened her little pochette bag and took out eleven dollars from the money Henry had given her. "I don't have exact change."

Miss Hunter blinked and forced a smile. "Well, we'd like to get to know a little bit about you first. We don't accept anyone without an interview."

"Oh, I'm . . . I'm sorry," said Irene. "I suppose I beat the pistol on that, didn't I?"

"Which of you . . . ?"

"Millie. Mildred Martin. Ask her anything you like."

"Me?" Millie's head spun toward Irene, eyes glassy with unspilled tears.

"Of course, you," Irene murmured. "You didn't think I'd move in here and leave you at Ringa's, did you?"

"But I don't want you to have to stay in that awful place!"

"I'm gone all day at the typing pool. I promise, I won't even notice. Besides, I've stayed in plenty of worse places."

Millie reached out and gripped her hand. "I'd rather stay with you," she whispered.

"Absolutely not," Irene murmured. "If you're here, I can visit." She turned to Miss Hunter, who'd politely averted her gaze but had certainly heard the whole interchange. "I can, can't I?"

"Of course you can. Anytime you like, up until curfew at nine o'clock."

◇ ◇ ◇

When the interview was over and Irene had paid the first week's rent, they walked back to the boardinghouse in the fading light. "I suppose I can move in on the weekend," said Millie.

"Nothing doing. I don't want you hanging around Ringa's all day. That place is a modern-day Greek tragedy. You're going to the Studio Club first thing tomorrow morning."

"I wouldn't stay at Ringa's all day. I could walk around like I did today and maybe sneak into the flickers again."

"And what if you get caught?"

"I won't."

"You think you won't, because you always think things will turn out all right."

"And you always think they won't."

"I have a lot of experience with things not turning out, Millie. And so do you, if you'd just stop and consider for a minute. Maybe it'd keep you from doing the next dumb thing."

Millie didn't respond, only kept trudging along in step with Irene.

Irene stopped. "I'm sorry. That was an awful thing to say."

"I deserve it," murmured Millie, looking down at her shoes, ugly boots that were all she had to wear, after she'd dropped her t-strap pumps on the beach.

"No, you don't deserve it at all. I just . . ."

"Worry."

She always knows, thought Irene. Worry had been Irene's near-constant state, since . . . since she'd decided not to go home with her uncle? No, she hadn't really worried at all then. Hadn't cared enough to worry. When she became friends with Millie—that's when the worry had begun. "I'm trying to keep you safe."

Millie slid her hand into Irene's. "You're the best friend I ever had."

◇ ◇ ◇

That night as they lay in bed together, Millie curled a little closer and whispered, "Would it make you feel better if I got up in the morning with you and went back to the benches?"

"Are you sure you're ready for that?"

Irene could hear Millie's breath quicken. Finally she said, "Yes, I'm ready."

"I don't think he'll be there," said Irene. "He's already got a picture going; he won't be looking for extras."

"How do you know?"

"I saw him."

"What did you do?"

"I'll tell you what I *didn't* do," Irene muttered bitterly. "I didn't punch him in his ugly face."

Millie let out a little sound, and at first Irene thought it might be a sob. But then it happened again, and it was clearly stifled laughter. "Oh, Irene, let's pretend you did!"

◇ ◇ ◇

It was harder than Irene had thought to leave Millie sitting alone among the throngs of would-be extras. She looked smaller somehow, like a lost child waiting anxiously for her mother to find her. But Millie's mother wasn't coming. In fact, no one was coming for her, now that Irene had to hurry off to work.

"Here's fifteen cents." Irene pressed the coins into her hand. "At lunchtime, go out and get us a sandwich at the drugstore up the street, and I'll come down and eat it with you. I only get twenty minutes, but at least we can talk a little."

She was the last one in at the typing pool, though not more than three minutes late, and Miss Clemente raised an eyebrow. It was a small thing, but the woman knew how to give it impact, and Irene worried she might get sacked for even such a tiny infraction. She sat in the darkest, most airless corner, at the typewriter with the sticking *n* key and had to stop to pull the type hammer back down every time *and* (or any other word including the misbehaving letter) was called for. That eyebrow had been the least of her punishment for tardiness.

Naturally, with all the stopping and starting, she didn't get her work done nearly as efficiently as she usually did. But by the same token, now that she regularly had an extra second to absorb the meaning of the words, she found herself thinking about the stories themselves a little more deeply. The synopses were the easiest to read as she typed. They were usually only a couple of pages and were condensed versions of the stories. The continuity scripts, on the other hand, were much longer and laid out every scene in detail: location, props, costume, inter-titles of dialogue, camera angle, even the amount of film the cameraman could expect to use.

Irene plodded along with her sticky *n* all morning until she came to a handwritten page that was nearly indecipherable, and this slowed her down even more.

Behind Her Socks?

If it had been a comedy, this might have been humorous somehow, but as Irene typed the synopsis, it was clear there was no humor intended. It was a love story.

Theodora and her older sisters live in poverty on the coast of England, and their only hope of survival lies with Theodora marrying well. She's out rowing her little boat when she capsizes. This is seen by Lord Bracondale, a dashing and wealthy young nobleman who dives in and carries her to shore. Attraction sparks between them before her sisters arrive to help her.

Duty compels Theodora to marry Mr. Brown, a wealthy but older and boring man from their village. They honeymoon in the Alps and go hiking. Theodora loses her balance and is soon dangling over a cliff by her climbing rope. Lord Bracondale, coincidentally vacationing nearby, climbs down the rope to her. They are lowered to the ground below and, while they await the rest of the group, rekindle their interest. He reveals his feelings for her and she for him. But she says she could never leave her husband. Their love seems doomed.

Theodora's husband goes on a business trip. She writes him a wifely letter, as well as one to Lord Bracondale reaffirming that, though he is her one true love, she will not leave her husband. She accidentally puts the letters into the opposite envelopes, and when Lord Bracondale reads his, he realizes the letter meant for him must have gone to the husband. He rushes to the husband's office, and they have a great fight. But Bracondale finally convinces the man his wife has done nothing to betray him.

Realizing that Theodora has been true to him despite lov-

ing another, Mr. Brown decides to join a safari and is killed in a hunting accident. Bracondale and Theodora can now be together.

It was signed "Eva Crown." This was the third synopsis Irene had typed for Miss Crown, and she noticed that, messy handwriting aside, they tended to be a cut above other writers' work. There were always added twists or details that made the story feel more gripping. This one, however, seemed a little . . . it was good, but maybe it hadn't been thoroughly fleshed out yet.

Irene rose and approached Miss Clemente. "I'm sorry, but I've done the best I can deciphering the synopsis—figuring out the surrounding words makes that a little easier," she told her. "But I just can't get the title."

After turning the paper this way and that, Miss Clemente finally admitted she couldn't make head or tail of it, either, and huffed an annoyed sigh. Irene didn't know if it was meant for her or for Miss Crown, but she certainly knew who would take the brunt of it.

"Should I . . . make something up?"

"No, you should not *make something up*," Miss Clemente sneered. "You will go and find Miss Crown and get to the bottom of this. And if I find out you've been out running about the lot like a headless chicken, flirting with the crew, then you won't be long for this job. Have I made myself clear?"

Irene plunked down on the bench next to Millie and was surprised to find her wide-awake, not napping, as she often had when they sat there together.

"Oh, thank goodness," Millie said. "I thought noon would never come."

"Well, it's not quite noon, yet, but I have an errand to do, so I thought I'd come by and remind you to go out for that sandwich."

Millie held up a paper sack on her opposite side. "I went hours ago. I saw Wally coming down the line, and hightailed it. Just the sight of him . . ."

"Oh, Millie, I'm so sorry. I really thought—"

"It's not your fault."

"We're moving you into the Studio Club tonight, and you can stay in your room all day, if you want."

"It's expensive though, isn't it?"

"Not really. Not much more than Ringa's, which is pretty cheap."

"And we know why, don't we."

"That's not your concern anymore."

"But the money *is* my concern. You can't take it all on your shoulders, Irene. I've been on my own for three years now. I'm not a child."

This was true, of course. But Irene couldn't help but think that Millie's survival may have been less about her good decision-making and more about her good looks, uncanny ability to inspire the help of strangers, and random luck. She glanced down and caught sight of Millie's battered ankle boots. They looked utterly ridiculous with her flowered cotton dress.

"We'll be fine," Irene lied. "And the first thing I'm doing with my paycheck is buying you a new pair of shoes."

◇ ◇ ◇

It took Irene a solid half hour to track down Eva Crown. Apparently she moved around quite a bit, because wherever Irene went she was invariably told, "Oh, you just missed her."

What is she, a leprechaun?

The only reason Irene found her at all was because she was sitting in a canvas chair with her name actually printed across the back, in front of an empty set that appeared to be some sort of ancient bedchamber made out of fake stone. She was hunched over a stack of slightly crumpled pages, scrawling what looked to be hieroglyphs in the margins with a leaky pen.

No wonder, thought Irene with irritation.

"Miss Crown?"

She didn't look up. "Yes."

"Miss Crown, I've been typing your latest synopsis."

"Thanks very much." She flipped the current page to the bottom of the stack and went at the next page with a vengeance.

"I'm having a bit of trouble . . ."

"With?"

"The title."

"What about it."

"I have no idea what it says."

Miss Crown chuckled and finally looked up. "You wouldn't be the first."

Her eyes were pale blue, and her brown hair was tucked under a pretty straw hat. She had a warm smile, and Irene thought she was lovely in a sort of Great Plains pioneer way.

Irene offered her the handwritten page.

"Well, it's perfectly clear to me that it's called *Behind Her Socks!*" Miss Crown let out a ringing laugh that invited Irene to laugh right along with her.

"It's sure to be a hit," said Irene with a grin.

"An absolute sensation! Because who doesn't want to know what's behind other people's socks?" She let out another laugh and shook her head. "It's supposed to be *Beyond the Rocks*, by the way.

Did you at least like the story, even when you thought it had such an absurd title?"

Irene nodded. "Yes, it's very good."

Miss Crown's gaze leveled at Irene, and she stopped smiling. "But?"

"Oh, no, not at all," said Irene. "It's wonderful."

"It's an early draft."

"Of course."

"So you could tell?"

"No, I—"

"What's your name?"

"Irene, but—"

"How old are you, Irene?"

"Twenty-one."

"I see no ring, so I assume you are unmarried?"

"Yes."

"Boyfriend?"

"No."

"How many romance novels have you read in your life?"

"I couldn't count—"

"You go to the movies very often?"

"As often as I can afford to."

"Irene. Last name?"

"Van Beck."

"Irene Van Beck, you are my ideal moviegoer. I write *for you.* Do you understand?"

"Yes, ma'am."

"Please don't call me ma'am. I'm not that much older than you. Well, I'm a bit older. Call me Eva."

"Okay."

"Irene, can you do me an enormous favor?"

"If I can, I'd be happy to."

"Can you give me one little idea—anything at all—that will improve this script?"

Irene smiled. Wandering around the lot in search of its creator, she'd thought of several.

"Ah! I knew it," cried Eva.

"Well, I was thinking that when Theodora and Lord Bracondale get lowered by the rope onto the ground, it's sort of . . . flat. You know, they're safe, and they're chatting, and it's romantic and all but . . ."

"Keep going."

"I thought that if maybe there were a ledge in the cliff, and they narrowly make their way onto that. And it's not clear right away how or when they'll be able to get off . . ."

Eva nodded. "It heightens their fear and thus their emotional connection, and creates an actual—"

"Cliffhanger."

Eva narrowed her eyes and shook her pen at Irene. "Don't think for a moment you'll be credited for coauthorship."

"Oh, no, I'd never—"

Eva smiled. "I'm kidding. I mean, you're *not* getting credit, but I didn't really suspect that you'd ask." She rooted around in the pocket of her dress. "You will accept a tip, though, because that was very helpful, and it's above and beyond your duties." She pulled out two dollars and held them out to Irene.

"Miss Crown, I don't . . ."

"What did you eat for lunch today, Irene?" She was still holding out the money. "Please be scrupulously honest."

"I split a cream cheese sandwich with my friend. She's out on the benches."

Eva put the two dollars into Irene's hand. "Tomorrow you can each get your own, and it won't have to be cream cheese. In fact, you should have enough for a pretty good dinner, too."

Irene slid the bills into her pocket. "Miss Crown?"

"Eva."

"Eva, I have one more idea, and that's my tip for you, for being so nice. Would you like to hear it?"

"Of course."

"You have Theodora putting the letters in the wrong envelopes herself. But maybe someone offers to mail them for her. A woman who wants Lord Bracondale for herself, and she purposely switches them to ruin Theodora."

Eva Crown smiled. "You know you've made more work for yourself, don't you? You're going to have to retype that whole synopsis and incorporate those ideas."

"I was going to have to do that anyway," said Irene. "Unless you really want to call it *Behind Her Socks*."

◇ ◇ ◇

The next day a book waited for Irene on her typing/sewing table when she got back from lunch: *How to Write Photoplays* by John Emerson and Anita Loos. Inside on the frontispiece, John Emerson's name had been crossed out with a note that said, *This is all Anita's. John is just a barnacle husband.*

The main message took Irene a little longer to fully decipher.

Irene Van Beck, Girl with Many Ideas,

    Read this book, and get to work.

        With confidence in your future,
          Eva

22

◇ ◇ ◇

Women are not in love with me but with the picture of me on the screen.
I am merely the canvas upon which the women paint their dreams.
Rudolph Valentino, actor, producer

enry was beginning to feel as rich as King Solomon himself with all the money he'd been earning on *The Queen of Sheba* set for the past month. Fifty dollars a week was more than he'd ever made in his young life, but also more than his father and grandfather had ever made. If they could see him now... Of course, he liked to think his grandfather *could* see him from whatever spot he'd negotiated for himself in the afterlife. As for his father, well, Henry couldn't care less. At least that's what he told himself. But if he was honest, and his vindictive side showed, the only thing he'd like better than waving all that money in his father's face would be to punch the old bastard right in the *kishka*. Or worse.

He'd often wondered why his mother, a kind though passive person, had ever married him. Had she been bullied into it somehow? Her own father, the only grandfather Henry ever knew, would shake his head dolefully whenever the subject of his daughter's choice in matrimony came up. But that's all he did. He certainly never offered theories, other than the one time he'd said, "She likes to cook; he likes to eat." True. But what kind of explanation was that?

◇ ◇ ◇

Henry thought he might steel himself to look for apartments again on Saturday, but the prospect, instead of filling him with happy anticipation, now filled him with dread. How many more of those signs were out there? And how many buildings had no signs but shared the sentiment nonetheless?

He'd gotten friendly with the other two chariot drivers over the last several weeks. He preferred Gert Turner to any of the other extras—her brashness was entertaining and belied her basic dependability. Gert wouldn't let you down even if it were in her own best interest. Henry wasn't sure he could say that about anyone else he'd met—Ray and Charlie, the chariot drivers, least of all. It wasn't their fault; it was only that the three of them were all about the same size and general degree of tall-dark-and-handsomeness, as Gert would put it. They were in direct competition for every future roll. In fact, when Henry took a particularly hard fall once during filming, he saw the look of interest—more like veiled hope—on their faces. He was being paid twice what they were. If something happened to him, one of them might get his job.

The handmaidens were off shooting some other scene, and it was just the three of them, waiting as usual for their next set of instructions. Ray liked to play gin and always had a deck of cards with him. Neither Charlie nor Henry liked it quite so much, so they took turns getting beaten by Ray.

"Say, who wants to head over to the Hollywood Hotel tonight?" Ray said as he shuffled the deck, riffling it perfectly between his cupped hands.

"For dinner?" asked Henry. As much as he felt like a rich man these days, he was still careful with his money. He had Irene and Millie to consider. An overpriced meal at a swanky hotel was not at the top of his financial priorities.

"You can eat if you want to," said Ray. "I just go to dance. Lots of stars, lots of beautiful not-quite-stars."

"I'll go," said Charlie, who looked at Henry.

"Why not?" said Henry. He could use a night out. Maybe it would improve his dark mood.

They met in the ballroom and were lucky to get in. Henry had heard it was popular, but he was unprepared, both for the crowd of people and for their identities.

Ray nudged him and pointed with his chin. "Mae Murray."

"The Girl with the Bee-Stung Lips," Charlie replied.

"So they say. The only thing stinging them now is that martini."

The Hollywood Hotel was of course operating under the same Nineteenth Amendment as the rest of the country, and for all its owner, Miss Almira Hershey of chocolate fame, knew, she was complying with the letter of the law. Unfortunately for Almira—though fortunately for her guests—her eyesight was going, and she could no longer tell that patrons openly brought their own refreshments. It was particularly easy for the stars who stayed in the hotel upstairs to pour clear drinks such as vodka or gin and bring them down to the ballroom in water glasses, with Miss Hershey none the wiser.

Charlie, Ray, and Henry sipped their smuggled drinks and continued to scan the crowd, an activity that was shared by almost everyone there.

"Valentino," murmured Charlie. "Must have just come down from his room."

"How do you know?" asked Henry.

"He lives here. A lot of them do for a while. They like to be in the center of everything. He can make an entrance and show off his tango without even leaving the house."

When the band started up, Ray said, "Here we go boys, the ladies await," and headed toward the girl with the blondest hair and reddest lipstick.

Henry hesitated, his head spinning a little with the alcohol he rarely drank and the swirling pitch of the music.

"You don't dance?" asked Charlie.

"No, I do. I guess I'm just looking for the right girl."

"One's about as right as the next." Charlie waded into the crowd.

◇ ◇ ◇

They danced and drank and laughed for a few hours. Ray thought he saw Gloria Swanson, but if he did, she wasn't there long. As in cards, Ray was an enthusiastic dancer and never stayed long with his friends before he saw the next girl he wanted to foxtrot around the floor.

Charlie was less so. Occasionally Henry caught sight of him with some girl in his arms, but Charlie never seemed to talk much, or even make eye contact.

Shy, thought Henry. He could be a bit reticent himself.

The crowd was just starting to thin, and Henry was finishing his last drink and thinking it was time to go when Charlie said, "There's a place I know up the street. It's a little quieter."

"What about Ray?"

"He just left with blonde number forty-seven."

"I'm beat," said Henry.

"Just one. You should come." Something about the way he said it sparked Henry's flagging interest. He really was tired. Or at least he had been.

They walked for twenty minutes or more, crossing down to Sunset and heading west, where the storefronts came fewer and farther between and the lemon trees up the hill spread their tangy scent into the night air.

"Down there is the Garden of Alla, Nazimova's place," said Charlie offhandedly. "You ever hear about her parties?" Alla Nazimova was a sultry Russian actress who'd recently starred in *Camille* with Rudolph Valentino. She played, coincidentally or not, a sultry French courtesan who throws lavish parties.

"I heard she has them," said Henry. "Not what goes on there."

"I think it's anything goes."

"But you've never been."

"Five-dollar-a-day extras don't generally get invited."

"So where are we going?"

"There's a little . . . well it's a sort of speakeasy nearby."

"Is it a speakeasy or not?" Henry was starting to wonder why he'd agreed to hike all this way, and he especially didn't like how cagey Charlie was being.

"It serves booze, which is currently illegal in the land of the free," Charlie replied testily, "so I suppose it qualifies."

They came to the last block of storefronts on Sunset before the lemon trees took over. The stores themselves were dark, but there was a muffled tinkle of music playing somewhere nearby, and as Charlie led the way around to the alley and down a set of steps, it was as if someone took the blanket off the piano. Charlie knocked. The door opened.

The room was dimly lit and filled with smoke, as most speakeasies were, of course, but the scent of the smoke held a slight spiciness that Henry recognized from telling jokes in the cheaper bars in Harlem and Hell's Kitchen. Tobacco with a little marijuana thrown in.

There were tables, but most of the patrons sat along the cushioned benches that ran around the inside of the room. There was a dance floor, but no one was dancing, and the music didn't

◇ ◇ ◇

Two musicians joined the pianist on the tiny stage, a bass and a horn player, and they set aside the jazz to begin a George Gershwin piece, "Boy Wanted." There was no singer, but it was a popular song, and Henry knew the words.

> *I've just finished writing an advertisement, calling for a boy.*
> *No half-hearted Romeo or flirt is meant, that's the kind I'd not employ.*
> *Though anybody interested can apply, he must know a thing or two to qualify . . .*

As Charlie made his way back from the bar, several couples, all men, got up to dance, holding each other and swaying unselfconsciously.

"I need to go," said Henry.

Charlie sighed. "You really don't."

"I've had too much to drink and I'm all . . ." Henry waved his hand around.

"If I've upset you, I'm sorry."

Henry looked up at him. "No, it's not your fault. It's just . . ."

"I know." Charlie sat down with the two drinks. "Do you mind if I stay? I've been waiting to get here all night."

"Not at all. I can find my way home."

"I'll see you tomorrow?"

"Of course."

Henry wended his way through the tables, which had begun to fill while he'd sat reviewing his brief romantic history. As he passed a group of men, all talking and laughing, one face was familiar.

Edward Oberhouser.

23

When in doubt, make a western.
John Ford, director, producer, writer

Sitting on a bench at Olympic Studios, Millie stared down at the scuff on her new shoes. They weren't brand-new, of course. Irene had taken her shopping for them three weeks ago with the money she'd gotten from that lady writer.

"You can't spend that on me," Millie had protested. "We need it for when you move into the Studio Club. Or at least spend it on yourself, since you earned it. Say, you could get a new hat!"

"I don't want or need a new hat," said Irene. "And you need shoes."

That was admittedly hard to argue with.

"Besides," she went on, "this is what my uncle would call star-shine money. It just dropped out of the sky, and so we have to do something special with it."

Two-dollar shoes didn't really qualify as "special," in Millie's shopping experience. They qualified as ugly and poorly made. But that wasn't what caught Millie's attention. "Your uncle?" she said mildly, so as not to scare Irene off the subject. "Where is he now?"

"I don't precisely know. We don't really keep in touch. Now, I saw in the paper that Baker-Hertzler on Hollywood Boulevard is having a dollar day on Saturday. They probably don't have shoes for a dollar, but there are sure to be some bargains."

As Millie surveyed them now in the September sun, they were no bargain, with their military heels and utter lack of any kind of adornment. Not so much as a button. But they were a vast improvement over the boots she'd been wearing in Southern California in August, so she was grateful. She was genuinely grateful for everything Irene did, and everything Irene was.

In fact, Millie wondered if she might be a little bit in love with Irene. Not so much in a stable-boy-hayloft kind of way, but in the truest, best way. She missed Irene all day long, as she trudged around Hollywood, getting her name registered on the extra list of every studio, large, small, or completely fly-by-night. She'd been to the Poverty Row studios around Sunset and Gower, and to Mayer and Metro-Goldwyn, touting her ability to ride a horse and drive a car—they all seemed to perk up at that. And now she lived at the Studio Club, where they could call and leave a message if they wanted her. But it had so far come to nothing except sore feet.

And she missed Irene all night, in her new twin bed that she had all to herself. It was the first time she'd slept alone since she'd joined Chandler's Follies, and she did not like it one bit. Irene had always let her snuggle up against her back as they were falling asleep. At first Irene used to ask, "Are you cold?" which Millie sometimes was, but that wasn't the whole reason, or even the main one. Millie would say, "A little," because she didn't want to lie, just to fib a tiny bit. And then Irene stopped asking.

Because she loves me, too.

The knowledge of this—evident in all the ways that gruff, practical Irene put reason and self-preservation aside time and again on Millie's behalf—was what kept her trudging in ugly shoes up and down the boulevards of Hollywood.

Because sometimes, she just didn't want to anymore. Actually most of the time.

It wasn't turning out for her. The tea set money—the only financial contribution Millie had made to this whole endeavor—was gone, and Irene was struggling to pay for them both on her paltry nineteen dollars a week. Henry had been helping out, which they thought she didn't know, but she did. She saw him slip some money into Irene's hand once, and another time into her purse.

And she was so lonely. Irene and Henry were gone all day, of course, and so was that sassy Gert Turner who Henry had introduced her to. She bunked in another room and went out a lot in the evenings. She often invited Millie to go with her, but Millie didn't have any money.

There were evening classes she could take at the Studio Club—tap dancing and oratory and understanding Shakespeare—but she was so tired. She didn't know why sitting on studio benches all day was so exhausting, but by the time she left in the late afternoon, she always felt as if she'd dug a whole field of potatoes.

Sometimes she thought it was that business with Wally that made her feel so worn-out and demoralized. But it had been a month ago. Shouldn't she be over it by now?

Irene came by almost every evening, and they often went to the movies, sitting up in the nickel seats. Henry came with them if he wasn't doing a night scene from that Bible movie he was in, or if he wasn't too tired from working all day and then getting woken up in the night from some thunderous snorer in the men's dorm at the YMCA.

Irene said going to the movies was "an investment" because it gave her ideas. She had a little notebook now that she scribbled in all the time, and she'd frown and knit her brows if some notion was giving her trouble. Sometimes she studied Millie or Henry in a strange, detached way and then scribbled some more, and then they would both yell at her not to write about them. Millie loved being with Irene, but sometimes Irene was so distracted, it was only a little bit better than being alone.

Worst of all, with the loneliness came the memories of that night, when she had struggled with all her might, only to be easily overpowered. She didn't sleep well anymore, and when she woke gasping in fright, there was no Irene.

Ugly and scuffed. Her life was turning out just like her shoes.

She had started thinking about all the farms there were on the outskirts of town and how she might go back to a life of picking beans and shoveling the cow manure out of the dairy barn. Maybe she could even find a place with horses.

"Mildred Martin! Is there a Mildred Martin out here?"

Millie blinked and looked up. People were swiveling around to see who the lucky girl was. Suddenly another girl a couple of benches down raised her hand. "I'm Mildred Martin!"

The older woman who'd been calling out turned toward the girl. "Horse rider?"

Millie was confused at first—was there another girl here with the exact same name? What were the chances? Or maybe . . . the realization was dawning on her that maybe someone else was desperate enough to pretend to be her, to take her job.

Oh, let her have it.

But then she thought of Irene and how angry and disappointed and just *sad* she'd be if she ever found out. Irene wouldn't show her sadness, of course. But it would be there.

Millie stood up. "*I'm* Millie Martin," she said to the girl. "I can jump a horse over a hedge at a full gallop. Can you?"

The girl sat back down.

◇ ◇ ◇

By ten in the morning, Millie was in the back of a car, headed to Olympic's Back Ranch, wearing a costume that a little angry man named Albert Leroux had given her. Made from a dark blue calico print, it had long sleeves and a high collar and swung down from the cinched waist to just above her ankles. It was a little big on her, which she was glad of. It would make it easier to straddle the horse. Her father had allowed her to ride in pants, though this had scandalized her mother. But since her mother never left the house, Millie had done as she pleased. The dress came with a white muslin apron and matching bonnet.

"Thanks for taking me," she said to the back of the driver's head.

"That's what they pay me for. I just brought the other girl over to St. Vincent's."

"St. Vincent's?"

"Hospital."

"Was she sick?"

"Broke something. Collarbone, shoulder, I'm not sure what. But by the sound of her, it hurt something terrible."

"How'd she do it?"

"Fell off a horse. She said it was skittish, didn't like the gunfire, so it reared up. Something like that. Hard to understand her through all that caterwauling."

◇ ◇ ◇

Millie was taken by cart out to the set, which was on the farthest edge of the lot on a rocky hillside dotted with brush and trees. Where the land flattened out, there was a cabin with a little yard and vegetable garden. There were even clothes hanging from a clothesline. The camera was set up in front with the crew clustered around it.

Millie stopped for a moment and took a deep breath to steady her nerves.

I'm here. And I'm making money. And I get to ride a horse!

As she approached, a few heads turned in her direction.

"There's the girl."

"About time."

"She the right size?"

"She'll have to do," said a man in a tan suit and knee-high brown boots. A megaphone swung from his hand. "Where's Wally? Wally! Get the girl ready!"

Millie turned to ice under the hot California sun when she heard his voice.

"Russell! Com'ere for a minute, wouldya? We gotta get this new girl sorted out."

He was coming toward her now, another man beside him with shoulder-length black hair and nothing but a square of cloth over his parts. Millie felt herself go blurry, the edges of her melting away into the dirt.

Don't faint, she told herself. *If you faint now, they'll haul you off to St. Vincent's like that other girl.* She bit at the inside of her lip until she tasted blood.

Wally didn't seem to know it was her at first, all covered up as she was with the high-necked dress and the bonnet hiding her black hair.

The bastard doesn't even recognize me. She felt her temperature rise. *He did what he did, and he can't even remember to what girl!*

"The Injuns swarm the house," he was saying, "and you're off in that paddock over there with the horses, and you—" He stopped suddenly and stared at her. "How'd you get in here?" he growled.

She didn't trust herself to respond, could barely find her voice.

You. Need. This. Job.

She gritted her teeth to quell the shaking. "Registration called for me."

"You told them you could ride."

"I can."

"I doubt it."

The Indian spoke up. "We'll see soon enough. Meanwhile, everyone's waiting."

"Then *you* tell her what to do," Wally said and strode off.

Millie exhaled. *Don't faint. Don't faint.* She took some sips of breath.

"Appears you two know each other. Some sort of romance gone wrong?"

Millie looked up at him, his eyes so dark they were almost black. "It was no romance, believe me."

His face changed then, and she couldn't really have said how. She might have thought his molars clenched, but they didn't. "Do you need to sit down?" he asked.

"If I sit down, I'll lose my job, won't I?" she murmured.

"Probably."

"Just tell me what to do."

He walked her back to the paddock, murmuring instructions the way her father's trainer would whisper to a spooked horse: a constant stream of mostly monotone words, many of which ended in question marks. "You're going to see me coming, right? And then you're going to mount that horse over there—can you do that? And then you look over your shoulder at me a bunch of times, like you're scared, okay? Like I'm terrifying."

"You're not terrifying."

He smiled. "Not now. But I can act like the hounds of hell. Just don't forget I'm acting."

"Isn't that what actresses are supposed to do? Pretend the actors aren't acting?"

"Let's just get the timing right in the first few takes, and then we'll worry about making it look real."

Millie stood where she'd been told, among the horses. There was an old gray Arabian with its concave nose and swaying back. He was the first to come over and say hello as she held her hand out flat so he could lick the salt from her palm. She wished she'd had an apple or lump of sugar to make friends with, but this stately gentleman didn't seem to require such tokens.

The Appaloosa came next, absolutely beautiful with his white coat and leopard spots. He was a bit more standoffish and declined to lick her hand, but his ears faced her, so she knew he was interested. The Indian would ride this one, of course, a classic Indian horse. Millie found herself a bit jealous. He'd be willing to jump, she could tell, but he wouldn't lose his head.

The sleek brown quarter horse, the one she was to ride, wouldn't even greet her.

"Oh now," she chided. "Don't be like that. We all need friends."

The horse lowered her head to the ground and nibbled some weeds.

"Those don't even taste good, you faker." Millie made a little whickering sound, and the horse looked up. "I do actually have to ride you, I'm afraid, so start getting used to the idea."

It was half an hour or more that she stood there waiting for her take while the Indians snuck up on the farmhouse below the paddock about fifteen times in a row. After a while she sat on the fence in a spot where the house blocked her view of the crew, specifically Wally. She was grateful for the time to collect herself and get acquainted with her equine cast mates.

How long had it been since she'd ridden a horse? The farm she'd worked on had only had two plow horses, and they certainly didn't need exercising after a day in the fields.

It had been since home. Her father had sold her lovely American paint horse when she was about to be shunted off to Miss Twickenham's. "There'll be no one to ride her," her father had said. "It's not fair to the horse."

Fair to the horse? she'd wanted to scream. *What about me? How is any of this fair?*

But she'd been too stunned to say anything. And Calliope was gone the next day. The day after that, so was Millie.

◇ ◇ ◇

The camera was suddenly being moved, and the herd of crew members went with it, around the side of the house, aimed at the paddock and at her. Then the director approached.

"Herbert Vanderslice," he said, his voice so deep she imagined it might be what a walrus would sound like if it spoke English.

She held out her hand to shake. "Mil—"

"Now you'll be standing with the horse over here, just having a nice time petting him. And then he"—Vanderslice gestured toward the Indian—"you—"

"Dan Russell," the man said quickly.

"Yes, well, you sneak around that side of the house toward her, crouching, sneaking, hands out." Vanderslice acted this out, and it seemed quite silly, this man in his expensive tan suit and stiff straw hat, stalking along like a thief. Millie knew she shouldn't laugh, but it was so much nicer to feel silly than faint from stress. She cut her eyes toward Dan Russell, who responded with a frown. Chastened, she folded her lips in and bit down hard.

"Then you, miss—"

Calliope whickered. Millie whickered back. Calliope took a step forward and so did Millie. The horse reached out her long neck, and Millie slid her hand a little closer. In a swish of the horse's lips, the sugar was gone.

"Cut!" called the director. "Very good, very good! We'll use that!"

Millie looked over at Dan Russell, leaning up against the shady side of the house, arms crossed against his bare chest. "I didn't know they were filming!"

"Be glad they were," he said. "A take with only you in it is more than atmosphere work. Your pay will go up. Now let's get this next one done."

"Okay, but terrify me this time, will you?"

"Will do."

24

Motion picture writing is as practical a profession as
plumbing, only the plums are bigger.
John Emerson and Anita Loos, in How to Write Photoplays

Over the last three weeks, Irene had taken Eva's confidence in her very seriously. She dragged Millie to the movies every other night and went without lunch to afford it; when she got home, she always made herself write a five-hundred-word synopsis, the standard studio-recommended length, of the plot points. On the weekends, she borrowed copies of plays, such as *A Woman of No Importance* by Oscar Wilde, from the Studio Club library and wrote out summaries of the action. She read the newspaper every day, and the latest copy of *Photoplay* magazine. She had practically begun to dream in five-hundred-word format.

Perhaps most useful was the fact that Irene was actually being paid to read (and then type) scenarios and continuity scripts all day long. She studied them as she tapped away and kept a running list in her notebook of the ones she hoped would be chosen and the ones she deemed too flat, undramatic, rehashed, or out of step with popular interest to make the cut.

"Your speed is decelerating," Miss Clemente warned her one morning.

on the servants' entrance gate. She was out there in the dark with her employer's baby who had the croup, walking him in the cool night air to soothe him.

> The criminal was sent packing when he heard a particularly harsh cough. "I do believe he thought it was the bark of a watchdog!" the nanny stated to the police.

This was not even worthy of a one-reeler, Irene knew. Though the drama was high when the nanny heard the intruder, that was it. There was only one point of conflict, and it was resolved almost immediately by the baby's coughing fit.

But what if the baby hadn't scared off the burglar? What if he'd grabbed the baby from the nanny's arms . . . and . . .

It had to be something unexpected, something that would make the audience gasp in fear and then in surprise.

What if the criminal was a father with children of his own? They'd had croup before, or maybe one of them even had it that very night. But his baby was sickly because it didn't have enough to eat. He needed to steal to feed his family . . .

Why would he grab this other baby? Irene frowned and stared out at Ringa's overgrown shrubs and patchy lawn.

To soothe the poor thing himself! The nanny wasn't doing a very good job. Or it wasn't the nanny . . . it was the baby's very young mother who didn't know what she was doing. And she'd been left all alone because her husband was dead. No! He was out carousing!

Oh, this is getting good, thought Irene.

And then she had to laugh. Here she was in the middle of the night by herself, gripped by the drama of her own made-up story, and she couldn't wait to find out what would happen next.

◇　◇　◇

After only a few hours sleep, she woke bleary-eyed and nudged an elbow out of her armpit. Jane (or June, or whoever it was who shared her bed now) was a sprawler. Not a cuddler, like Millie, but the kind who invariably got a limb on you. Irene rose quickly, relieved to disentangle herself, but dreading breakfast in equal measure. There were more girls than ever squeezed into the rickety house, and meals were like feeding time at a third-rate zoo, with each hyena snarling and grabbing for what few scraps she could get her paws on. Irene was ready to storm the Studio Club and evict someone bodily, if that's what it took to get a spot.

Far more than her own comfort, though, she was concerned about Millie and how much time she spent alone. Millie wasn't a time-to-herself person like Irene was. She was a more-the-merrier person, and since the incident she'd been particularly fragile. Instead of gradually returning to her usual upbeat, silly self, she seemed to be withdrawing even more, getting quieter, more afraid. Irene decided she would risk Miss Clemente's wrath and take a little longer with Millie at lunch. Maybe she could get her laughing somehow or distract her from her dark feelings by the story of the croupy baby and the fatherly burglar.

But at lunchtime, Millie was nowhere to be found. She always made her rounds at the other studios early in the morning so she could be at Olympic in time for Irene's lunch break, picking up a bottle of Royal Crown ginger ale and a cream cheese sandwich for them to split on her way. She'd found a drugstore that sold them for a nickel, so the whole lunch only cost a dime. Not that they had a dime to spare these days.

Irene waited at the benches, then took several laps around the studio, but there was no sign of her.

"Irene Van Beck."

She spun around at the sound of her name, and there was Eva Crown, wearing a green cotton dress with a small blue ink stain on one thigh, right where the bottom of the interior pocket must have lain.

"I hope you and Anita Loos have been getting along well. I see her peeking out of your little purse there."

"Oh, yes, she's brilliant. I can't thank you enough."

"Your note was very nice. I feel fully thanked. And have you been doing any writing yourself?"

Irene smiled. "Actually . . . I've been driving my friends a bit mad, scribbling in my pad all the time, writing down ideas and details. They're sure they're the main characters of every story."

"Get used to *that*," Miss Crown said with a conspiratorial eye roll. "It's the human condition to think we're all a little more interesting than we actually are."

Irene gripped her purse strap and forced herself to say, "I . . . um. I've been working on something."

"And?"

"And, I think . . . I think it might not be . . . completely terrible."

"Well, that's a glowing endorsement! I can see it in large script across the movie poster now." She gestured in the air. "Might Not Be Completely Terrible!"

Irene felt herself flush. "I guess it's hard for me to judge."

"Oh, now. I'm just teasing you. And yes, it's hard for any writer to objectively judge her own work, but we do get a feeling about it, don't we?"

Hesitantly, Irene nodded.

"All right then, what's your feeling?"

"I think it's good."

Eva leveled her gaze at Irene. "How good?"

◇ ◇ ◇

It was one of the most fitful afternoons Irene could ever remember. Between worrying about Millie and what trouble she might have gotten into and wondering what Eva Crown was thinking about her synopsis of "A Baby's Cry," Irene's stomach felt as if it were filled with molten lava.

After work she hung around the lot, hoping to intercept one or preferably both of them. A truck stopped just inside the gate, and Irene watched as several cowboys, Indians, and a pioneer family climbed out. Suddenly Millie hopped down, a muslin bonnet bobbing against her back.

She's an extra—not wandering aimlessly around Hollywood or loafing with that Agnes! Irene felt relief flood her.

Millie caught sight of Irene and headed toward her at a trot. Then she stopped suddenly and turned back toward the truck. A man came up behind her, naked from the waist up. Millie took his elbow and tugged him around next to her. He had short black hair and was holding a black tangle in his hands. A wig with a piece of cloth tied around it as a headband. Irene could just make out his face as they came closer. Dan Russell.

Millie was beaming. "Irene, I worked!"

"That's wonderful!"

"This is Dan Russell. He plays the Indian who captures me. And I got to ride a horse again! A mean one—well, not mean really. Just unhappy."

Irene held out her hand to him, and he shook it. "Irene Van Beck."

"Pleasure." His gaze was strange, she thought. Intense.

"We're taking him to dinner," said Millie.

Irene's mouth dropped open slightly. *With what?* she wanted to ask.

Millie laughed. "Well, to be truthful, he's taking us, but as soon as I get paid, we'll give it right back to him." She turned to look up at Dan. "You trust us for the money, right?"

Dan chuckled. "Yes, I trust you."

It was agreed that they would meet at a restaurant Dan knew of called The Cottonwood at seven-thirty. That would give Millie and Irene time to go to the YMCA and round up Henry, then head over to the Studio Club so Millie could wash and change.

"You should change, too," Millie said as they headed down Sunset toward the Y. The village of Hollywood was so used to seeing people in strange attire, hardly anyone blinked an eye at Millie in the long calico skirt with the bonnet swinging from her hand.

"I only have one other summer dress, and it's about as fresh as this one."

Millie frowned. "You know you're a lovely girl, right?"

"Where did *that* come from?"

"It came from facts, Irene. You're lovely. You shouldn't act un-lovely so people will leave you alone."

"I don't!"

Millie shrugged, as if Irene's protest didn't change the truth. Then, in typical fashion, she moved on to the next subject that sprang to mind. "Dan's nice, don't you think?"

Irene was still ruminating on the previous subject. "What? Oh. I only met him for a minute."

"Well, he's nice, believe me."

Maybe that was what had brought on the comment about acting "un-lovely"—Millie had a little crush and she didn't want Irene to embarrass her. At least this guy seemed like he might not be a monster. Irene remembered how he'd walked away when Wally was bragging about what he'd done. But of course Millie had no knowledge of that. Maybe her judgment was improving.

"What makes him so nice?" Irene asked and was stunned by Millie's answer: Wally on the set, nasty and accusatory; Dan helping Millie calm down, showing her the ropes, helping with the misbehaving horse.

"I would've lost that job inside of a minute if it weren't for him."

He knew, thought Irene. He understood how scared Millie was—and why—and he went out of his way to be kind. In a world that always seemed so full of Chandlers, Barneys, Mama Ringas, and too many Agneses to count, chalk one up for the quiet heroes.

When they got to the YMCA, Henry was just coming out the door, looking suave in a new suit and recently cut hair. He smelled good, too. When they told him why they were celebrating, his face fell. "I'm so sorry. I promised some friends I'd meet them at the dance at the Hollywood Hotel."

"Friends?" said Millie, obviously disappointed.

"Just a couple of guys from the set. I'd rather be with you two." He hesitated, the dilemma playing out on his face. "It'll probably be a bore." He sighed. "But I said I'd go."

The restaurant was at the corner of Hollywood Boulevard and Ivar Avenue, and it was a far cry from Musso & Frank, with its mahogany paneled walls and leaded glass bar cabinets. The exterior was brick with two plain bay windows and a wood-frame door in the middle. Above in pale green paint on a dark brown background were the words THE COTTONWOOD. Inviting but not fancy. Irene suspected Dan had chosen it so as not to run up Millie's bill.

He was waiting inside the door, standing quietly with his hands clasped behind his back, his short black hair freshly washed and slicked back from the tan skin of his face. He wore a nondescript brown serge suit, white cotton shirt, and green wool tie. He was either not trying very hard to impress them, or it was his only suit. Or both.

Millie laughed and patted his arm. "I'm not used to seeing you in clothes!"

The host waiting to seat them put a fist up to his mouth and coughed. Dan shot a warning look at the man, who then turned away.

"I don't generally wear the breechcloth when I go out to dinner. It tends to make the ladies blush and the men want to fight me."

Millie grinned. "It didn't make *me* blush."

"You're an actress," he said. "The work requires a certain open-mindedness."

Millie leaned toward Irene and whispered, "I'm an actress!"

"You are now," she whispered back.

They were seated at a small round wooden table in one of the front windows. Mismatched but pretty cotton napkins sat under the forks, and a thin vase with dried purple flowers was the only table decoration. The placed smelled of freshly baked bread and roasting meat. Savory, homey smells so different from what Irene was used to at Ringa's. She liked the feel of it, unassuming and yet confident about what it had to offer. It was a little like Dan himself.

The menus were small printed paper cards with much of the usual fare: lettuce salad, mashed turnips, baked chicken, corned beef and potatoes, and the like. But there were also some things Irene had never seen.

"What's good here?" asked Millie.

"I always get the roast mutton and the blue corn dumplings. Reminds me of home."

"Where's home?"

"Arizona," he said. "The cook is from there, too."

"What took you from Arizona all the way to Hollywood?" said Millie, and Irene worried that Dan Russell didn't like being interrogated, no matter how innocently it was meant.

"The train," he said. "How about you? Where were you ladies before life brought you to the flickers?"

"Oh, we were in a burlesque show," said Millie. "That's where we met, right, Irene?"

Irene's face went hot, and it was all she could do to keep from kicking Millie under the table, except it was so small she'd likely end up kicking Dan, or toppling the whole thing over, little purple flowers and all.

"It's all right," murmured Dan.

"What?" said Millie. "Burlesque?"

Irene cut her eyes at Millie, a *shut-up-would-you?* look.

"Dan's an actor," said Millie, "which, as we all know, requires a certain open-mindedness."

Dan chuckled. Irene just hoped her flaming cheeks wouldn't light anything on fire.

"It's not like we *wanted* to be in burlesque," Millie went on. "More than anything we wanted to get *out*, but that wasn't so easy to do, until Irene decided we should jump off a moving train."

Dan caught Irene's eye. "Stunt women, too? That's some list of talents."

Irene shook her head and sighed. She was already planning the talking-to she would give Millie on the walk home.

"It wasn't so bad," said Millie. "We just got kind of banged up and scratched. Irene's knee swelled, but it was much better the next day, even after we had to run for our lives from the burlesque show owner's henchman. That was my fault entirely. I stole his silver tea set."

The waiter came, and they all ordered mutton and blue corn

dumplings, Millie barely pausing to say, "Yes, me, too, please," before she resumed the saga of their escape.

Surreptitiously, Irene watched Dan watching Millie. He didn't seem the least bit appalled, though he was clearly well versed at keeping himself to himself. But no, he seemed genuinely to enjoy Millie's performance, as she giggled her way through the part about *The Gypsy and the Runaway Bride* or pumped her arms a little when describing how they bolted willy-nilly for the train, shaking her finger as she imitated Henry yelling something foul in Yiddish at Barney.

Dan was charmed, Irene decided. She had to admit it was understandable. She herself had been utterly charmed by the wild-yet-guileless Millie Martin.

When the story was over, and Millie was tucking into the mutton that had gone almost cold on her plate, Dan turned to Irene and said, "So you're a writer."

Irene nearly choked on her dumpling. "No, I . . . well, I'm hoping . . . maybe someday."

"Millie told me you write in a notebook all the time, practicing to be a scenarist."

"I do scribble a lot. As a matter of fact . . ." Why was she telling him this? She shouldn't brag when it would likely come to nothing. ". . . I submitted a scenario to one of the head writers today." She put her napkin to her lips and compelled herself to slow down, stop talking about herself and her little story. She shook her head. "It's just a first try, and it will definitely get rejected, but at least it's good practice."

Millie let her fork drop onto her plate with a clatter. "Irene, you did it!"

Irene shrugged, but she couldn't help but smile. "I shouldn't have said anything."

"Now you *are* a writer," said Dan.

25

◇ ◇ ◇

Happiness often sneaks through a door you didn't know you left open.
John Barrymore, actor

---

enry climbed the steps from the speakeasy door and headed down the alley to Sunset Boulevard. He stopped to remove his jacket, loosen his tie, and lean up against the side of the building in the cool night air for a moment to collect himself. The combination of scotch and memories and, yes, he had to admit, the sight of men being openly romantic with one another, had him practically feverish with emotions that ran the gamut from shock to sadness to longing.

He had tried so hard not to be what his father had called him. To his everlasting shame, Henry had refused to speak to Sol when he'd come to visit in the hospital that next day. As if it were in any way Sol's fault that Henry's father was brutal. Or that Henry was what he was.

The look on Sol's face, so terrified that he might come face-to-face once again with the raging Mr. Weiss. But he'd come, hadn't he? He'd been far braver than Henry was on that day or any day since.

He'd never seen Sol again. Henry had quit school and gotten

a job laying bricks with his father, hating both the man and the job. All that cement, such a godawful mess. He'd dated girls and started fistfights and missed his *zayde* terribly. The old man, gone almost two years by then, might not have had much to say about such matters, but Henry knew without a moment's doubt that he would have served as the human refuge his grandson so desperately needed.

His mother, a quiet person, had gotten quieter. And then one night when his father was out, his mother had handed him a little muslin pouch with a string tie and said, "Go see your uncle Benny." The pouch had sixty-three dollars in it. To this day Henry wasn't sure where she'd gotten such a boodle. Had she stolen it? Had she siphoned it penny by penny from the money her husband gave her to buy food and household items over the years, anticipating just such an emergency? This was his mother's *knippel*—her stash of money that offered a small sliver of freedom from her husband's control. And she had given it all to her son.

Uncle Benny was living in a boardinghouse near Coney Island during his summer break, when many theaters were too hot to hold performances. He taught Henry some jokes and sent him off to the bars with a hat for people to throw change in. Henry would sneak back into his uncle's room to sleep in the middle of the night, until the two of them got thrown out.

"It's time to get back to work, anyway," said Uncle Benny, and he set Henry up with a traveling review, the owner of which owed him a favor.

Must have been a big one, Henry thought, because he still wasn't very good. Over time he improved enough that when the review closed, he'd been able to get himself hired onto a series of mediocre shows until he'd hit Chandler's Follies.

Henry straightened up and put on his jacket, his head still foggy with drink and memory. When he stepped from the shadow of the alley, a car was rattling down Sunset toward him. With the headlights shining at him, he couldn't see the car, but by the clanking of the engine and the occasional backfiring, he guessed it was an old flivver.

It slowed as it approached, and he wondered if the driver was lost and in need of directions, though there weren't many to give. Keep going east toward downtown Hollywood or turn around and go west toward the ocean were really the only two options.

The car stopped, and Henry stepped toward the driver's window. He heard the driver say, "Okay, but make it quick." Then the back door opened.

The next thing he knew someone had socked him in the jaw. Henry staggered back, and in that moment he wanted only to ask why. What had he done to provoke this attack? But he had been in enough fights to know that, no matter the reason, he'd better come back swinging if he didn't want to end up facedown in the dirt.

His first punch landed on the side of the fellow's head with a crack, quickly followed by the sound of stunned pain from the recipient as he went down. But suddenly there was another man coming toward him from a different angle whom he could see a little more clearly by the car's headlights: stocky, in a coarse cotton shirt, with a crooked nose, and messy hair to match.

"Faggot can hit," the man muttered to his friend.

Oh, thought Henry. *That's why.*

He barreled into the man, wanting only to knock him over so he could run. But even several inches shorter, the thug had at least thirty pounds on Henry and only staggered back a few feet. He pummeled Henry in the gut until Henry delivered an uppercut to the chin.

He heard voices behind him coming from the alley, but he had no idea who they were or whether they might help or join in. He turned to bolt, knocking squarely into the other man who had gotten back up. He hit Henry in the chest so hard, he went down on one knee.

Ah, shit, he thought, because once you're below the other fellow, it's so much harder to hit back.

The man raised his foot and kicked Henry in the chest. "Fucking faggot actor," he growled as he stood over Henry, now splayed out on the ground. "Take your faggot friends and go back to New York!"

Henry threw his hands up over his head and curled on his side to protect his gut. He heard shouting and someone saying, "Get in, get in!" The gears screeched, and the old car pulled away, spraying him with road dust.

"My God, are you all right?" The voice was beside him, and Henry slowly uncurled himself.

He groaned as he tried to sit up. "Nothing ice and aspirin won't fix."

He was still trying to right himself, the stabbing pain in his ribs making that a goal he had to accomplish slowly, when the voice said, "Henry?"

Henry looked up and squinted into the face of Edward Oberhouser.

Now in the back of Oberhouser's car, which his driver had run to fetch when they'd come upon the melee, the director asked, "Are you sure you won't go to the hospital?"

"Honestly it's not that bad," Henry assured him. "There's nothing to stitch, so they won't do anything except clean me up, which I can easily do myself."

"Sounds to me like this wasn't your first fight, especially with the way you were able to hold off two large men."

"No, not my first." Henry shifted painfully on the soft black leather seat, trying not to grimace. "Hopefully my last."

"I don't mean to pry."

Then please don't, thought Henry. The less said about all of this—the whole strange night—the better. But what could he do? It was likely that Oberhouser had saved him from far more damage, showing up and calling out like he did. "Not at all," said Henry.

"I'm just wondering if this was a random attack . . . or was it possibly someone who was looking for you? Perhaps you owe money? Because it's nothing to be ashamed of. Many, many actors are forced to borrow if they don't find work right away. I might be able to help—"

"Oh, no, thank you, but it's nothing like that. They didn't know me."

"I see. I thought that might be why you were so adamant about not reporting it to the police."

How could anyone be so dense? wondered Henry. Didn't he know what kind of bar he'd been in? Of course he did. The very fact of it was clear from every dancing couple. The police would never help someone who'd been coming out of a place like that. Did the director think he was immune somehow because of his position? Or did he imagine that Hollywood was an entirely different planet, where that kind of threat didn't exist?

"Mr. Oberhouser—"

"Please call me Edward."

"Not Obie?"

"Oh, Lord no. I absolutely hate that. Obie," he scoffed, "like I'm some sort of mutt begging for food at the screen door."

"You do know everyone calls you that."

"Yes, I know. I let it go because it makes people think I'm chummy enough to have a nickname. Which I'm not, actually.

But friendships, even the appearance of them, are what make the cogs of Hollywood turn. Pictures are made—or not—based on alliances. You'll see that soon enough."

It wasn't lost on Henry that Edward was choosing to reveal this bit of personal information to an extra he'd only known for a month, which actually *was* chummy. He hoped to return the kindness by warning him about going to the bar again.

"Edward, I don't mean to bring up something that generally isn't . . . discussed." At this he shot a glance at the driver, who appeared to hear nothing, but who Henry was sure could hear everything. "Based on the comments those fellows made while they were trying to beat the stuffing out of me, they did it because of the . . . the establishment I'd just left. The one you left only minutes later."

A dark look passed over Edward's face. "Because we're homosexuals."

Henry's pulse began to race at hearing such words spoken aloud, and his immediate reaction was to deny it, as he'd done his whole life. But it seemed pointless. Edward knew. He also seemed to feel no qualm about including himself in the category or proclaiming it at normal volume for his driver to hear.

"Yes," said Henry. How strange it felt to hear the admission come from his own lips!

"Well, it's no surprise, I guess," said Edward.

Henry was dumbstruck by the man's casual tone, as if the possibility of getting beaten up was just the price of admission for allowing your proclivities to be known. As if it were worth it.

"There's the general, you know . . . revulsion." Edward said this as if this were a mere irritant. "And then there's the industry."

"What about it?"

"Well, when filmmakers first started coming out to Hollywood ten or fifteen years ago, it was practically like one of those

Gold Rush towns that popped up—rustic, a little dangerous. They thought of themselves as he-men, braving the Wild West to get the shot. As pictures got more sophisticated and started making real money, the New York crowd took notice. The artists came. Since then there's always been a bit of a standoff between the straight shooters, as they like to call themselves, and the so-phisticates." He gave this last word a meaningful emphasis.

"So that's what he meant when he said go back to New York," said Henry. "I'm actually from there, so I wondered how he knew."

"I grew up outside of Cleveland," said Edward with a wry smile, "but apparently we're *all* from New York."

"I don't think these fellows were movie people. The one I could see was dressed for manual labor—a farmer or a dock worker, maybe."

Edward nodded. "Thugs, then. The kind who feel like handing out a licking and think we're the easy prey." He smiled. "They were in for a surprise with you, though, weren't they? I'll have to keep you in mind for my next picture with a fight scene in it."

Henry smiled. Maybe the bruising had been worth it if it generated more work. "I'd be happy to oblige. But I . . . uh . . . I hope I can trust you not to mention . . ."

"Of course." Edward nodded thoughtfully. "I'd forgotten."

"Forgotten?"

"What it's like when you first get here and you assume you have to be as desperately secretive as you've always been."

"And you don't?"

"Well, you have to be discreet, of course," said Edward. "But Hollywood is like no other place in the world for people like us." He smiled. "You'll see."

Millie snorted at this. "What took you from Arizona all the way to Hollywood?" She affected a lower voice and answered herself, "'The train.' Ha. *That's* a story you're not telling."

◊ ◊ ◊

With Dan standing in front of her, Millie didn't see Wally approach, and when he came into view only a few feet away, he had a look on his face like he'd just been forced to eat a rotted fish head. She startled at the sight of him, and Dan turned around quick, hands up, ready to fend off whatever threat was behind him.

"Back off, Geronimo," Wally snarled.

He took that wide stance he had and barked some orders in their direction. "You take off on the horse"—he flicked a finger at Millie—"then you follow after her and catch up and grab her off that horse and carry her toward the trees. Then you get shot and drop to your knees. You get me?" Without waiting for an answer, he stalked back down toward the camera.

That woozy, cotton-headed feeling came over Millie, as if the world around her wasn't quite real.

"Let's pretend that didn't happen," Dan said somewhere near her. "Let's act like no one talked to us, and we can just decide for ourselves how to play the scene."

Millie was good at pretending things were better than they were. She'd been doing it all her life. "Okay," she breathed.

◊ ◊ ◊

They practiced the chase slowly a couple of times before the camera crank started turning, trotting the horses single file until Dan nudged his horse to catch up to her. When they were side by side, he said, "Now, I'm going to have to wrap my arms around you pretty hard to make sure I don't drop you down between the horses. I'll pull you across to my lap and then we slide off on the downstage side of the horses." Millie nodded, and Dan got hold of her and pulled her toward him and onto his thighs.

She suddenly went stiff in his arms.

"What's the matter?" His mouth was right by her bonnet.

"It's . . . It's what he did that night . . . grabbed me and pulled me onto his lap."

Dan didn't say anything for a moment, and Millie worried that he might have gotten tired of her and her problems, weak and scared like some boring little fraidy-cat.

"Take off the bonnet and look at me so you know it's not him."

She did as he said, and it helped. It was Dan, sweet and kind. Not the monster.

"But I wouldn't take time to pull off my bonnet while I'm being kidnapped," said Millie. "Wait, I know! I'll keep it untied and let it fly off my head when we're galloping."

"Smart girl."

Millie liked that very much. Of all the things she'd been called in her life, smart had never been one of them. Maybe being an actress was something she could really be good at.

Dan swung his foot over the horse's haunches and slid down onto the ground with Millie in his arms, carrying her like a bride toward a thicket of woods. "You okay?" he murmured.

"Quite comfortable. You must carry women around like this a lot," she teased.

"I believe you're my first."

"Well, don't let me be the last. I promise, it's a hit!"

A laugh burst out of him so hard it made her bounce against his ribs, which got her giggling, too. She felt his grip on her slide a little, and she yelled, "Hey, don't drop me!"

There was a sound a little ways off, and Millie looked up to see the crew and a few of the extras looking over at them and laughing. Except Wally. He still had that rotted-fish-head look.

They practiced the sequence with more and more speed, and then the camera rolled—quite literally. The crew hoisted it onto the back of a truck, tied it down, and drove along beside Millie as she rode, the cameraman cranking madly. All went well until the truck hit a bump and the poor guy flew off and landed in the dirt!

Everything came to a halt. Everyone stared at the man lying flat on his back in the dusty road behind the truck. "You okay?" yelled a fellow leaning out the driver's-side window.

The cameraman lifted his head. "Camera okay?"

"Yeah."

"Did we get the shot?"

"We got the shot."

He rose slowly and dusted himself off. "Lash me in for the next take," he said, and they started filming all over again.

The horses cooperated beautifully, as did Millie's bonnet, flying off at just the right time. Dan had to grab her roughly, but she could see his face and knew he regretted the unpleasantness. The scene ended with Millie in his arms, and it was all they could do to hold their frightened/fierce expressions until Vanderslice yelled cut. They fell apart with laughter at the end of every take.

Next it was time for the close-ups: Millie's terrified face as she sees Dan approaching; Dan pulling Millie off the horse; Millie staring up at him in horror as he prepares to carry her off into the forest. Dan had to hold her for a long time as they filmed each take from several different angles. "What did you have for lunch?" he teased. "Rocks?"

"I ate everything and went back for seconds," she said. "I knew you wanted to build up those muscles."

"Enough talking," huffed Vanderslice. "I'm trying to make a picture!"

As annoyed as he was during each take, he seemed quite happy when it was over. "Such a fresh young face," he said. "The audience will gasp at that iris shot, mark my words."

"Iris shot?" said Millie.

Vanderslice held his cupped hands out facing each other and then closed them in around her face. "Till all we see are those big, terrified eyes."

The next take was Dan's death scene, and this made Millie nervous. How would she manage on the set without him? And even if Wally walked off a cliff somewhere and was never heard from again, Dan was such good company during all the waiting between takes.

"Call for Mr. Gibson!" Vanderslice bellowed into his megaphone.

Soon a man walked toward them, not terribly tall, a bit on the stocky side. He wore a red plaid shirt, blue vest, and green pants tucked into boots with the biggest spurs Millie had ever seen. There was a gun belt at his waist and a red bandana around his neck. On his head sat a cowboy hat so big he could have stashed his lunch in it.

To make him seem taller, she thought.

He shook hands all around and seemed to take in stride the deference he was paid as one of the biggest western stars in the pictures.

"He seems nice!" Millie whispered to Dan.

"He's still going to kill me."

"Oh, I hate the thought of it," muttered Millie.

Dan chuckled. "You'd better act like you *love* the thought of it. You're in the middle of being kidnapped, remember?"

The scene of Hoot riding in and shooting all the other Indians was done. Dan was the last and the worst of them. With Dan still holding Millie in his arms, Hoot was to draw his six-shooter and fire into Dan's back.

"Well, that doesn't make sense," Millie said to Dan while he held her and they waited for Hoot to saddle up. "He could easily shoot me in the process."

"They're blanks, Millie."

"Yes, I know they're blanks, Dan. But the audience is supposed to think they're real bullets and he's a real cowboy."

"He actually is a real cowboy. He was a wrangler, and then he was a rodeo star."

"Well, I know spurs, and believe me, those are right out of the costume department. They look like buzz saws."

"It's the movies, Millie. The audience needs to be able to see the spurs. And they'll know he did the right thing by shooting me when you run back to your mama at the cabin."

Millie sighed. "Okay. But I don't like it."

Poor Dan had to pretend to be shot and drop to his knees in the dirt holding Millie about twelve times before Vanderslice was satisfied, by which time Dan's knees and shins were a mess of blood and dirt. "I'm so sorry," she whispered to him every time. "I wish I were lighter."

"You're light as a cloud, Millie. It's just a tough shot. Don't worry, it'll heal. Besides, all this attention on you means a little more on me, too. I'm getting paid better because of you. Now tomorrow, act like Hoot just saved you from a horrible death, will you please?"

◇ ◇ ◇

As they headed toward the truck once the scene was done, Vanderslice stopped them. "Miss—"

"Mildred Martin," Millie interjected.

"Miss Martin, would you be so kind as to report to Stage Eight on Friday morning at nine? We'd like to screen test you there. Of course, we've already gotten some excellent footage here, but we'll want indoor shots and some of you emoting for different types of films."

"Of course! Thank you so much, Mr. Vanderslice!"

He turned to Dan. "And uh—"

"Dan Russell," said Millie.

"Yes, we'd like you at Stage Twelve at the same day and time."

"A screen test," said Dan, barely concealing his shock.

"You did some good work out here, Russell." Vanderslice waved a hand around, indicating Dan's breechcloth, and added, "Leave all this at home. We know what you can do as an Indian. We'll be looking for other things."

On Friday morning, Millie woke up in her room at the Studio Club and stared at the ceiling, reviewing the little film she'd made in her head of all the advice Irene, Henry, Dan, and Gert had given her.

It began with a scene of her and Dan riding the truck back to Hollywood the previous afternoon, talking about how to make the most of their screen tests. His title card said:

> *Make friends with the crew. They always know things the director doesn't tell you, and they make a lot more decisions about the shot than they get credit for.*

The next scene featured Gert helping Millie practice applying all of her many new face paint products. Gert and Henry had taken her all the way to Max Factor's House of Makeup that evening, a little shop in downtown Los Angeles. "He's the one all the stars go to," Gert had said. Millie's new makeup box held flexible greasepaint, Supreme Liquid Whitener to lighten any freckles or blemishes, Color Harmony face powder, lip color, eyeliner, and mascara.

On the trolley back to Hollywood, Millie told Gert all about performing *The Gypsy and the Runaway Bride* with Irene and Henry in Flagstaff and how she'd gotten a case of the giggles right in the middle of it. Gert had laughed, but Henry had only shaken his head. He was just irritable, Millie decided. That bruise on his face from tripping on a buckle in the sidewalk must have been aching.

In her film now playing on the ceiling, Henry's title card said:

> *Follow the director's instructions to the letter, Millie, and try not to get silly.*

The last scene featured Irene, of course. Her title card was the most important, so Millie had placed it next to last in her little film.

> *Pay attention to the story—it will tell you what to feel and be your map for what gestures and expressions to use.*

But there was another card, something Irene had said when she'd left her at the door of the Studio Club, before she'd begun her slog back to that awful Ringa's. It was:

> *I'm proud of you, Millie. You're a beautiful, talented girl, and I just know the director will love you.*

◇ ◇ ◇

Millie went early to the studio to have a few moments to make friends with the crew, as Dan had suggested. When she got to Stage Eight, there wasn't much of a crew, only a short, barrel-chested man fussing with the camera and adjusting the lighting this way and that by inches in front of a set with only a small table and a telephone.

"Good morning," Millie said, in her friendliest tone. "I'm Mildred Martin. I'm here for the screen test."

"Wilson Grimes," he said, holding out his hand to shake. It was surprisingly soft for a hand that spent all day cranking a camera. "Nice to meet you."

"I'm glad I got here early," said Millie. "I'm new at this, of course, so I wonder if you could let me know a little bit about what to expect."

"Why, sure," he said. "When the director gets here, he'll give you a scene to play. He might have you do it several times, with different gestures and expressions. Then we'll head to one of the outdoor stages to see how the sun likes your face."

They chatted a few moments more, and then he suggested they do a quick practice. "Go over by the table and pretend to answer the phone, and I'll see what we've got."

She did as she was told, and he squinted through the camera lens. "Don't tip your chin down quite so far, I'm losing your eyelashes. Okay that's better." He came around and adjusted the light stands again, then went back to the camera. "Much better. All right, now with a telephone in the shot, I guarantee he'll ask you to react to some bad news. You want to try that? And it's okay to talk out loud. Makes it more realistic."

Pay attention to the story, Irene had said. But there was no story. She'd have to imagine some bad news. What was the worst thing she could think of? Irene being hurt—or even killed!

She took a few steps back and then headed toward the

phone as if it were ringing. With the receiver at her ear, she said, "Hello . . . yes, this is Mildred Martin . . . Irene Van Beck? Why she's my very best friend in the whole world! . . . What's that you say? A trolley? . . . She was hit?" Millie bit her lip, afraid to ask the next question. "Is she . . . is she all right? . . . No! . . . No! . . . She can't be! How could she be . . . dead!"

Saying the words felt so real and so horrifying that Millie burst into tears, her body convulsing with uncontrollable sobs, and she had to grab onto the table to keep herself from sinking to the floor.

Wilson Grimes's face emerged from behind the camera, eyes wide. "Boy, howdy," he murmured. "Wish I'd been cranking for that one."

He loved it! A grin broke through Millie's tears.

"Huh," snorted someone off to the right. "Where'd you learn to blubber like that—the correspondence school of expression?"

27

My whole career has been devoted to keeping people from knowing me.
Lon Chaney, actor, director, writer

Henry didn't know what to expect when he arrived on set the day after Edward rescued him from the thugs and drove him to the YMCA in his expensive car. His stomach felt as if it had munitions stored in it, and if Edward said one word, the whole pile would blow.

But Edward didn't say a thing. Nor did he treat Henry any differently. If anything, he kept his distance.

Wilson Grimes, on the other hand, pointed out with smirking jocularity that Henry needed more greasepaint and powder to cover the shiner under his left eye. "Mix it up, did ya?"

"Little bit." Henry hid his embarrassment with a touch of feigned swagger.

Wilson chortled and slapped him on the back.

On Friday they rehearsed Sheba's big exit from the palace to begin the journey back to her kingdom, including the full cast of extras, horses, and chariots. Edward warned them all that he wouldn't waste film until they had the scene down to the last hoofbeat.

Henry was glad for the distraction; it would keep his mind off wondering how Millie was doing at her screen test. The two months she'd spent without work had been so hard on her—and Irene—and he worried about them both. Irene would never abandon Millie, but how long could she go on making barely enough to survive on herself, much less for two people?

Henry directed his thoughts back to the task at hand. Edward had given him a note to hold his shoulders back a bit more but remained his ever-professional self, and Henry was relieved that there seemed to be no reason to worry that Edward would reveal him in any way. It was as if nothing had happened between them at all.

Good, Henry told himself. *As it should be*. But a soft little voice inside him whispered that it had been nice to share such confidences and hoped that Edward thought so, too.

Rehearsal was going well. Betty Blythe was resplendent in her virtual nakedness, and Henry had to admit that however coarse or alcohol-soaked she might get, the woman knew how to make it look good on film. Fritz Leiber also appeared to have recommitted himself to his art, setting aside his wit and maintaining his kingly bearing even between takes.

By the late afternoon, they were working on a part of the scene where Betty and one of her handmaidens—Gert Turner, Henry was happy to see—were wringing their hands over her unexpected pregnancy as they prepared to leave. The rest of the extras were set loose to roam the lot, and Henry took the opportunity to stretch his legs with a walk behind the "palace," where a small herd of guards in their metallic costumes were smoking and rolling dice in the dirt.

Farther along, a handmaiden was slipping a sandwich under

the canvas siding that surrounded the set. When she saw the look of confusion on Henry's face she hissed, "My husband's out there and he hasn't had work in three weeks, so mind your own potatoes!"

Beside a tree he saw his chariot-driving friend Ray kissing one of the blonder handmaidens with an ardor that the poor girl could hardly keep up with, as her dark red lipstick migrated from her chin to the tip of her nose.

They were all called back, and at last they were ready to put the whole sweeping scene together. Betty began her regal procession from the palace doors, but Edward yelled cut before she'd taken more than three steps.

"Present my compliments to the two gentlemen at the back," he called peevishly through his megaphone, "but unless those cigarettes are rolled in papyrus, they are historically inaccurate. And someone give that chariot driver's face a dusting. I don't know how, but he's gotten lipstick on his forehead."

A titter rippled across the set, but the laughter was not energetic. The cast knew Edward's waning patience was not something to be fooled with. After a long day that was the culmination of a hell of a week, Henry himself was looking forward to enjoying a beverage at whatever blind pig he happened upon first. He'd likely round up the girls, as well, and get all the details on Millie's screen test. He dearly hoped it had gone well.

Edward must have been reading his thoughts, because once the rehearsal was over, with the usual pandemonium of cast, crew, props, and equipment heading for the exit, he strolled casually toward Henry, nodding and smiling at the scurrying masses.

"I wonder if you might like to join me for a drink tonight," he murmured when he was certain no one was in earshot.

Henry waited for the now-lit bombs to detonate in his stomach. But it didn't feel like explosions . . . so much as butterflies.

Edward, with his aquiline nose and regal bearing. And very lovely hazel eyes. His restraint. And his lack of it.

"Oh, I, uh . . ." Henry stammered. And then he felt it. The grenade of his own shame and anxiety going off. "I'm sorry, but I already have plans."

"Another time, then." Edward's smooth face did not register the slightest disappointment, but Henry knew it was there. Edward had been brave enough to make his interest known. Henry, on the other hand, was the coward once again.

As he watched Edward's tall frame recede, more fuses igniting in his gut, Gert Turner walked up and hooked him by the arm. "Drinks?" she said.

"And lots of 'em."

28

No amount of dialogue can express the sweet, sincere
and invariably speechless emotion we call love.
Norma Taldmadge, actress, producer

Irene sat at her typewriter, distracted by her desperate hope that
Millie might receive a positive review for her screen test. They
needed the money, of course—they already owed Henry so
much, not to mention two dollars to Dan for the dinner he'd paid
for at The Cottonwood—but more importantly she was worried
about Millie's spirits. She'd been so low, and working had made
her so happy. As vulnerable and gullible as she was, if she went
back to haunting the streets and alleys of Hollywood . . . Irene
didn't like to think about who might get their hooks in her.

Irene was doubly distracted by the fact that she'd heard nothing from Eva Crown. Honestly, how long did it take to read a
couple of paragraphs, anyway?

When the door to the typing pool opened, Irene didn't look
up. Miss Clemente had gone off to deliver some typed continuity
scripts, and Irene assumed it was her. Then she heard a little gasp,
as if the person who'd opened the door couldn't breathe.

Millie's face was smudged and wet, with eyeliner striping
down her cheeks. Irene jumped up and hurried across the room,

aware that all the other typewriters had suddenly gone silent. She guided Millie out to the hallway and closed the door behind her. Millie collapsed against her, and Irene had to hang on to her to keep her from sliding to the floor.

"My God! What happened!"

Millie was crying so hard she could barely inhale, but she finally gasped out, "Wally."

"Where? What did he do?"

"Screen test."

"Where the hell was Vanderslice?"

Millie swiped her eyes against the shoulder of her dress, leaving muddy stripes of white, tan, and black. "He was at Dan's test," she panted.

"And *Wally* directed your screen test?"

Millie nodded.

Irene grabbed her by the shoulders. "Did he hurt you?"

"He . . . he just . . . scared me!"

"How? How did he scare you?"

Her sobbing had become little gasps she struggled to speak around. "He was so . . . mean. He said awful things. I tried to stay calm, but he . . . he got too close to me and I . . . I panicked." She started to cry again in earnest. "I ran away. I was so afraid he would touch me!"

Irene pulled Millie into her arms. "You're safe now. You never have to go back there."

Over Millie's shoulder, Irene saw Miss Clemente, stopped midstride, watching them.

"I'm sorry, Miss Clemente. My friend—"

"Your friend shouldn't be here in such a state."

"I'll work through my lunch and powder room break to make up for it."

"Just take her home."

◇ ◇ ◇

Irene hurried back to the typing pool just as the other girls were leaving for lunch. She tugged an old handkerchief with fraying edges from her purse and dabbed at her damp forehead and neck, nodding her gratitude at Miss Clemente, who hadn't left yet for some reason.

Irene sat down and stared at the typewriter a moment, willing herself to concentrate. Then she rolled in a piece of fresh paper, pulled a handwritten page from the stack, and began to type.

"What was all that about?" Miss Clemente demanded.

Irene looked up. "My friend was just upset. Thank you for letting me—"

"I could see that. Why was she upset?"

"She had a screen test, and it didn't go well."

Miss Clemente opened her purse and squinted into it, looking for something. "You asked if the director had hurt her."

How could Irene explain that one? And why was Miss Clemente asking so many questions?

"You used his first name."

"She had a date with him about a month ago, and he . . . well, he wasn't nice."

"She seemed terrified." Miss Clemente's glare remained trained into her purse, as if she might find the fountain of youth in there. Or at least some magic cream to smooth all those pockmarks.

Irene shook her head. "It's my fault," she said bitterly. "The next day I confronted him, and I guess it made him mad, because he took it out on her."

Miss Clemente's gaze rose from her purse, small brown eyes blazing.

◇ ◇ ◇

That evening when Irene came down the stairs from the typing pool, there was a figure leaning against the wall in the shade of the building. "Dan! How did it go?"

"Seemed all right. I guess we'll have to wait and see." A shy pride belied his casual tone. "How'd it go for Millie? I went to Stage Eight, but they must have finished before I got there."

"Not that well." Irene met his gaze. "The director was hard on her."

"It wasn't . . ." A fury ignited behind his eyes. "Don't tell me it was Wally." Before she could even respond, the heel of his palm suddenly slammed against the wall. "He scared the hell out of her on set," Dan seethed. "And he enjoyed it, the son of a bitch."

Irene's stomach sank. "She didn't tell me."

"Vanderslice loved her. He only wanted to see me because he wasn't sure of me. He was sure of *her*, though. He said the screen test was just a formality. Something to show the producers. She had it sewn up—until that bastard came along."

"I have to go. She's waiting for me." Dan didn't ask if he should come, too, only got in stride with Irene as she hurried silently toward the Studio Club.

But Millie was not waiting for her. The house director said she'd left hours before. A trickle of anger bubbled through Irene's anxiety. Wasn't it just like her to go off and do something foolish, and not consider the consequences? *Just like the damned tea set.*

At that moment, Gert Turner came down the curved staircase. She smiled at the sight of Irene, then her smile faded. "Well, you look like you just grabbed the wrong end of the poker."

"Have you seen Millie?"

Gert shook her head. "What's the rub?"

"She had a screen test today. She'd had a date with the fellow who directed a while back, and he wasn't . . . gentlemanly. Wasn't happy about her getting a screen test, either."

"Son of a bitch scared the hell out of her, and she bolted," said Dan.

"Jesus," Gert breathed, and shook her head. "This town . . ."

"I just want to find her. She's not exactly the queen of common sense."

Gert squinted in thought. "I was about to meet Henry for a drink. You two take Hollywood Boulevard, and we can take Sunset. Whoever finds her, meet back here."

"Gert, you don't have to—"

"What am I supposed to do? Drink and laugh like everything's jake?"

When they got to Hollywood Boulevard and headed west through town, Irene told Dan he didn't have to come. "I'm sure you have better things to do on a Friday night, and you live around here, don't you? I can manage. I'm used to fending for myself."

"I know you can fend for yourself, Irene. But it's getting dark, and I'm worried about her, too."

Irene stopped. "Why? Why are you the least bit concerned about any of this? You met her, what—three days ago? She's not your problem."

He leveled a look at her that made her hold her breath for a second. "She's not yours either," he said after a moment. "But here we are."

As they neared Cahuenga Boulevard and passed the Nash automobile dealership, they saw a crowd of people on the sidewalk by the new Security Trust and Savings Bank. There was a movie camera and crew members filming three young men dressed in military uniforms.

"Someone's always filming here," Dan commented.

"Why's that?"

"Big, new fancy building, close to the studios. The crew can walk back for lunch." They scanned the onlookers for any sign of Millie, without luck. They stopped in at Kress Drug on the opposite corner, with its long lunch counter and countless unguents, ablutions, and salves, but the place was empty save for an older couple sitting on stools at the counter sharing a sardine sandwich, and three teenage girls sniffing the perfume bottles at the end of the aisle.

They crisscrossed their way down Hollywood Boulevard, dodging Model Ts and sporty coupes, Dan checking a diner on the north side of the street while Irene scanned a hat shop on the south. They both went into the Iris Theatre, bought the cheapest nickel tickets, and then crept along the outer aisles, searching for Millie's face in the coruscated glow of flickering light.

A few blocks down, the finishing touches were being put on a huge new theater painted to look like an Egyptian tomb. Mama Ringa's was a couple of blocks north. Could Millie have gone there looking for her?

She had to tell Dan to wait in the overgrown, sun-scorched yard.

"Not even on the porch?"

Irene shook her head, and Dan tugged the wide brim of his black felt fedora down a little on his forehead and crossed his arms. She nearly ran Mama Ringa over in her haste to get up to her room to see if Millie was there.

"What in the . . ." Ringa muttered as she staggered back a step. "Where are you stampeding off to?"

"I'm sorry, but I'm looking for Millie. Have you seen her?"

Ringa looked away. "She and Agnes went out."

"Went out where?" Irene demanded.

Ringa waved her away. "Wherever girls go on a Friday night."

"Where do *your* girls go," Irene hissed, "to their everlasting disgrace?"

"Watch yourself." Ringa's voice was full of quiet menace. "I can fill your bed in the time it takes to say 'Pack your bag.' Girls like you are a dime a dozen."

◇   ◇   ◇

The Hollywood Harem was on the outskirts of West Hollywood. "It's just dancing," Ringa often said with that motherly smile she twisted off and on like the wheel handle of a garden spigot. "A pleasant way to earn a few extra dollars."

The name alone had been enough to make the fine hairs on the nape of Irene's neck stand at attention. Then she'd learned it was a "closed" dance hall, meaning closed to women who didn't work there. Only men could get in, the kind who wanted or needed to pay for dances, instead of going to a normal hall and simply asking a girl to dance for free.

"That's a good hike from here," said Dan when she told him.

"Agnes must have paid for a cab. Millie doesn't have a nickel." Though with her looks and a share of the ten cents she'd get for each dance, she probably had plenty of nickels by now.

"I'll flag one down. And I'll pay for it. I know your situation."

"You work pretty steady now?"

"Cowboys and injuns." He hit the last word with a hint of derision. "America never tires of them."

The Hollywood Harem was doing a brisk business by the time Dan and Irene arrived at eight o'clock. Of course, Irene could only know this from the stream of men entering. She wasn't allowed to go in and see for herself, and for this reason alone, she was grateful for Dan's help.

As she stood on the sidewalk, arms crossed around her, more

building up the hill on Ivar Avenue. Dan's studio apartment was small but uncluttered, with a little wooden table up against the window, sections of the *Hollywood Citizen* fanned haphazardly across it by the breeze. An upholstered love seat with carved wooden legs sat against one wall, and Irene guided Millie to sit down.

"This is nice," she said and let her head loll against the sofa's back.

It was awful to see her like that, and Irene just wanted her to stop talking in that airy, wraithlike way and go the hell to sleep. But there was no bed. Irene wondered if Dan curled his sizeable frame into the love seat each night.

There was a large weaving on the wall with intricate geometric patterns and loops at the top corners that hung from hooks. He released one of the loops and let the weaving hang from the opposite side, revealing the outline of a Murphy bed in the wall, which he pulled down. It was sloppily made with sheets and a thin blue cotton blanket.

"She needs to sleep," he said.

"Okay," said Millie. She rose and drifted to the bed, lay down with her shoes on, and was unconscious in seconds.

Irene stared at Millie's peaceful features for a moment and burst into tears.

How would this ever work? How could they continue to survive on her thin salary, with Millie likely to wander off and do something foolish any day of the week? Irene couldn't abandon her. She couldn't. But she couldn't keep going like this, either. She pressed her hand over her mouth, embarrassed and overcome, and when Dan approached, she shook her head. He stopped, but he didn't retreat. "It's been a long, hard day," he murmured.

One of the longest and hardest. Irene had had longer and harder, of course, but not for a while. Not, if she remembered correctly, since she'd met Millie.

"Why don't you lie down with her and rest."

Irene shook her head again. She thought she might drown in her own wet sorrow if she lay down. And she was mad at Millie. Or just scared. It was all a jumble.

Her weeping slowed, and Dan passed her a handkerchief, as gray and threadbare as her own. He pulled Millie's shoes off and slid them under the bed. Then he tugged the top sheet and blanket out from under her and tucked them around her limp form.

Irene watched him do this, unflustered, as if none of it really surprised him. This was the world, his actions seemed to say, and he was a full-fledged citizen.

He pulled a chair out from the table for Irene and then went to root around in the icebox. She slumped down into the old wooden chair, scratched up but surprisingly sturdy. He put down two glasses of water and a plate with a hunk of cheese and roughly sliced bread. Holding an apple in his hand, he pared off the bruises and sliced it onto the plate.

He sat down heavily in the other chair and nodded toward the food. "Go on," he said.

"I'm not sure if I'm hungry."

"You are."

She inhaled a sniffle. Maybe she was. And whether she was or not, it felt good to be fed. The apple slice was cold and sweet on her tongue, and he cut her a wedge of cheese to go with it. "You must have younger brothers and sisters," she said.

"I do."

"Where are they? Arizona?"

He cut a piece of cheese for himself and wrapped a slice of bread around it. He looked up at her before he took a bite. "The Navajo Reservation."

She knew he was waiting for some sort of reaction, but she was too exhausted to have one. What was it like on a reservation? She had no idea. "You must miss them."

talked about himself all night, she would be happy to sit back and listen.

She took another sip of her tea. "Tell me about the school."

◇ ◇ ◇

The Phoenix Indian School was far away. "More than just miles," he said. "The physical distance was the least of it."

He'd been a prime candidate at the age of seven, with paler skin than most and a "reputable" father. "He was a bronco buster, mind you," said Dan. "Not exactly a state senator." But it wasn't his line of business they'd cared about. It was the color of his skin. It made the fine folks at the Bureau of Indian Affairs feel that his son would have a better chance than most at assimilation because, as they'd said, being American was in his blood. "Their version of American, of course." His mother had wept when he'd been taken off to the school. His stepfather was all too happy to see him go.

"The first thing they do is cut off all your hair." Dan explained that for the Navajo, long hair wasn't a fashion choice. Brushing the hair with bundled stiff grass and tying it into the traditional bun at the nape of the neck was part of the tribe's spiritual practice. "You can't accomplish it yourself. You need another person, your mother or a relative, to do it for you." It further connected people to one another. At the tender age of seven, a newly shorn Dan was convinced that his mother would not recognize him, and he was now an orphan.

"But you wear your hair short now," Irene said.

"Living here, it's easier to go out and not have people stare. Also, I can take a non-Indian part if the opportunity arises." He'd grown his hair out when he went back to the reservation as a teenager but had it cut and made into a wig when he came to Hollywood.

"That wig you wear is your real hair!"

He grinned. "So I can have my cake and be a Navajo, too."

◇ ◇ ◇

He'd allowed her to ask all kinds of personal questions for hours, but he'd never asked any of her, though he'd left spaces for her to be forthcoming if she'd cared to be. She was anxious enough without going into all that. She wanted only to be transported from her current situation to the fascinating life of Dan Russell and dreaded the thought of leaving.

"I should probably wake her up and get us out of here so you can get some sleep."

"It's past midnight!"

"Dan, we can't stay here. You're a single man, and this is your bedroom. It's unseemly enough that we came here at all."

"We just dragged your friend out of the Harem in a drugged-up haze, and you think coming here is the unseemly part?"

She must have been beyond tired, because his annoyance—and his logic—made her laugh. Of course he was right. "Yes, but where I come from—"

"And where is that, exactly?"

"Van Wert, Ohio."

He crossed his arms. "Tell me what the good people of Van Wert would say."

She couldn't stop chuckling. It was suddenly all so ridiculous. "They would be *mortified*, and I would *not* be invited to help plan the church suppers or so much as walk my neighbor's *dog* for fear of corrupting him."

"Irene, have you consulted a map lately? Because this is not Van Wert, Ohio." He pointed out the window. "This is Hollywood, California, where you'd have to run naked down Sunset on a Sunday for anyone to glance up from the latest *Photoplay* magazine."

She laughed until her eyes watered and she had to dab at them with the handkerchief he'd given her hours ago for a very different sort of tears. She shook her head. "I am so tired."

"Go to bed."

"Your neighbors won't be scandalized?"

It was his turn to laugh. "Trust me, they all *know* where they live."

She took off her shoes and slid under the covers with Millie, watching with half-closed eyes as he undid the wall blanket from its remaining hook, lay down on the braided rug, and covered himself. "I hate that you have to sleep on the floor."

"Good night, Irene."

"Good night, Dan. And thank you."

◊ ◊ ◊

It could only have been a few hours—the sun hadn't even risen yet, though the sky was softly lightening—but Irene felt strangely well rested, as if for that brief period she had let every last worry, every care she'd ever had or anticipated for the future, float into the ether.

With her cheek at the edge of the mattress, she gazed down at Dan Russell lying on his back on a braided rug on his own floor, hands resting across his chest.

Savage Indian.

It's what her aunt would say. She had a particular love of westerns and had taken Irene and Ivy to the local movie house regularly. Irene had seen so many "savage Indians" attack Conestoga wagons and God-fearing farmers it was a wonder she wasn't terrified to face a real one.

But she wasn't. Not remotely. She'd had a good feeling about Dan from the moment she met him, and his "savage-ness" had been fully refuted by his protectiveness of Millie and unflagging kindness to Irene over the course of such a strange and horrible evening. He'd had every reason to pass judgment on them, these burlesque girls, one of whom had taken drugs and danced for pay. But instead he'd welcomed them into his home, offered food and drink, and given up his own bed to sleep on the floor.

And he'd talked to her, told her the stories of his life, though some were undeniably painful, and he still didn't seem sure if he'd always made the right decisions. He'd opened his heart to her. As Millie had over and over, and Henry, too, with his endless support and generosity. Somehow they'd oiled the rusty hinges on her own heart.

Savage Indian, indeed.

His eyes fluttered and he gazed up at her, a smile slowly warming his face. "Well, that's a nice way to wake up," he murmured.

Without thinking she slid her hand off the mattress and down to him, and he took it and held it against his chest. She could feel the reliable thumping beneath it as they each lay in silence and stillness, at arm's length. After a few moments he raised her hand to his lips and kissed her palm, never taking his eyes off her.

The tenderness. Dear God, she'd never felt the likes of it. Filling every inch of her. Cutting all the ballast that had weighed her down for so long.

She found herself sliding off the edge of the mattress toward him. His arm opened to fold her in, and she curled herself against him, needing as much bodily contact as she could manage while fully clothed and lying on a braided rug, with her best friend snoring in the bed above her.

"I want to know everything about you," he whispered.

"Okay," she said. "I'll tell you."

pumping out flickers and reaping the profits, without interference from sermonizers and moralists.

◊ ◊ ◊

When they arrived at the studio, the faces of crew and actors alike were so mournful, there might as well have been a funeral dirge playing. Film industry morality had always been in question; that was nothing new. But if someone as successful, rich, and well liked as Fatty could be accused of such a heinous crime, well, it looked like judgment day had finally come.

The paper had reported on his several nights as a guest of the California penal system, after which he'd been handed over to a grand jury by zealous prosecutor Matthew Brady. There were the articles on the reaction from around the nation. The Women's Christian Temperance Union, still basking in the glow of having foisted Prohibition on the nation, felt they were up to the task of crushing immoral behavior wherever it raised its bejeweled head.

Closer to home, at the Methodist Church on Hollywood Boulevard, the pastor railed against the film industry as "a community of jazzers," whose only interest was in "eating and drinking and wearing clothes and more clothes—and less clothes—and more jewels and trying to drive faster and seeking hungrily for fresh sensations and bizarre things." They were "moral lepers, lounge lizards, mashing parasites and lip-sticked women."

On set, the crew went about the business of preparing to re-shoot scenes that hadn't come out to Edward's satisfaction. The mood was somber, but he soldiered on with his characteristic good manners and attention to detail. The village of Hollywood might be commencing to drive a silver Bentley straight to hell, but Edward Oberhouser had a picture to make.

At the lunch break, Henry made his way casually toward Edward, who was scanning an inked-up copy of the continuity script Eva Crown had handed him. No one else was in his immediate vicinity, and Henry told himself no one would bat an eye at an actor—not a star, of course, but someone with a part and lines to say—asking the director a quick question. Nevertheless his heart pounded as if he'd been cornered in an alley by a gang of thugs.

"Mr. Oberhouser?"

The director looked up, face placid. *His* heart wasn't pounding, Henry felt certain of that. And yet his gaze caught on Henry not as an employer ready to manage some trifling question of an employee, but as . . . a person. An acquaintance. Even someone with whom he'd shared a notable experience. It gave Henry courage, and he began again.

"Edward."

The man blinked, and his face colored ever so slightly. "Yes?"

"I wondered if I might take you up on that drink tonight."

◇ ◇ ◇

They met at The Valley Quail, which was far enough south on Highland Avenue not to be a Hollywood favorite, and yet not so far that Henry couldn't easily walk there. He appreciated the director's thoughtfulness in the choice. It was fairly nondescript, a notch above a diner. As Henry waited outside, he began to get the distinct feeling that more people were going in than the place might be able to accommodate. He hoped they'd get a table. And yet, when he peered inside, several were empty. The phone booth in the back, however, seemed to be getting a lot of use. There was even a line forming.

Edward's car pulled up, and in the waning light, with no fresh injuries to distract him, Henry was able to fully appreciate the vehicle. It was a subtle navy blue, not the ostentatious champagne color that so many stars seemed to prefer. Henry had failed to notice the canvas roof when he'd ridden in it the previous week, or the high whitewall tires with thick wooden spokes.

Edward emerged and shook his hand, noticing Henry's interest in the car. "It's a Packard Twin Six. Twelve cylinders. It's not too flashy, but it's got a lot of power."

Just like its owner, thought Henry.

The driver didn't even glance at Henry but kept his eyes trained forward before pulling away to park somewhere. He'd clearly been hired for his ability to behave as an extension of the car, blind and deaf to anything but the road.

Henry held the door to The Valley Quail open for Edward and followed him as he strode straight back to the phone booth. He held a hand up to Henry, entered, and closed the folding door. Then he opened it and cocked a finger, inviting Henry to join him.

Two men in a phone booth together?

Henry balked, but Edward tipped his head, insistent. And then he disappeared.

Henry took a hesitant step forward, and suddenly a man's voice growled, "In or out? I'm not holding it open till the cops come." The back panel of the booth seemed to have been pried back. Henry stepped through into another world.

The room was small, crowded with about a dozen small round tables, the walls hung with tapestries as a sort of decorative soundproofing, he suspected. It smelled of smoke and drink, of perfume and food, and of humans enjoying themselves just a tad more than they might have without the tingle of secrecy.

A makeshift bar took up the length of one wall, and Edward stood ordering drinks. He looked over his shoulder at Henry and motioned for him to get a table. And then he smiled.

Edward was happy.

He had a stately sort of handsomeness even when scowling, but with that joyous little grin on his face, he was the most beautiful thing Henry had ever seen.

◇ ◇ ◇

They were several drinks in, talking about this and that, exchanging chitchat about the studio and eventually boyhood information, nothing much more revealing than place of birth, siblings, parents still alive or not, when Edward asked, "And what brought you to Hollywood?"

Henry gave him the whole story—performed it for him, really—about Irene and Millie, the three of them jumping off the train, the silly play they concocted, and running for their lives from Barney. Edward laughed or shook his head in wonder at all the right places, and Henry found himself thinking, *This is a date.*

He'd had many dates before, of course, when he was trying so hard to like women. He'd fed and entertained them, kissed and petted them, and even taken one to bed, which had been disastrous. In her mind it confirmed that he was the man for her, while at the very same time it confirmed for him that he never wanted to do anything like it again.

This is a date, he thought. *The one I never dared to hope I could have.*

◇ ◇ ◇

After dinner, the car magically reappeared, and Henry wondered if the evening was over. If so, he couldn't complain. It had been the most enjoyable dinner he'd had in a long time—possibly ever. But

Edward said, "Have you been up in Laurel Canyon? It's a beautiful night for it. We could put the top down."

They drove the lonely road up to Lookout Mountain, and Edward pointed out Tom Mix's log cabin on the hill. It was such a quiet spot, the sky noisy with stars, and sitting with Edward so near, Henry almost forgot the reason he'd suggested they get together in the first place.

"I need your advice on something."

Edward turned his gaze from the sky to look at Henry. "Of course."

"My friend, Millie. She's in a bit of a bind."

Edward's face, so serene, suddenly lost some wattage. "Oh."

"I'm sorry," said Henry, flustered. "Have I said the wrong thing?"

"No, not at all." Edward's voice was slightly flat. "Young actors and actresses always need help of some form or another."

"I didn't . . ."

"Didn't what?"

Words wouldn't come. Henry shook his head.

"Didn't come out with me tonight so I would help your friend?" Edward prompted.

"Edward . . ."

The director was silent for several seconds and then he said gently, "How can I help?"

It's time to stop all this cowardly nonsense, Henry thought. *It really is time.*

"I came out with you because I want your help, it's true. But I do want to be here. With you. And if the only reason I was brave enough to do it was because I told myself I was helping a friend . . . well, that's embarrassing. Truly. And Millie, you know, she's so . . ." Henry clenched his hands in frustration. "But she has this way of making you feel like you would jump off a ship in the middle of the ocean to save her. Which is exactly what this feels like to me—like I'm bobbing around in the sea without a life jacket." He shook his head. "I suppose I should thank her. As maddening as she is, she got me here."

Edward's gaze never wavered, but he remained silent.

"Actually," Henry whispered, "I'm having the night of my life."

He leaned forward, slowly, watching those lovely hazel eyes for any reluctance, and seeing none, pressed his lips to Edward's.

30

◇ ◇ ◇

On Saturday morning, when Millie woke in a strange apartment with Irene sleeping next to her, she thought, *Isn't this fun. I wonder where we are.*

It came back to her in pieces. The dance hall. Dan showing up. At first she'd thought he wanted to dance, and she was so relieved, because he wasn't grabby or bad-smelling like the others. He'd be nice to dance with. Then suddenly she was outside and Irene was there. That look on her face . . .

Even in the wobbly, cotton-headed state she'd been in, Millie had seen the pain she'd caused her dear friend. Remembering it now, remorse crashed over her and she almost gasped at the weight of it. She'd been remorseful for many things in her life . . . at least at the time . . . at least for a while. But this was different.

When Irene began to stir, Millie could hardly wait to tell her. "I'm sorry. I'm so sorry, Irene. You were so worried, and I just wanted to help out, but I shouldn't have done it like that."

Irene pushed a lock of hair out of her eyes. "What time is it?"

"It must be almost noon. See where the sun is? Whose apartment is this, anyway?"

She heard movement on the other side of the bed. "It's mine," said a man's voice thick with sleep. Dan sat up from the floor, and his cheek was creased in the strangest little braid pattern.

In fact, there was a braid pattern on Irene's arm, too.

Dan gave Millie a nod and then smiled at Irene, and her cheeks went pink.

Something had happened between them. Millie wasn't entirely sure what, but she thought it must be good. She knew she shouldn't say anything, but she couldn't help grinning and giving Irene a secret little nudge.

Irene's face suddenly went flat with anger. "Millie, there is *nothing to smile about. What you put us through last night—*"

"I know! I'm so sorry—"

"You know? *You know?* How could you *possibly know?* You were so drugged up you barely knew your own name!"

"It's true, but even in such a"—Millie waved her hand around searching for the word—"such a *state*, I could see you, Irene. I could see your face and how upset you were. And I promise I will never forget it. I will never put you through that again."

This seemed to take a little starch out of Irene's fury, but she wasn't ready to let it go. "Millie, I swear—"

"You don't have to swear, you just have to know that I've learned my lesson, and I'm so, so sorry, Irene. Truly. And Dan, you, too. You both have been so good to me and I will never let you down again."

◇   ◇   ◇

She would never let them down again . . . but that didn't mean she wasn't tempted to go back to The Hollywood Harem the following night with the twenty or so tickets she'd found stuffed in her pocket and cash them in. That was about a dollar's worth of dancing right there, and she was entitled to it.

But if she did that she knew there would be additional temptations: the first would be to find another one of those very, very nice cigarettes that Agnes had shown her how to smoke. It had made even boring things seem fascinating, like the pattern of dandruff on one man's shoulders or the way the lights hanging from the ceiling seemed to move, even though she knew she was the one moving. The second temptation would be the money she could make if she stuck around to have a few more dances.

"Things have a way of cascading with you, Millie," her father had often said. "One little misstep leads to a bigger one and a bigger one after that." She didn't know why that was, but there seemed to be some truth to it. This time she was determined to keep that first domino from falling.

On Sunday, she and Irene had searched the papers for jobs, anything Millie might be able to do. On Monday, she applied for several maid positions. But she had no experience, and one very blunt wife informed her that even if Millie had super-human cleaning powers, the woman wouldn't hire her because she was too pretty and would "distract" her husband.

There were too many young women in Hollywood looking for jobs that required no skill. The skills Millie did have—farm and stable work—those jobs all went to the many young men who were also scouring the area for work to hold them over until their big break in the pictures finally came. She was told she was just too dainty to muck out stalls.

Things brightened up considerably on Thursday, though. For Irene, at least.

Millie returned to the Studio Club that afternoon, feeling terribly dejected after another round of fruitless job hunting and in danger of breaking all her promises to everyone.

Irene must have run all the way to the Studio Club and back during her lunch break, because when Millie checked in at the club office, as she now did from habit rather than expectation that anything good might await, there had been a note:

> Meet me at The Cottonwood at seven. I have good news, and it involves dress shopping!

Millie looked down at the one she was wearing. It had once been her best day dress, Nile green in crepe rayon with a boat neck, three-quarter sleeves, and an inset sash around her hips. It had been washed so many times now that the sheen had gone fuzzy and the hem of one sleeve was beginning to fray to a rather appalling degree. The need for new dresses was clearly at a critical state, yet she knew it was the last thing Irene would spend money on. Something was either very right or very wrong.

Millie walked up to The Cottonwood and caught sight through the window of Irene and Dan sitting together at a table inside. Dan had apparently just teased her about something, because he was grinning like the cat that got the cream, and Irene went a little pink and flicked the back of her hand against his arm. Her gaze never left his face, though. Nor he hers.

Millie was staggered by the love she saw between them. She had known something was up at Dan's apartment—a crush maybe? Even a kiss?—but Irene was still angry about the Harem, and Millie hadn't wanted to push her luck by prying for details.

This, though. This was more than a crush, and at first Millie was just so glad. Irene deserved to be adored by the whole world! But then it suddenly occurred to her that if Irene started wanting to spend her free time with Dan—alone for at least some of it—

that would mean less time with her. She felt her throat tighten like a string bag at the thought of it.

Don't be greedy, she told herself and stepped inside.

Irene spied her and extended her arm to beckon her over. "Millie!"

I still belong to her. Millie let out a little sigh of relief and went over to kiss Irene on the cheek and nod and smile at Dan. "Now, what's all this about dress shopping?"

Henry and Gert were fast on her heels, and when they were all seated and anxiously awaiting the news, Irene pulled twenty-five dollars out of her purse and waved the bills in the air like little green flags. "I sold my first scenario."

A cheer went up, and handshakes and kisses were exchanged.

"I'm so happy for you, Irene." Henry's eyes shone with pride.

"And I'm so happy for *you*, Henry Weiss, because you're finally going to get your loan repaid!" Henry crossed his arms resolutely and shook his head, but Irene was so happy, she just laughed. "Also, dinner tonight is on me."

Millie was delighted to see Irene feeling free to be so generous, but she had to wonder. Once she reimbursed Henry and Dan, paid for dinner, and socked a few dollars away for next week's rent, that money would be gone. She leaned over and whispered in Irene's ear, "We don't have to get dresses. Let's wait until you sell the next one."

Irene grinned and patted Millie's hand. "That's very practical of you."

Millie nudged her with her elbow. "I *am* sometimes, you know!"

Irene raised her voice to address the group. "The very wise Millie Martin is concerned that I'm going overboard with spreading around my boodle. So I guess I should tell you that I have even better news. I was recommended for a job in the Scenario Department reading submissions to suggest for production. They'll teach me how to write continuity scripts, too. I start on Monday at thirty-five dollars a week."

◇ ◇ ◇

When Millie arrived home that night, she was still smiling. The stars seemed to be aligning for her wonderful friend, both romantically and professionally. Millie still felt desperate to get a job somewhere, but at least she didn't have to worry quite so much.

As she passed the office on her way up to bed, Miss Hunter called out, "There's a message for you." Her homely face seemed particularly bright. "Mr. Carlton Sharp's secretary called to say he would like to meet with you in the Olympic Publicity Office tomorrow morning at nine."

Millie frowned. "Did she say what he wanted?"

"She didn't," said Ms. Hunter. "I suppose the only thing to do is go and find out."

◇ ◇ ◇

Most of the buildings on Olympic's lot had the architectural appeal of a car barn. They'd been thrown up hastily as the demand for pictures rose and overran the available set space. But the corporate offices were in that grand pillared building with the enormous iron lanterns they'd seen on their very first day in Hollywood. Millie had never been inside before, separated as it was from the ongoing fray of production.

In the lobby she approached the reception area and was told Publicity was on the second floor, next to Vice President Louis Manning's office. The heavy oak door with CARLTON SHARP, DIRECTOR OF PUBLICITY stenciled in gold stood ajar, and Millie peeked in.

and we"—he glanced at Manning—"Olympic is prepared to recompense you for your . . . inconvenience. As long as you sign a statement denying any culpability on the studio's part and promising that you will not go to the papers."

Go to the papers? Millie thought. *And say what? That I allowed a man I barely knew to force himself on me, so I can be publicly shamed on top of the private shame I already feel?*

She stared at him.

He stared back, but then he cut his eyes once again to Manning. "A hundred dollars."

"A hundred dollars?" Millie said, confused.

"Two hundred. And another screen test. Wilson Grimes said you were the best fresh talent he's seen this year, until the other man entered the room."

"You're offering me two hundred dollars and a screen test to keep me from talking to the papers." Millie thought hard about this. "It's because of that horrible business with Fatty Arbuckle, isn't it?"

Mr. Sharp's mouth twitched. "Not at all. There is no murder in this case. There may not even be a crime. It's your word against his, and these things never actually make it to court."

He was right about that. But these men weren't worried about a court case; they were worried about her going to the papers. Very worried. And the longer she didn't take them up on their offer . . . the higher it went. Which suddenly made her feel a lot less worried. She smiled, and Mr. Sharp flinched.

"A thousand dollars," Mr. Manning suddenly growled from across the room. "Now come over here and sign this statement before I change my mind."

Afterward, Millie was handed an envelope and told to report to Stage Six on Monday for her screen test. The men were suddenly in great haste to shuttle her out the door.

"But how did Mary Pickford know? She doesn't even work for Olympic."

Mr. Sharp let out an exasperated sigh. "One of your friends at the Studio Club reported it to the director, who addressed the matter with Miss Pickford. She's a patroness of the club, or didn't you know that?"

Just before the door closed behind her, Millie heard him mutter, "Dumb Dora."

She didn't care. She had a thousand dollars in her hands. And a screen test.

PART 2

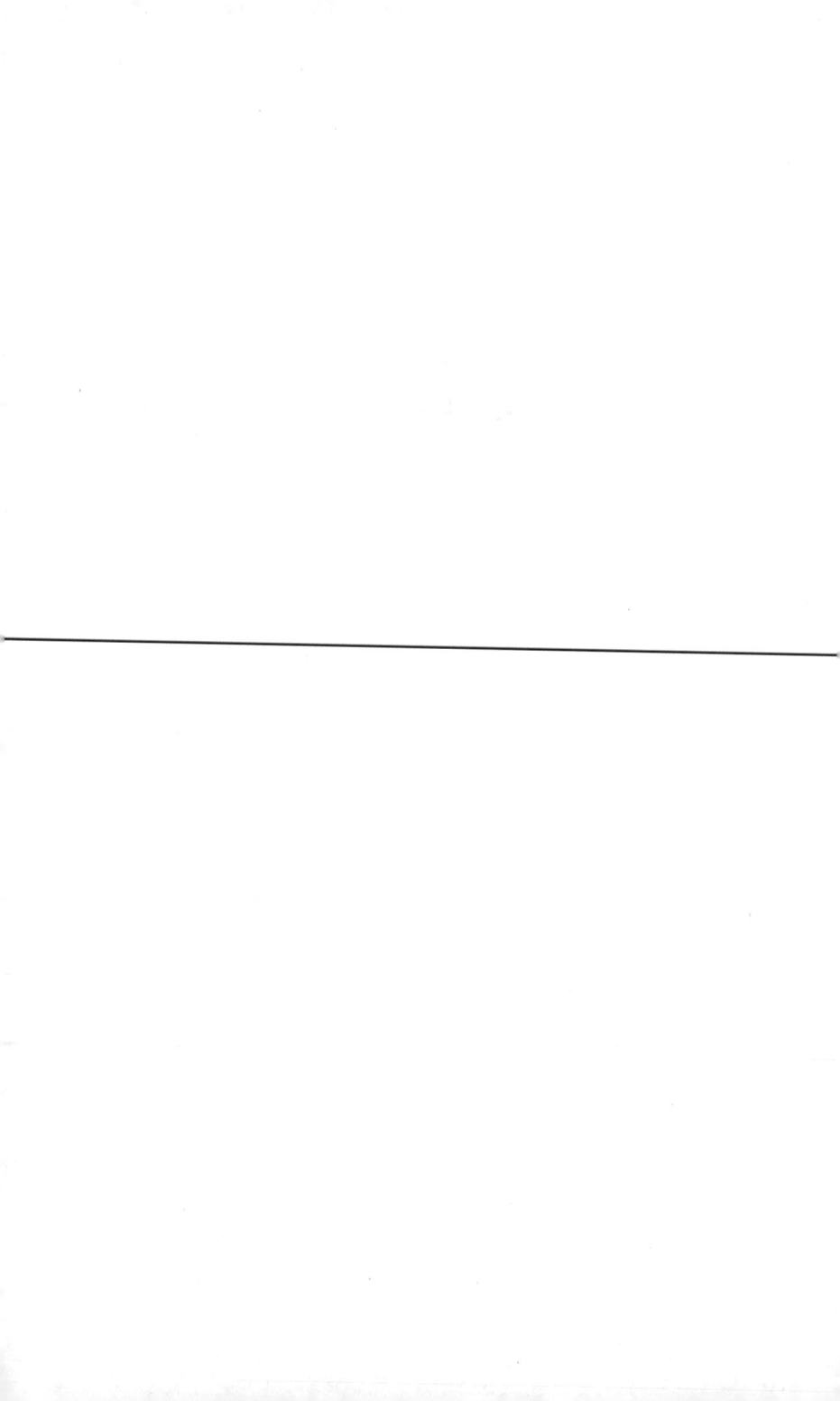

In February she landed the roll of the young mother in *A Baby's Cry*, and that night the five friends howled their glee in half the speakeasies in Hollywood. Irene and Millie working together as scenarist and female lead—it had been beyond imagining six short months before when they'd been jobless, penniless, and living in squalor at Mama Ringamory's.

Henry might have had a chance at the male lead, if he hadn't already landed the roll of the title character in a romantic comedy called *Husbands for Sale*. Dan and Gert hadn't had quite the same meteoric rise but worked steadily and comfortably as extras or minor secondaries.

That March morning, on the set of her very first flicker, Irene brimmed with gratitude for all their successes.

Herbert Vanderslice, who'd been assigned to direct *A Baby's Cry*, was not nearly as grateful, however. Irene had heard him muttering about getting placed on a dull domestic drama "with about as much action as an embroidery circle." The scuttlebutt around the studio was that Vanderslice had been coming in late and over budget with the sprawling western pictures he preferred to make. Studio head Abe Tobiah had finally put him under house arrest, with a picture that would be shot almost completely on the main lot, making it easier to keep an eye on production costs. That picture, for good or for ill, was *A Baby's Cry*.

◇ ◇ ◇

Millie was still in bed when Irene had left that morning. At least Irene assumed she was in bed. Now that they had their own bedrooms, Irene had a strange feeling of losing track of her friend in the apartment they now shared at The Hillview on Hollywood Boulevard. It had been built by studio owners Jesse Lasky and Sam Goldwyn specifically for actors and actresses, who were considered undesirable tenants by many landlords. A short walk to Olympic Studios, it was four floors with a lovely courtyard in the middle of the building, an elevator, and even its own garbage incinerator. The basement was meant for rehearsal space, though it was more often the site of parties.

Separate bedrooms had taken some getting used to after so much time sharing a bed, and it wasn't rare for Irene to wake to the sound of Millie snoring there beside her. On the other hand, Millie's social life had expanded exponentially. She made friends with virtually everyone on every picture she worked on and she went out a lot, especially when Irene spent time with Dan. Sometimes they didn't cross paths for days.

"She's a born hobnobber," Dan said. "And someone falls in love with her every day of the week."

Irene didn't like the sound of that. "She's no vamp!"

"Of course not. She's just absurdly likeable. And very . . ."

Irene crossed her arms. "Very what?"

"Very pretty."

Irene fired off a warning look. Dan slid his arms around her waist and murmured in her ear, "Not as beautiful as my Irene, of course, but she's okay if you like that sort of thing."

Irene smiled. "What sort of thing, exactly?"

"The sort of thing that makes your eyeballs fall out."

"Excuse me, is this Stage Four? I know I'm a bit early." Irene and Wilson looked up to see a young man standing at the edge of the platform. He had thick, sandy blond hair, soulful brown eyes—the type they called cow eyes—and a deep dimple in each cheek.

You could carry spare change in those dimples, thought Irene.

"Nothing wrong with early," Wilson said, cutting his eyes at Irene. "You're Jack Dennis, our burglar."

"Why, yes!" The young man strode forward, leading with an outstretched hand to shake. He was wearing a bedraggled, ill-fitting suit and a plaid shirt with no tie. "You must be Wilson Grimes. I've heard all about you. And I'm just mad about your pictures, of course."

Wilson gave his hand a hard pump, nearly destabilizing the boy. "This is Irene Van Beck. You've heard all about her, too, of course."

Jack opened his mouth to speak but just ended up nodding and smiling instead.

"Incorrigible," Irene hissed at Wilson. To Jack she said, "I'm the scenarist. This is my first big picture, too."

Jack let out the breath he'd been holding and laughed. "Are you as nervous as I am?"

She smiled. "Maybe even more so."

Millie came in behind Jack, wearing a much flimsier night-gown than the script called for. It was sleeveless, with a low neck, and made of a pearl-colored silk satin that clung and shimmered all the way down to her calves. She was playing a new mother, for goodness' sake, not a bride on her wedding night.

"Irene, can you check my makeup? Am I supposed to be wearing lipstick this dark?"

Millie had always done her own makeup from her little kit, and she was quite good at it. But as the star of the film, she now reported to the makeup department.

"Vanderslice made a few changes to the continuity last night," murmured Wilson.

"I'll say." Irene shook her head. "Millie, did you bring your kit so we can fix it?"

But Millie didn't answer. She was looking at Jack Dennis, her face lit with interest. "Hello."

Jack's eyes went even wider than they normally were. Irene wondered if Dan had been right, and his eyeballs might actually fall out.

"Hello," he said. After another moment, "I'm Jack Dennis."

"I thought maybe you were. I'm Mildred Martin, but my friends call me Millie, so I hope you will, too." Spying Wilson, she gave him a wink.

Absurdly likeable. Dan had been right about that, too.

Several crew members began to filter in, and Millie made a point to introduce herself to each one and learn their names. "Dan taught me that, by the way," she murmured to Irene afterward. "He said they can tell you things the director might not let you in on. Your sheik knows his onions."

Irene tried not to roll her eyes. Since the movie *The Sheik* had come out the previous year, catapulting Rudolph Valentino to the peak of stardom and women's fantasies, people had begun using the term to mean a handsome man, particularly if he was someone's boyfriend.

"Did he say anything about underwear?" Irene whispered. "Because I think he would tell you to wear some."

"First of all, I tried it with drawers and a camisole and it utterly ruined the line. And second, Dan would never be so crass as to talk about underwear with me." Millie nudged her. "I hope he talks about it with you, though."

No, she and Dan didn't *talk* about underwear . . . but they had recently become rather familiar with each other's undergarments, specifically how quickly they could be discarded.

In many ways their courtship had been backward. After that first night in his apartment, curling themselves around each other on the braided rug and revealing things they'd kept locked away from almost everyone else on the planet, it had felt strange to go on dates. To do mundane things like choose a movie or discuss

"Well, you're not meant to look quite so interested, Connie. Remember, you have another woman waiting for you, with whom you'd much rather be."

"Yes, but wouldn't the audience think I was off my trolley for not taking this girl for a quick roll first? I mean *look* at her, for the love of Christ."

Millie clasped her hands under her chin, tilted her head, and mugged a silly grin. Chortles erupted from the crew; Vanderslice, however, was not amused. The shot took seventeen takes because he was never fully satisfied with Conrad's level of interest in his wife, which ranged from listless to lewd, nor with Millie's level of sultry attractiveness, which ranged from high to higher.

"See why he got grounded?" Wilson murmured to Irene.

"Yes, but why do the rest of us have to take the punishment, too?"

Wilson patted her shoulder. "You're new around here, aren't you."

The baby, an adorably pink and pleasant child named Rosemary, who was bright-eyed and ready all morning for her first paying job, passed out like a drunken sailor in the afternoon. Nothing could rouse the poor exhausted infant, which made it tough to pull off the scenes in which she was supposed to be crying and miserable.

Her mother was clearly nervous about being fired. She pinched Rosemary in the thigh several times, but this only made the baby lurch momentarily and then fall right back to sleep, and left ugly red marks on her legs.

Wilson put a stop to it. "We can just as easily do those scenes tomorrow," he assured the distraught mother.

"It will put us behind schedule!" Vanderslice whined.

"Not if we do a couple of tomorrow's scenes today."

Irene had to admire Wilson's restraint in not pointing out that the director himself had put them behind schedule hours before and made the baby wait too long for her nap.

They decided they would shoot the scene where Jack breaks in and Millie first sees the intruder. The prop man gave her a baby doll to hold, which would be spliced with takes of the live baby once they shot those the next day.

If it was possible, Jack looked even more handsome for having had some of his smooth edges roughed up a bit by the makeup girl. He no longer looked like a college freshman at his first football game. He looked like a man who'd been around the block a few times.

Irene had rewritten the thief's backstory over and over, finally hitting on his being the oldest son of a widowed mother with several younger children, whom he'd helped raise in his father's absence. He worked as a bricklayer—Henry had given her wonderfully colorful details—but his cruel boss had denied him his wages, and his family was about to be evicted and thrown into the street.

When the husband leaves (without a "quick roll," much to Conrad's chagrin), there was to be a title card for Millie that read, "DON'T FORGET TO LOCK THE DOOR, DARLING. I'VE HEARD THERE HAS BEEN SOME THIEVERY IN THE AREA."

Conrad clearly leaves without any concern for the door. Thus Jack is able to enter without a sound. He sneaks into the living room and reaches for a silver candlestick. Startled by the baby's loud coughing, he knocks the candlestick to the floor. A distraught Millie comes running down the stairs, babe in arms, hoping it's her husband so he can fetch the doctor.

The young mother and the thief catch sight of each other and freeze, staring.

Irene—along with everyone else on set—froze, too. The take was absolutely flawless.

"And cut," Vanderslice said quietly, almost reverently. Even he could find nothing to complain about.

Then Jack and Millie burst out laughing. He strode toward her and knelt, taking her hand and kissing it. "Your servant, ma'am," he intoned in a British accent.

She plunked herself down on his knee and giggled. "Aren't you the cat's pajamas!"

Oh, Lord, Irene thought as the crew cracked up around her. *He's Millie in pants.*

32

◇ ◇ ◇

he premiere of *The Queen of Sheba* was on March 31, only
two weeks away, and Henry did not have a tuxedo yet.

"You can borrow one of mine." Edward sat sipping coffee
in his pajamas and reading the *Hollywood Citizen* at his kitchen
table. "We're about the same size."

"I'd take you up on it," said Henry, kissing the top of his head
as he went by on his way to the percolator, "but my *zayde* would
spin in his grave if I wore another man's suit to a formal event."

"But he wouldn't mind you wearing another man's pajamas?"

Henry smiled. "Strangely, we never discussed it."

Edward folded the newspaper and gazed up at Henry. "I wish
we could go together."

"Acclaimed director Edward Oberhouser cannot be seen taking a lowly extra to his sure-to-be-a-hit film, never mind a male
one."

"You've already starred in a picture."

"The public doesn't know that. *Husbands for Sale* won't be out
for two months."

"My point is you're no lowly extra anymore. You're Henry Weston now." The studio had determined Weiss to be too "ethnic," and almost before Henry knew it, he had a new last name.

"Thanks to you."

"Thanks to your own talent!"

"And your friendship."

"Ah, well," scoffed Edward, "ninety percent of the people in the business got here through friendships of one sort or another."

"How many through our sort?"

Edward reached out and caught Henry's hand. "Only the luckiest ones."

◇ ◇ ◇

It had taken a long time for Henry to feel comfortable staying the night at Edward's apartment in Westlake. In those first few months, even dating a man seemed so foreign to him that he'd often told Edward he had other plans when he didn't.

Stranger still, he was suddenly noticing men! He'd tamped down his interest for so long and so completely that once the lid blew off, his desires flew out like a prank snake from a fake can of peanuts. Hollywood was disturbingly full of handsome men, and Henry sometimes found himself so distracted he could barely walk down Sunset without running into a streetlamp.

He'd visited more establishments that catered to individuals of his variety, too. *Research*, he thought as he struggled to know this side of himself. He'd kissed a few other men, including Charlie, but it never felt quite right. No one filled his heart like Edward.

Fortunately for both of them, Edward was a patient man.

"I grew up in the Midwest," he'd reminded Henry once. "There's fear in me that I'll take to my grave."

"It doesn't show."

"Yours doesn't either."

"Because I work hard at making people think I'm not afraid of anything. You just live your life!"

Edward smiled. "I'm older than you. I've had ten more years to cast off the self-loathing. And I don't live in front of the camera and on movie magazine covers like the stars do. As long as I'm not too obvious about it, I can do as I like."

"I'm going to take up directing," grumbled Henry.

Edward had patted his hand. "You'll be wonderful at it."

◇ ◇ ◇

"I suppose you'll be with your gang for New Year's Eve," Edward had said to him at the end of December, over dinner at the Pacific Dining Car in Los Angeles.

"Actually, Gert went home to Binghamton for the holidays to see her sisters. Irene will certainly be with Dan—they don't seem to spend a minute apart—and wherever Irene goes, Millie goes. Eva Crown is throwing a party at her place up in the hills."

Edward's gaze was mild, undemanding, and he said nothing. In fact his silence seemed as if it might last indefinitely.

Henry fiddled with his dinner napkin. "Do you have plans?" he asked finally.

Edward shook his head. "Quiet evening at home."

Henry had thought he would go to Eva's party, but as he sat there across from Edward, pretending to have a work-related dinner, he knew now that he would not be happy at Eva's. He'd be imagining beautiful Edward alone, sipping a drink, listening to his phonograph. And he'd be desperate to get there. To be in Edward's calm, loving presence.

"Maybe I could come by," he said.

"That'd be nice."

"I could pick up dinner."

"The Valley Quail packs up a good meal." It wasn't lost on Henry that Edward had suggested the restaurant where they'd had their first date.

"I'd stay for midnight, if you weren't too tired," said Henry. "Silly to be alone at midnight if you don't have to be."

"I won't be too tired."

"Of course it's hard to get a cab at that hour."

"I'll have my driver take you home."

Henry could feel his breath coming in and out, time slowing down, the moment upon him. "Or I could stay."

Edward, so patient, so yielding. Without the slightest change in expression, Henry could feel the man's love flood across the table, and it was all Henry could do not to lean over the remnants of the meal and kiss him.

"That would be lovely," Edward said quietly. "But if you change your mind, that's all right, too."

"I won't change my mind."

And he hadn't.

◇ ◇ ◇

The tuxedo arrived in the nick of time for the premiere of *The Queen of Sheba* at the end of March, and a little part of Henry was disappointed. He would have liked to wear one of Edward's. They wouldn't be able to touch each other all evening, and that tux would've felt like a secret embrace.

The premiere would be held at the newly built Egyptian Theatre on Hollywood Boulevard. Henry and Gert had strolled by on opening night, when tickets to the premiere of *Robin Hood*, starring Douglas Fairbanks, cost the princely sum of five dollars! And he had been inside several weeks later to see that same movie, though they'd only had to pay the still-quite-steep price of seventy-five cents for gallery seats. Orchestra tickets were a dollar and a half.

But now, at the premiere of *The Queen of Sheba*, his orchestra tickets hadn't cost him a nickel. Walking down the red carpet of that instantly famous courtyard with Gert on his arm, searchlights crosshatching the sky, the creases of his new tuxedo so sharp he could almost hear them snapping as he walked, Henry felt as if he'd wandered into someone else's life. Someone far more glamorous, of course, but also someone to envy. In his whole life, he'd never felt remotely enviable. Until now.

He and Gert didn't inspire the gawping stares that Betty Blythe or Fritz Leiber did, of course, but Henry could hear the crowds cordoned off to either side murmuring, "Who's that?" and "Aren't they a handsome couple!"

Gert heard it, too. She cut her eyes up at him with a look of amusement, as if she were in on the grandest secret. *We're no better than any of them*, that look seemed to say, *but we keep scrapping. And here we are.*

There was an unspoken agreement between them. Neither asked too many questions about the other's love life. Gert dated here and there, but always circled back to Henry for any important events. She'd canceled a date with a ridiculously handsome supporting actor a few weeks ago because Henry had just found out he'd gotten the lead role in *Fox Trot on the Congo*, a comedy about a society couple who goes on safari, and she wanted to be there for the celebration with Irene, Millie, and Dan.

They took their seats in the orchestra section, which were several rows back from Edward, the two stars, secondary leads, and studio muckety-mucks. Sid Grauman certainly knew how to make movie watching seem like a trip to Buckingham Palace, or in this case, King Tut's tomb. The stage was flanked by four mas-

"He's colored."

Henry's eyebrows went up.

Gert put her hands on her hips. "Well that's a laugh, coming from you."

"No, it's just . . . you're so . . ."

"White?"

Henry felt his cheeks go warm. "Yes, I suppose that's what I was thinking. To be honest, it's hard to imagine."

"Well, it's hard to imagine you kissing a fellow, so there we are. Both of us kissing the wrong people. People other people don't want to imagine us kissing—or anything else, like just living our lives, for instance."

Henry put a hand on her shoulder. Gert Turner, quite a woman. He wished he *did* want to kiss her. "Where is he?"

Her face broke a little, and he could see a pain so familiar that he felt it in his own skin.

"I don't know. What's the point of keeping in touch?" she said. "But I just wish I knew if he's . . ."

"If he's happy?"

"If he's alive."

33

◇ ◇ ◇

It was simply a case of California, the glamour of the Southern California moonlight and the fascinating lovemaking of the man . . . I honestly believe that Rudolph would have married any woman with an automobile.
Jean Acker, actress, on marrying then little-known actor, Rudolph Valentino, while she was in a relationship with actress Alla Nazimova

"If you don't come out with me tonight, I'm going to go up into the hills and throw myself off the Hollywoodland sign." It was two weeks into filming *A Baby's Cry* and Jack's penchant for flirting had been fully revealed.

"Are you playing a cripple in your next film?" said Millie. "Because you'd only break your legs."

Jack was standing very close, his breath tickling against her hair. He smelled absurdly good. "Yes, but it's so remote up there; it'd be too far to drag myself to food or water."

"A skinny cripple then." The smell was outdoorsy, she decided, almost like a hayfield. She wanted to press her nose against his chest and inhale.

The baby reached up and patted her mouth, and Millie kissed the soft little palm. This, too, smelled heavenly, so human but pure, without the body odor and bad breath of teenagers and adults. And that impossibly smooth skin. Millie took every opportunity to gently rub her nose against little Rosemary's cheek, which made the baby giggle and snuggle against her.

"Cut!" yelled Vanderslice. "I cannot get these close-ups if you two keep talking! And for the love of all that's holy, could you *please* stop making that baby laugh, Mildred. She's supposed to be on death's door."

Millie looked down at Rosemary and whispered, "You don't look like you're on death's door. You look like you're ready to live a long and happy life, full of kisses and biscuits!"

The baby gurgled happily. Vanderslice threw his megaphone on the floor.

◇ ◇ ◇

On Friday, Jack picked her up in a little black three-passenger Buick coup.

"Well, my goodness!" said Millie, giving the hem of her silvery-blue dress an extra little swish around her knees. "Where on earth did you get this?"

"Hop in, and I'll tell you all about it."

He began with the fact that he hailed from Manhattan in New York City.

"You don't happen to know our friend Henry Weiss?" Millie interjected. "He grew up in a neighborhood called the Low East."

"I think you mean the Lower East Side, and no I wouldn't have known him. My neighborhood was a few blocks north of there."

"That doesn't sound very far."

Jack smiled. "Doesn't sound like it, but it is."

He'd been enthralled by the moving pictures since he'd seen his first at the age of twelve and had wanted to be a part of it in any way he could. His parents were of a different mind, however, refusing to pay for acting lessons or even let him get a job as a movie palace usher.

"Why on earth not?" said Millie. "That's a great job for a kid."

"My family was . . . comfortable. My brothers and I didn't need jobs, and we would never have been allowed to, as my dear mama would say with her hanky at her brow, 'receive the filthy nickels of the unwashed Bolsheviks.'" Jack chuckled. "And they wonder where I get my dramatic flair."

He had made them a bargain, however. If he completed his senior year of high school at the Collegiate School with straight A's, he would be allowed to work in the film business. He had never studied harder in his life, before or since, and his father had held up his end of the bargain. His business connections had landed young Jack in the business office of Paramount-Artcraft Pictures down on Seventh Avenue in Manhattan.

"It was about as exciting as a spinster's diary—except on the days the actors and actresses came in to renegotiate contracts and complain about directors."

His father soon offered him a new bargain. If he stayed for one year, he could try out for stage work in New York. "He was waiting me out, hoping I'd lose interest in the flickers."

"So you stayed for a year—"

"Not on your life! I talked to anyone who came in the door, just to see what they were about—Mae Murray came in all the time—"

"Mae Murray!"

"The very same. Everyone said the movie business was moving to the coast, and I should come out here. So I told my old man, the deal's off. I'm going to California with or without your blessing. I'd ride the rails like a hobo if I had to. Mother nearly cast a kitten, but in the end, they saw me off at the station and put some dough in my pocket, enough to buy a car and get along for a while."

"And now you're starring in a picture for Olympic!"

"And taking out the prettiest girl on the lot."

"Taking her *where*, I'd like to know."

tic "Song of Love," and he held her loosely, comfortably against his chest. She tipped her chin up and asked him, "Have you ever loved a girl?"

He considered this, blinking down at her, and she suddenly regretted the impulse. It was practically an invitation to say something sappy or untrue, and she didn't want that. She had simply wondered and spoken her curiosity aloud.

"I don't think I ever have. Did you ever love a fella?"

She smiled. "Nope."

He grinned back at her. "We're birds of a feather."

"And we're flocking together," she said happily and put her cheek against his shoulder, smelling that hayfield scent of his, even despite all the expensive perfume wafting around them.

He's nice, she thought. And handsome, charming, and good smelling, of course. But the nice part—that was the important thing, the part she hadn't paid enough attention to with that monster, Wally. She was smarter than that now, and also smart enough to know that things could still go wrong, but the chances were at least better that they wouldn't.

They were driving back from the party at three in the morning when he said, "I'll take you back to your apartment."

Hearing the question in it, she said, "Is the evening over so early?"

"I could come up," he offered.

"I wouldn't want to wake Irene."

"I could show you my house."

"I'd like that."

He reached over and slid his hand into hers, intertwining their fingers. His skin was so soft she knew for certain he'd never held a tool or leather reins in his life, and that all of his spoons had been silver.

◇ ◇ ◇

He'd rented a one-bedroom bungalow on the edge of the Hollywood Hills from a little-known actor who hadn't gotten the breaks. The fellow had gone back to New York but couldn't bear to part with the house "in case."

"In case what?" Millie asked.

"In case a miracle occurs, and Hollywood suddenly regrets spitting him out."

It had its own tiny yard and several lemon trees obscuring the neighbors on either side. Inside it was tidy, except for the unmade bed she could see in the other room, and a chair covered in several articles of clothing—a green vest, some sock garters, and a gray silk bow tie. The closet door was open, and Millie was impressed at how full it was. Jack was no starving actor, and between his ambition and family connections, she suspected he never would be.

He brought out glasses of lemonade, and they sat on the sofa, talking for some minutes before he said, "Would it be all right if I kissed you?"

Would it be all right? Millie had known this would be the likely course of events, yet now, with the moment upon her, she felt an electric shock of fear that seemed to surge at her from out of the dark. Would it *actually* be all right?

"I don't want to be manhandled."

The seriousness of her usually sunny face made him sit up straight. "I am a gentleman," he said, as if startled at having to affirm something so unassailably true.

"I don't need you to be a gentleman," Millie said. "I need you not to grab me if I don't want to be grabbed."

He blinked at her, trying to parse the meaning of her words. She took his hand and opened it, drawing her fingers across the palm, and then took it to her face and kissed it very gently. He tipped his head, his face softening at the tenderness of the gesture. She offered him her open hand, and he did the same. Then he let his lips graze the inside of her wrist. He raised his eyebrows in question, and she nodded.

Yes, this might be all right.

◇ ◇ ◇

For a boy who was in such a hurry to get where he was going, Jack was remarkably unhurried in his lovemaking. When they were on the set together, she could sense him reacting to her, rather than simply pantomiming his half of the story. Their acting had a give-and-take to it, and this carried over to the bedroom. He listened, he paid attention . . . and then he ran those soft hands up her thighs and over her hips and slipped her dress right off.

She had moments of anxiety: when he wanted her to sit on his lap, or later when he lowered himself on top of her in his bed. But she didn't have to do anything more than give him a little push to make him reverse so she was on top.

"Was that all right?" she asked afterward as she lay spent and warm on his stomach.

He ran a finger down her spine and murmured, "I think that may now be my preferred mode of travel."

◇ ◇ ◇

"I thought you were sleeping!" Irene looked up from the breakfast table when Millie came in the next morning. Her tablet of paper was, as usual, fighting for space with the plate of whatever meal she was eating. "Where've you been?"

"With Jack."

"You two have been out roaming around all night?"

Millie smiled. "No, not roaming around. Staying in one place."

"His place."

"It's quite nice. He's lucky he's got family money." Of course Millie had had family money, too, but that had been a long time ago. A lifetime ago.

"Are you . . . are you okay?"

Millie sank down into one of the kitchen chairs and took a piece of Irene's toast. "I'm fine. Relieved actually. I didn't realize it, but I've been smelling that bastard for almost a year, and now I don't smell him anymore. I smell Jack."

Irene looked relieved, too. "What does he smell like?"

"Hay."

Irene burst out laughing. "Oh, Millie, you're part horse!"

"I think I just might be." She grinned at Irene. "What does Dan smell like?"

Irene shrugged. "I've never really thought about it."

"Come on now," scoffed Millie. "You know what the man smells like."

"Tea, I suppose. Greenthread tea."

"I knew it. We both have men who smell like plants." She took a bite of Irene's toast, but then remembered something else and put her fingers to her lips to hold in the crumbs. "Henry was at Mae Murray's party!"

"Gosh, I haven't seen him in a couple of weeks. Was he there with anyone? I've been wondering if he might have a girl he's spending time with, and that's why he's not around as much. I'm pretty sure it's not Gert. They like each other, but there's no real spark."

"I only saw him with Beryl Tate, and she's twice his age. Maybe he's got someone but he's not ready to introduce us. We're his family now, so that would mean it's serious."

"Well, whoever it is, I hope she's nice."

"And good enough for him. Henry's just so good, isn't he?"

Irene smiled. "He's wonderful."

34

◇ ◇ ◇

Don't be afraid to make a mistake. Your readers might like it.
*William Randolph Hearst, American newspaper publisher, whose
chain of publications printed as fact many damning
falsehoods about Roscoe "Fatty" Arbuckle*

"Have you seen this?" Irene asked Dan.

They were up on newly built Mulholland Drive for a spring picnic. The spot was breezy but warm under the late-April sun, with a spectacular view of the burgeoning city. They had finished a lunch of roasted chicken, buttered beets, and tapioca, and Irene lay on her back perusing the latest edition of *Ladies' Home Journal*; the short stories and serialized novels it printed were first-rate, and she always made sure to read and consider whether they would make good film scenarios.

Dan dozed on his side snuggled up around her, arm across her waist, thigh against her hip. They often slept this way on the nights they stayed together, having determined by trial and error that this was the precise configuration that suited them both best.

In fact, Irene noticed she now slept fitfully on the nights when the warmth of his strong, sinewy body against her was absent, and this worried her. She didn't like to feel dependent, and she wasn't ready for the change that would place his comforting presence beside her every night.

The name of that change was marriage, and as much as she loved him, she also loved her life just as it was: working hard, earning an enviable living, making her own decisions. Back in Ohio she would already be on the express train to spinsterhood, but here in Hollywood, the rules were different—mainly because there weren't many. She could live with her best friend, sleep with her lover, and come and go as she pleased. The only thing that might one day change her mind was a desire for children. But she had no interest in that now, and Dan was quite responsible in his duty to ensure they always had prophylactic supplies. As a well-paid twenty-two-year-old with a job she adored, she couldn't imagine a more ideal arrangement.

She knew Dan was tired—he'd gotten a role as a cattle rancher in a western and spent his days chasing lost calves down ravines and hauling hay around a barn. He came home happy and exhausted. She hated to rouse him, but she knew he'd be interested. "It's Zane Grey's latest, called *The Vanishing American*. It's about a Navajo boy."

She handed the thick magazine to him and watched his eyes trace the text.

The boy, Nophaie, is kidnapped by white horse thieves and abandoned far from his tribe. He's rescued and taken east by a well-meaning white woman who puts him in white schools. In college he falls in love with Marian Warner, a white student, then returns to his tribe and invites her to visit. In his letters he rails about how the white government agents bamboozle and intimidate the Navajo into giving away their best land.

"Huh," Dan snorted. "Well, it's true to life, I'll give him that."

Marian heads west and is finally reunited with Nophaie. He shows her his world, his hogan home, his place of prayer, and then admits a terrible truth: he has lost his faith. The white man's education has made him question his Indian spirituality. Marian decides to stay and work at a school for Indian girls, and she tells Nophaie of the corruption of the white government workers and Christian missionaries, one of whom has licentious desires for a lovely Indian girl. Marian wants Nophaie to kidnap the girl to protect her from this hideous fate.

> *. . . the ruin of Indian girls by white men employed on the reservation was the basest and blackest crime of the many crimes the white race had perpetrated upon the red.*

Dan looked up from the page, eyes flat with anger. "Don't waste your time. They'll never make this into a flicker."

"Why ever not? It's got everything! Romance, great visuals, a gripping story of good versus evil—"

"The red man's good versus the white man's evil. Think of almost every cowboy and Indian movie you've ever seen, Irene. It's always the other way around."

"Maybe it's time for a more realistic view. I think people will be fascinated."

"They'll think it's a lie and they'll be infuriated." He handed her back the magazine and closed his eyes again.

◇ ◇ ◇

Eva Crown was frowning, which wasn't unusual. She was exacting about everything, from the width of a leading man's tie to which adjective best described a flapper's laugh—was it self-indulgent or was it actually more haughty? Sometimes Irene wanted to scream, *Oh, for cripes' sake, it doesn't matter! Regardless of what we write, the actress playing the flapper will interpret it as she likes, then the* fruit at the screen." Suddenly there was a funny little twinkle in her eye. "And . . ."

"And what?"

"Well, I'm just thinking out loud here, but if the studio loves this story as much as I do . . . and if *A Baby's Cry* does well . . . You might ask to direct. You've definitely got that in you, Irene—not just the skill, but the personality for it."

A laugh burst out of Irene, half-thrilled, half-disbelieving. "You mean I'm bossy!"

"Yes, you're bossy. In a good way—a great way. Actually I prefer the term commanding." Leave it to Eva to quibble over the descriptor. "There are a lot of women directors, you know. They don't let us do the westerns, but who wants those anyway? The domestic dramas, though, and the romances—the seats are full of girls and women, so they trust that a woman director knows best how to cater to those audiences."

Reason number 957 why Vanderslice shouldn't have been foisted on A Baby's Cry, thought Irene.

"Why haven't you ever directed?" She regretted the words as soon as she uttered them. What if Eva wanted to, but the studio heads wouldn't give her the opportunity?

"Oh, they've asked me, and I've been very tempted. Just to have that much control over the process would be so satisfying. But I don't really like . . . people. Dealing with stars' egos, keeping the crew motivated to do the grueling hard work, making sure the extras don't wander off . . . Not for me. I'm happier locked in a room alone, scribbling away about my imaginary friends."

Irene's brain twirled with visions of bringing her stories to life just as she saw them—not as some other director interpreted them. She would be the maestro conducting the whole orchestra, not just the violin section. She knew she could do it . . . and that she'd love it.

"Also the money's better," said Eva. "*Much* better."

35

◇ ◇ ◇

The picture was nearly finished, but there was no way
of shooting around Wally [film star Wallace Reid]. He just had to
be there, in front of the camera. So the company, not wanting to lose
the investment entirely, sent the studio doctor with an ample supply of
morphine to the location, where he injected Wallace to the extent
that he could feel no pain whatsoever and he was able to finish
the picture. But afterwards he was thoroughly hooked.

Karl Brown, cameraman, writer, cinematographer

Henry was the first to admit he had been a pretty mediocre stand-up comedian. He wasn't all that good at writing jokes, and he'd never quite gotten the rapid-fire timing down for telling one after another. But when it came to saying funny things other people wrote, and incorporating them into an ongoing story, it turned out he was far above average.

His good looks were also very camera friendly, and he filled out his first tuxedo in a way that women couldn't quite get enough of. In fact his leading lady on *Husbands for Sale* had done virtually everything short of holding a knife to his throat to get him to sleep with her. Henry was beside himself with the stress of it until Edward suggested he tell her he was secretly married, but that his wife was in a tuberculosis ward, and the studio insisted on keeping it hush hush.

"And sew them back together again, Henry boy. That's the important part."

"You Turner girls aren't exactly slaves to social convention, are you?"

She grinned up at him with unabashed pride. "Not one bit."

Filming for *Fox Trot on the Congo* began in June, and Henry regretted not having more time to spend with Gert. He did not regret Irene's absence from his life, however, or at least that's what he told himself. He tried not to stew on it, but in his worst moments he was sure she was utterly repulsed, and their friendship, as life changing as it had been, was now over.

Edward had a different view. "It took you twenty-four years to accept yourself, and it's still a work in progress," he said matter-of-factly. "How can you possibly expect her to learn of it, understand it, and embrace it, all on the spur of the moment?"

"She's avoiding me!"

"You avoided you, too."

Henry had other things to distract him from these dark ruminations: Edward had been chosen to direct *Fox Trot on the Congo*, and the concentration it took to pretend they had a strictly professional relationship, and not a particularly friendly one at that, was exhausting. They were extra careful not to be seen together off set, too, and this relegated Henry to sneaking into Edward's apartment late at night and sneaking back out before dawn.

Making matters worse, there were whispers that the leading lady, one Hazel Hampton, was a dope fiend. From her weary, washed-out look before makeup worked its magic, Henry suspected it was true.

"Why on earth did you recommend her?" he asked Edward late one night.

"Because she's a brilliant comedy actress, for one thing, and for another, she's the reason I have a career at all. My first big hit was with her, and she carried that picture, let me assure you. I was a bit of a hack, and she was kind enough to show me how to make a picture that was funny, but also complex and subtle. *She* directed *me*."

Friendships. It was what he always said.

"Okay, but you're certain she's off the stuff now?"

Edward looked away. "No. I'm not certain. We've talked endlessly about it, and she knows this may be her last chance to pull herself together and keep working. I've paid off her debts to those sharks, and I only hope she's smart enough not to press her luck with them again."

"How did she ever get on it in the first place?"

"The same way so many of them do. A stunt gone wrong. She was supposed to be jumping from one moving car to another, and she tripped and fell out. Her back got wrenched up something awful. They put her on morphine to ease the pain so they could finish the picture."

"Finish her career is more like it."

"The studios are just starting to see that stunt people save them money. And of course it's all about the money. If there were no such thing as movie stars, whose names do so much to sell the product, they'd just go on treating actors and actresses as disposable. I'm convinced they'd prefer it, actually. You stars wouldn't be able to command such high salaries."

Henry was, in fact, becoming a star. Though fairly low budget—in part because he was unknown and had only been paid a flat five hundred dollars—*Husbands for Sale* was a surprise hit, and with Edward's help, Henry had negotiated a contract for four hundred a week, whether he worked or not. As proof of his bankability, *Photoplay* magazine was now angling for any and all information about the man behind the tux. Henry was terrified.

"Carlton Sharp will make something up, don't worry about that," Edward said. "The next thing you know, you'll be an avid yachtsman with a penchant for saving stranded baby seals."

"I've never been on a boat in my life."

"And it couldn't matter less."

Filming was not going well. The story revolved around a wealthy couple who goes on safari, gets separated from their tour, and stumbles upon a society in the middle of the jungle that is just as ostentatious and party loving as their own—only more "African," of course. The couple becomes so endeared of the tribe that they create a big ruse to protect them from the outside world when colonialists threaten to invade.

On the days when Hazel was "well," her comedic chops could not be matched, and Henry watched and learned from a master. On the days when she was "a little off," he could barely get a reaction out of her, no matter how boisterous and silly he became.

He and the rest of the cast and crew waited while Edward took her on long walks to buck her up. Production costs rose. Lou Manning, vice president in charge of production, stepped in. Edward was beside himself over the fate of his friend, and nothing Henry could say would comfort him.

"Sweetheart, they had to do it. She couldn't—"

"For heaven's sake, Henry, don't you think I know? I've been in this business far longer than you, so please don't lecture me on—"

"I'm not lecturing. I'm only saying—"

"Well, don't." They sat in doleful silence for some minutes in Edward's dimly lit parlor.

"She really was something," murmured Henry, and Edward burst into tears.

In the hour before dawn, Henry lay with his arms around Edward, who had slept fitfully for the few hours since they'd gone to bed. Edward's breathing changed, and he rustled slightly.

"Sweetheart," whispered Henry. "Is it too soon to suggest a replacement for Hazel?"

"Unfortunately, it's not. We're so far behind schedule as it is."

"I was thinking . . ."

Edward rolled over to face him. "I know," he murmured. "I'll talk to Lou, and we'll get her in for a test. Today, if possible."

into her skin like she was scrubbing a dirty floor. "Then, of course, I'm trying to write new scenarios so I can keep my job. You're off with Jack, so you don't see how hard I'm working."

Millie came up behind her and rested her chin on Irene's shoulder so she could see her in the mirror. "Something's upset you."

Irene took a breath and held it for a moment, then thought better of whatever she was going to say and let it out. "Not at all. I'm just irritated. I could kill that Vanderslice! I could strangle him with his damned silk bow ties until his eyes bug out."

Millie laughed. Irene was usually sensible, but when she wasn't, she was so funny!

"He's just mad because he's older than you, and he's been in the business a lot longer, and he's a man, and you're *still* better at telling stories than he is."

Irene spun around to face Millie. "You really think so?"

"Wilson was ready to accidentally run him over during a trolley shot." She dabbed at the one spot of face cream that Irene hadn't obliterated.

"It'd be nice if he could manage it before Vanderslice gets me fired. He's still higher up the ladder than I am."

"You won't get fired."

Irene snorted. "It could happen."

"You're too smart and talented to fire." Millie followed Irene into her room, turned down the side of the bed Dan sometimes slept in, and climbed in.

Irene laughed. "Something wrong with your bed?"

"Yes, as a matter of a fact there is." Millie grinned sleepily at her. "You're not in it."

◇ ◇ ◇

The next morning, Millie woke with Irene's unhappiness still on her mind. It wasn't just Vanderslice, she felt certain of that. But Irene wouldn't reveal anything further, and Millie knew not to push. The only thing to do was lie next to her and be comforting, like a favorite pillow.

Millie would have liked to stay snuggled up behind Irene for the rest of the morning, but she knew she really ought to be at the set early. They were screen testing her for a new picture. Something about a maid, which sounded like loads of fun. She'd *had* maids, of course, but she'd never *been* one before, so this was her chance to know what it was like.

She went into her room and opened her top dresser drawer, rooted around for a garter belt, and pulled out her sanitary belt instead. She stood there for a moment, staring down at the straps lying across her palm.

Well, that's funny, she thought. *I haven't used this in a while.*

37

◇ ◇ ◇

Love is a fire. But whether it is going to warm your hearth
or burn down your house, you can never tell.
Joan Crawford, actress

Irene had come so close to telling Millie about Henry. She was
desperate for someone to talk to about it, to help her understand how someone so kind and good could also be a depraved
pervert. That's what her uncle had always said about men with
that particular compulsion. It's what everyone said, and not just
the Bible thumpers who called it an abomination and worse.
Homosexuality was a sin, of course, but it was also just . . . wrong.
Wasn't it?

She knew there were homosexuals in Hollywood. Everyone
knew. But that didn't mean she knew what to make of it. Until
now, she hadn't had to make *anything* of it. She had just put the
whole concept out of her mind and ignored whether some fellow
in costume or set design might be of the "lavender" persuasion.
But Henry was a leading man; his whole job was to love women.
At least on-screen. Apparently he was an even better actor than
anyone knew.

Had he been acting with her in those first few months in
Hollywood when they'd clung to each other for survival, an un-

spoken agreement not to complicate their friendship with romance? It was a shock to learn that it hadn't been a sacrifice for him as it had been for her. Because if she were truthful—if only with herself—a little corner of her heart had always been his, and she had thought he'd felt the same. Falling in love with Dan had been amazing, wonderful, exhilarating, . . . and terrifying. Telling herself she always had Henry was a sort of security blanket that allowed her the luxury of vulnerability.

She couldn't talk to Millie about it. For one thing, Millie loved everyone. She'd probably be surprised for five minutes, then say, "Oh, well," and go on with her life. That would be no help. But more importantly, Millie was so open. She was liable to mention it to the wrong person, and then Henry could lose his career. No matter how questionable his proclivities, Irene would never forgive herself if his life got upended because she told the wrong person.

Dan, though. He could keep a secret, and he'd been in Hollywood longer than any of them. He'd certainly come across men of that ilk, and he could help her figure out what to do. If anything.

Now she had two difficult things to discuss with him: Henry and the fact that she and Eva had submitted a synopsis for *The Vanishing American*. She decided to start with the easier of the two.

Dan laid the three-page synopsis down on her kitchen table. "You can't submit this."

Irene tried to stay calm. "Why not?"

"Why not? Irene, you *know* why not."

"It isn't an exact representation of Zane Grey's story, but no scenario ever is."

Dan's face went wide with fury. "It completely misses the entire point! You've got one evil white man, and you've made him look like some sort of rogue agent with a weak boss. It rosies up a whole system of government that, with help from supposed men of God, is bent on making us white or dead!"

But you are white.

She didn't say it out loud, of course. And she knew he was only half white. But in that moment, it dropped on her like an anvil that he would never be able to accept a watered-down version of this story because it was *his* story. In so many ways, he was Nophaie, caught between his own whiteness and his Navajo heritage, and in love with a white woman to boot. What made it worse was that Nophaie had chosen the arguably more valorous route of returning to his people to lead and help them.

Dan had gone to Hollywood.

He had occasionally revealed the conflicted feelings he had about this choice. The rejection he'd experienced from his stepfather for having mixed blood; the lack of opportunity on the reservation; his insistence on living on the lean side so he could send as much money home as possible. He was getting better and better parts now, playing all sorts of roles, making much better money. And while this confirmed for him that he'd made the right decision, paradoxically it also seemed to bring on more guilt.

"Please promise me you won't submit it."

Irene was stunned. She knew there'd be parts of it he wouldn't like, but it never occurred to her he would ask her to abandon it entirely. "Eva has it," was all she could think to say.

"Get it back from her. Tell her you changed your mind."

"It was a collaboration, so it's partly hers. Actually, as the head writer, it *is* hers."

He stared at her for a moment. "You knew this would happen, and you waited to show it to me till it was out of your hands."

There was a tiny kernel of truth to this. She hadn't anticipated that he would have nearly this strong of a reaction, but she did think that if he happened to have a negative response, it would blow over sooner if the decision to submit had already been made. The thought of directing had been too great of an enticement to leave it to chance.

"I wasn't trying to trick you, Dan. I actually hoped you might be happy to have *any* picture made that brings to light the plight of your people, and the way that even one bad government agent can affect so many lives."

"But the missionaries are all good."

"For godsake, you work in this industry, and you know that there is absolutely no way the studio is going to make a movie that offends churchgoers. Even so, the script shows the missionaries as not always aware of what's best for the Indians."

"But not as rapists. I would have thought you'd have a little more justice on your mind, after what Millie went through."

Now it was Irene's turn to be enraged. "How *dare* you throw that in my face to make a point! She's my dearest friend, and I did everything I could to right that wrong! You owe me an apology for that."

He crossed his arms. "And you owe me an apology for this fairy tale of a scenario."

"Well, you're not going to get it!"

"Neither are you." With that he stood and walked out her door.

38

◇ ◇ ◇

We did as we pleased. We stayed up late. We dressed the way we
wanted. I used to whiz down Sunset Boulevard in my open
Kissel, with several red chow dogs to match my hair.
Clara Bow, actress and original "It" girl

t was really so easy to ignore it. Millie felt nothing. No morning sickness, no thickening around her waist, no weariness or heartburn. She knew the signs because the girls at Miss Twickenham's Finishing School had loved to talk about sex and babies and what men looked like under their clothes. There was a lot of misinformation, of course. One girl swore a man's private parts expanded to the size of two baseballs and a bat. Millie knew this wasn't true, and she stirred up quite a lot of excitement when she told them exactly how she knew.

For weeks she thought maybe she wasn't pregnant at all. Although her monthly had always been regular and she was pretty sure it hadn't come since February. She'd started sleeping with Jack in March, and now it was June.

There was a little part of her, a small calm voice that said, *It's time to find out. Pretending everything is dandy when it might not be is the old Millie.*

So she made an appointment with a doctor in Los Angeles,

took a cab to his office, gave a blood sample, and congratulated herself for being so responsible. *This is what Irene would do!*

But when she called for the results, it was clear that congratulations were no longer in order. She felt so ashamed. How had she let this happen? How could she have jeopardized her career like this? Everything had been going so well! And now she was going to lose it all.

And not just her career. Honestly that was the least of it.

What would Irene say?

Millie was fairly certain that she and Irene would not have been friends at Miss Twickenham's. Irene would've been one of those girls who went to bed at lights-out, not snuck into the girls lavatory and sat around on the tiles talking about men's private parts. In fact, Millie wasn't entirely sure why they'd ever become friends at all. Irene had liked her for some reason, and Millie had never wanted to probe too deeply as to why. Maybe Irene herself didn't even know.

This pregnancy business, though. This was going to be a problem. Stripping aside, Irene was raised a small-town, churchgoing girl. True, she slept with her boyfriend and illegally drank alcohol on occasion, but everyone in Hollywood did. And Irene never got drunk, nor would she ever allow herself to get pregnant. For godsake, she never even jaywalked.

And what could Millie say? *I'm pregnant and I know that's bad, and I have no idea how to make it any better . . . but you should still be friends with me anyhow?*

She would throw herself on Irene's mercy. She would do anything Irene told her to do as long as they could still be together. As long as Irene would still love her and be her friend.

◇ ◇ ◇

Days went by. A week. Millie couldn't bring herself to do it. And not only because she was terrified of what Irene would say, but also because Irene wasn't herself. Something was very wrong. She was inside her own thoughts all the time, distracted. Unhappy. How could Millie load one more piece of bad news onto Irene's shoulders?

Not telling Irene gave Millie more time to think, which was not good, because the more Millie thought about it, the more she knew what she wanted to do. It gave her time to talk to Jack and come up with a plan. And it made her realize that no matter what Irene said—no matter how furious or upset or disgusted—Millie would probably go through with it anyway.

39

◇ ◇ ◇

Movies are written in sand: applauded today, forgotten tomorrow.
D. W. Griffith, director, writer, producer

~~Independence Day. Irene woke with a start. She'd been dreaming~~
of a speeding train with all the doors locked, taking her away
from everything she'd accomplished, everyone she loved.

It had been almost a month since she'd last spoken to either
Dan or Henry.

Vanderslice had found his revenge for her constant insistence
that he stick to the script for *A Baby's Cry*. He hadn't had her
fired—though Irene was sure he'd tried—but she'd suddenly been
reassigned to the editing department. She was now a cutter girl,
splicing together scenes like some seamstress in a garment factory
instead of creating new stories.

Eva had tried to have the decision reversed, but to no avail.
"I'm afraid you may have cooked your own goose," she said.

"How exactly did I do that?" Irene whined miserably.

"You fought for that script, and *A Baby's Cry* is far better because
of it. The studio chiefs are thrilled and they don't really care why it's
good. They assume it was his doing because he directed. The writer
always gets short shrift, Irene. Better you should learn that now."

Oh, she was learning, all right. Learning about getting your salary cut almost in half. Learning about sitting alone in a dark room, staring into a tiny lit screen until your eyes watered, toiling away on *other* people's work. Learning that while some directors got it done in a handful of takes, others shot as many as thirty— and they all looked exactly alike!

Learning that an egotistical hack like Vanderslice could play God with her life.

Irene still had Millie, though. Actually, now more than ever. Once *A Baby's Cry* had wrapped, Millie's relationship with Jack puttered along until it fizzled altogether. He was on another flicker now, filming "on location" in Sacramento, the river up there often used as a stand-in for the Mississippi. Millie was on a picture, too, a drawing room comedy about a maid who inherits a fortune, buys her employer's mansion, and hires him as a chauffeur because he was swindled out of all his money. It was filmed completely on set, and she was home every evening.

As Irene's eyes fluttered open, heart still pounding from the dream of the locked train, she realized Millie had crawled into bed with her once again.

"I have to tell you something," Millie whispered.

Millie often had flights of fancy to share, so Irene couldn't account for the warning pressure she suddenly felt in her throat. "What is it?"

"I'm pregnant."

Irene spun around to face her. "You think? Or you know?"

"I know. I went to a doctor, and he gave me a test."

"Millie, for the love of God! How could you suspect you might be pregnant, make a doctor's appointment, and go to that appointment, all without saying a word to me?"

"Because you've been busy and distracted and unhappy, and I didn't—"

"I am not any of those things!" Irene threw the covers back and got out of bed. She wanted to leave, to flee this new information, as if she could somehow disconnect herself from the knowledge that Millie, her roommate and dear friend—only friend at the moment—had done it again. Only this time, there was a baby involved.

But she couldn't leave. Where would she go? It was the middle of the night. She went over to the window and stared out at the jacaranda tree.

"I'm sorry." Millie's voice came out in a little sob. "I'm so sorry, Irene."

Irene turned to look at her in the dappled light of the street-light through the tree. "Why are you apologizing to me?"

"I know this is not the kind of thing you would . . . and you've got a lot on your mind, and I just—"

Irene closed her eyes, willed herself to calm down. Here was Millie, in a hell of a fix, and her big concern was how Irene would take it. The writer in her set itself on the task of scripting a solution to this crisis. Was the doctor a quack? Could the test be wrong? Could it have been switched with someone else's test?

She sat back down on the bed. "Millie, are you sure? Didn't you and Jack use . . .?"

"Well, um . . ." Millie sat up and gulped back a tear. "That first time was kind of a surprise, and he didn't have any, and all the drugstores were closed."

"Did you tell him?"

"Oh, yes. We talked about it."

"And?"

"And he offered to pay for whatever I want—to end it, or have it and put it up for adoption. He'll do anything."

"Except marry you."

"He was never going to do that."

"For godsake, it's his responsibility! In any other town in America, that's exactly what he'd be expected to do!"

"You're right, of course," said Millie, still penitent. But then she added "Except, well, this isn't any other town in America, is it? We can do almost anything we like here. We can sleep with people we aren't married to and drink like there's no law against it and make a lot of money even though we're girls. The usual rules don't apply."

Boy, was that ever true.

Millie's gaze searched Irene's. "Are you . . . are you disappointed in me? Are you angry?"

Of course she was! It was one more mess to clean up! But how could she be more angry with Millie than she was with herself? She had ruined her relationship with Dan, gotten herself relegated to the cutting room, and was avoiding Henry. So much had gone wrong in her own life lately, and the only person she had to blame was herself. Irene let out a long, hard breath.

"Millie, it was an accident. You didn't mean for it to happen, and you certainly didn't accomplish it all on your own. We just need to figure out how to handle it. Have you thought about what you want to do?"

"I like babies," Millie whispered, wiping her eyes with a corner of Irene's sheet. "I didn't know it before *A Baby's Cry* with that adorable little Rosemary, but I do."

"You want to keep it?"

Millie's face lit with a soft little smile. "Yes."

"So you want to have it and adopt it later, like Barbara did." Barbara was an actress they all knew who'd gone "away" long enough to give birth and get her figure back, and then several months later adopted a cute little boy she'd "coincidentally" met visiting an orphanage to make a donation. "And what will you do when you have to go on location for a month?"

"Well, I figure I'll do what all rich people do. Hire a nursemaid and pay her handsomely so she won't tell any secrets."

Irene sighed. "There's no getting around the fact that you have absolutely no idea how to raise a child."

"Well, I certainly know how *not* to raise one. I'll just do the opposite. I'll love it and listen to it and help it grow into its very own self." Millie's hand slipped onto Irene's elbow. "And you'll be the best auntie in the whole wide world."

I'll have to be, won't I? Someone would have to make sure the child went to bed before midnight and brushed its teeth more than occasionally and got registered for school before the age of ten. She looked at Millie, smiling like a grand prize winner instead of a poor girl who'd been knocked up and left by her boyfriend. At least there was no doubt this baby would be loved. Millie was made of love.

"You're sure you're not mad?" said Millie. "Even a little bit?"

"I'm sure." And she realized she wasn't, not even a little bit.

Millie hugged her so tight it actually made her laugh.

"You know you'll have to go somewhere when you start to show."

"It'll be fun! Like a vacation. Where should we go?"

"Oh, Millie. I can't go with you. I'll lose my job."

"You don't even like that job. Besides, you can get it back."

"No, I probably can't. I'm not a star like you. If I quit and go off with you, someone will take my spot before we've left the city limits."

"You don't have to work at all. I can pay for you, just like you did for me all that time."

"I like to work. I actually love it." She'd been writing synopses in the evenings and submitting them to the Scenario Department, hoping to earn her spot back that way.

"You love work more than you love me?"

"No, of course not. And if your life were in danger, I'd quit in a minute. But you're coming back, Millie. And if you have any trouble getting work again after your absence, I'll be on solid footing to support us. The three of us. We can't take chances with our income if there's a baby involved, right?"

Millie shook her head. She would not take chances. Other than the ones she had already taken . . . or might take in the future.

40

◇ ◇ ◇

He was my cream, and I was his coffee, and when
you poured us together, it was something.
Josephine Baker, actress, dancer, singer

enry and Gert sat in his tent on the back lot, where much
of *Fox Trot on the Congo* was being shot. She'd taken to the
role of the zany wife, her first big break, as if she were born
to it.

Henry stood and stretched his legs. "I was thinking I'd walk
over and watch the nightclub scenes. Want to join me?"

"Not really, but I suppose I should. Tongues will wag if I'm
alone in your tent for long."

"Oh, tongues are already wagging. Edward tells me Carlton
Sharp is cooking up an on-set romance for us, you know."

She grinned up at him. "I could do worse."

"Yes, you could be stuck with a man who *doesn't* love you, on
top of not wanting to sleep with you."

The set had been built among lush vegetation that required
constant watering in the dry summer months. The tribe revered
the great god Scott Joplin, and their orchestra—which looked remarkably like the band at any respectable nightclub, except that
all the players were black, and their tuxedos were trimmed with

bones and shells—played ragtime, jazz, and popular hits of the day. The African nightclub had a bit of the Cocoanut Grove atmosphere, with its palm trees and twinkling lights, though these were meant to be candles.

The players were rehearsing a new song, and Henry and Gert stood off to the side to watch. The horn section stood and blew a loud and happy trill, and one of the dancers who'd been hired for the take skittered out onstage. He was tall and broad shouldered with short pomaded hair, and he moved in a whirl of arms and legs, jumping higher than seemed possible for a mere mortal, and landing in a blur of tapping that had all the crew grinning and cheering him on. When the dance was over, he took a quick bow and jogged back offstage while everyone erupted into enthusiastic applause. Even the band members were clapping.

Gert, however, stood still as a pillar.

"What's wrong?" said Henry.

"Tip," she said. "That was him."

"That fellow? He's the one you've been in love with all this time?"

"Yes."

"Well, for the love of Mike, go to him!"

"What if . . . what if he's married or he doesn't remember me . . ."

"Gert Turner, no man who's ever kissed you, or even *met* you, has ever forgotten you."

Still she remained motionless, staring in the direction he'd gone. Henry took her by the shoulders. "I know it's been a long time, and it might not be the same. But, honey, you've got to go see, or you'll never forgive yourself."

He guided her gently but firmly by the elbow and led her around the back of the set. Tip was dabbing at his forehead with a handkerchief and nodding as Edward gestured and offered notes about staging.

"Excuse me, Obie," said Henry, and he could feel rather than see Edward cringe. "Gert here knows this gentleman from their vaudeville days and wanted to say hello."

Tip looked over at her, a polite how-do-you-do smile on his face. But then the impact hit, as if he'd suddenly been struck by a meteor of longing.

"Gert," he said softly.

"Hello, Tip."

"Obie, I had a question about that scene in which I fall off a cliff." There was no such scene, but Henry knew Edward would understand something was up. "Mind if I pick your brain for a minute?" He walked away, and Edward followed.

"Well?"

Gert closed the tent flap behind her, and her entire face bloomed into a smile the likes of which he'd never seen on her before. Gert never moped, but until that moment, he realized she'd never been completely happy, either. This was unalloyed joy.

"Is he married?" Henry prompted.

She shook her head.

"In love with someone else?"

Again, no.

"Still madly in love with you and missing you just as much as you've missed him?"

Her eyes went shiny, and she slumped onto the canvas chair opposite him. "What am I going to do? It's worse than ever."

"What did he say?"

"The first thing he said was, 'Is that your man?'" She chuckled. "I told him you were my best friend, and a homosexual Jew."

Henry's eyebrows nearly hit his hairline. "Glad you got that cleared up."

Gert?" he asked. "Please tell me she's coming to work tomorrow. I can't take another change in the lead actress."

"She's a vaudevillian—those birds are tough. Nothing stops the show." Henry took a sip of Edward's scotch. "Besides, Tip doesn't have any professional reason to stay in Hollywood now that his scene is done. He'll be gone in a day or two, and poor brokenhearted Gert will be all yours."

Edward smiled wryly. "You devil."

"Well, what about it? He could easily be worked into the script. Make him the king's nephew or something. Throw him a few more scenes. It'd be a drop in the bucket on production costs."

"You've turned out to be quite the romantic."

Henry took Edward's hand and brought it to his lips. "And whose fault is that?"

41

◇ ◇ ◇

The only thing I regret about my past is the length of it. If I had to live my life again, I'd make the same mistakes, only sooner.
Tallulah Bankhead, actress

In September, Millie got the call she knew would come.

"Thank you for meeting with me today, Mildred," said Carlton Sharp.

"Well, I wanted to see what this office looked like when I'm wearing a nice dress and decent shoes," she said.

His professional smile dimmed at the memory of their previous encounter one year ago in this room, but he tried to pass it off with gaiety. "Any different?"

"No, just the same. Except for me, of course. And you can call me Millie."

"Well, then, Millie, please call me Carlton." He gestured for her to sit down on the same sofa she'd sunk into when she'd been so certain she was in trouble.

"That's okay. I just finished a movie in which I played a cripple, and I've got a lot of standing to catch up on."

He seemed slightly confused, but nodded anyway. "Well, then I'll get to the point as quickly and politely as I can."

"She didn't just die from the flu."

Had Millie misremembered it? She could be forgetful some-times, but never about something like that. "Oh . . . I thought you said . . ."

"I *gave* her the flu, Millie. I got it first and I was quarantined. No one was supposed to come into that room except the doctor. But I thought I was dying and I wanted to see her one last time, so I called out to her, and she came. I was selfish and I gave my sister the thing that killed her." Irene's voice went weak and breathy. "I killed her."

Millie felt her friend's guilt like a physical blow. Tears came to her eyes under the weight of such an avalanche of remorse and sorrow. "No, Irene. No," she soothed.

"Yes," Irene whispered. "I did. You shouldn't wish to be my sis-ter, Millie, because I'm selfish and I hurt people."

She began to cry, but she kept talking, a torrential river of re-gret that had finally breached its banks. "I hurt Dan because I was so ambitious, I chose the possibility of a promotion over his feelings, and I hurt Henry because he told me he's a . . . a . . . he likes men not girls, and I'm such a country bumpkin that I didn't know what to think, much less what to say, so I just said nothing, and I don't think he'll ever trust me again. He shouldn't. Neither of them should. And it's a good thing you're leaving because nei-ther should you."

Millie wrapped her arms around her friend and held her close. "No," she murmured. "No, it's *not* good that I'm leaving, because all I want to do is stay here with you. But I made a mistake—a big one. A mistake so big it's a whole person. And it's not the only mistake I've made. You know that. You more than anyone, be-cause over and over again you saved me from those mistakes. Join-ing up with Chandler? Saved me. Having no job or money for two straight months? Saved me. Going off to dance with strange men and smoke special cigarettes? Saved me, and how! You've made mistakes, Irene. Welcome to Millie-ville. It's a lovely place as long as you have friends."

"But what about Dan and Henry?"

"You can try to fix those mistakes. Maybe they can be fixed or maybe they can't. But if you can't fix them, it's not because you're meant to be alone, Irene. You're meant to be loved."

Irene began to sob, and Millie held her and waited and thought about all the times Irene had pushed people away. Now she knew why.

Also she thought about Henry. Apparently he was a homosexual! Well, that was surprising but it also explained some things, like why he was never terribly interested in holding her hand, much less getting her into bed, which most fellows seemed at the very least to consider. But Henry liked men. *Okay,* she thought. *That's a good thing to know about a friend.* She was learning all sorts of things tonight.

Irene's weeping slowed to small sobs and sniffles.

"All is not lost," Millie soothed.

Irene stopped crying. "Is that a line from that maid flicker you did?"

Millie winced. It had sounded so natural when she'd said it on set. "Yes, but it's still true, even if a writer wrote it."

The smallest little chuckle came out of Irene. "I'm glad we earn our keep once in a while."

At 8:00 a.m. the car Carlton Sharp had ordered pulled up in front of The Hillview Apartments. Millie hugged Irene one last long time, and Irene could feel the hard bulge around her friend's midsection.

"Write to me every day," said Millie.

"There won't be something to say every day."

"Then make something up! That's your job, isn't it?"

The car door slammed, and Millie was on her way to a home for unwed mothers in some little town in the middle of nowhere called Las Vegas, Nevada. She'd probably charm everyone in a mile radius within an hour.

Irene went upstairs and sat in a chair by the window. It was foolish to cry, to miss someone so terribly only five minutes after they were gone. Her longing for Millie had taken that brief time to equal her longing for Dan. She had ruined that one but good, hadn't she? At least she would see Millie again, though not for a solid four months. She'd been friendless for years before she met Millie, but now she was spoiled by love. So much of it from so many directions.

And Henry. She had seen him here and there, crossing paths at the studio with a brief hello. But she hadn't known how to raise the subject that had stunned her into silence, and as time went on, she felt more and more awkward about it.

Everyone she loved was gone. Maybe she'd been foolish to love them in the first place. Because now there was nothing Irene wanted more in life than to stop missing people.

42

◇ ◇ ◇

The only things we really keep are the things we give away.
William Desmond Taylor, director, actor, producer, who was
shot and killed in the prime of his career. His murder has never been solved.

The party at the Garden of Alla was no garden party. Famed actress Alla Nazimova had purchased the forty-room mansion on the western end of Sunset a few years before and spent thousands renovating it, adding a pool in the shape of the Black Sea, which bordered her native Russia.

"Is that really the shape of the Black Sea?" Gert asked Henry.

Apparently the host, clothed in matching black silk camisole and harem pants, heard her, because as she passed by she murmured, "Darling, it is. But who cares? Get a drink."

Tip had left Gert in Henry's care soon after Edward's driver had dropped them off. He'd taken one look at the vast sea of white skin and asked, "Y'all sure about this?"

"It's Alla's," Edward said. "There are far more unusual things to see than a colored man."

And he was right. Most of the guests were in some state of disinhibition and undress, whether from the impressive variety of alcohol being served or from the marijuana cigarettes being passed around the pool. Jean Acker was there, and Bessie Love.

In the pool itself, two women had just jumped in naked and were kissing. Alla waved at them as she walked by.

Nevertheless, Tip went over to say hello to the jazz trio, three black men who were taking a break from entertaining the guests, enjoying cocktails brought to them by a white-coated waiter. The older men nodded and laughed and seemed to be poking fun at Tip. Suddenly they all looked over at Gert and smiled with approval. No one else seemed to care at all.

Edward came back with drinks. The jazz trio started up, and Tip returned. The four of them stood there, sipping their cocktails among the guests, not saying much, likely hoping, as Henry was, that the alcohol would soon hit their bloodstreams at a gallop.

Edward smiled at Tip and rested his hand on Henry's shoulder. Tip took one last glance around and slid an arm around Gert's waist. She grinned and leaned into him.

"At last," said Edward, raising his glass and making them all laugh at their own self-consciousness.

◇ ◇ ◇

It was a wonderful evening. Tip danced with Gert, spinning her this way and that, holding her close for the slow ones; they gazed at each other as if they were falling in love all over again. In the month since he'd turned up on the set of *Fox Trot on the Congo*, Edward had placed him in several more scenes and recommended him for small parts in other films. He was in enough demand as a tap dancer that he could perform in theaters around the Southwest and be back to Hollywood within a day or two.

When he went to refresh their drinks, Gert made her way over to Henry and Edward, who sat at one of the tables, holding hands.

"We've never danced together before!" she said still catching her breath. "Isn't he something?"

When Tip returned, they congratulated him on his skill. He ran the tip of his brown finger down the dimple in her pale cheek. "She could make digging ditches look good."

"You're a great lead," she said, eyes shining up at him.

"It's a good thing, too," he teased. He turned to the men. "I had to muscle her a bit in the beginning. The girl knows her mind!"

"And that's why we love her," said Henry, feeling loose with affection for all of them.

A breeze blew through the lemon trees, the jazz trio picked up again, and sitting there with Edward's hand in his, Henry thought he might just possibly be the happiest he'd ever been in his life.

Then Hazel Hampton stumbled in.

It wasn't clear where she'd come from—the house? The street? Edward groaned. "She's ossified."

"Let's get her a cab."

"She can't go back to her place. All the dope peddlers know where she lives, and in her state she's likely to buy anything."

Henry gripped Edward's hand a little harder. "I don't want this night to end."

"I don't either, sweetheart, but I also don't want her to die. There'll be other nights."

Henry let go. Edward kissed him, then stood and headed for Hazel.

Henry awoke in his apartment to a thumping sound, rapid fire, and for the briefest moment he wondered if it were his own heart. The pounding began again, and he stumbled through the dark to his door. It was Carlton Sharp.

"Put some clothes on."

"What? Why? How did you—"

Sharp averted his eyes from Henry's bare chest. "I'll explain in the car."

They sped down a very familiar route: the way to Edward's house. Sharp refused to give any straight answers.

"You tell me what's going on *right now*," Henry warned, "or I get out at the next stoplight."

Sharp turned to face him. "Edward Oberhouser's been shot."

Henry's vision wavered, oceans crashing through his head. Edward. Shot. Edward. Shot.

"It appears to be a drug deal that took a turn. Neighbor called the police. Police called me."

Henry began to shake. "Is he—is he—?"

"I need you to come into the house and help me gather up anything that might be . . . unflattering. Love letters, unusual clothing, certain things that a police investigation might turn up. You know what he has and where he keeps it. This is for Edward, you understand. You've got to do this for him."

The car pulled up in front of Edward's garden apartment, the sky just beginning to lighten around it. Henry didn't know if he could walk. Sharp jumped out on his side and hurried around to wrench Henry's door open. "For godsake, get out of the car. We don't have much time."

He saw himself approach Edward's apartment, but he didn't know how. His legs didn't feel attached to his body. Sharp opened the door as if he owned the place. Two uniformed policemen stood in Edward's front hallway.

"This is the friend. He needs to see," said Sharp, and the policemen stood back.

There sitting on the tile, his back collapsed against the hall table, was Edward. The front of his crisp white shirt was dark red, and a trail of blood ran from a hole just above one of the shirt studs. His head hung at an awkward angle from his neck, his eyes open but unseeing.

Henry lunged for him, but the officers caught him and held him back. "Whoa, there son," said one of them in his ear. "We're good enough to let you in before this goes public. Don't tamper with the evidence, or we'll never find who did this to him."

"HE SHOULD BE IN A HOSPITAL!" Henry bellowed.

"The only place he'd be welcome in a hospital is very, very cold," said the cop. "He was gone before we got here."

They lowered Henry to the floor, and he crawled the last few feet to his beloved.

"Edward," he whispered, though his throat felt as if he were being slowly strangled. He took the hand, only faintly warm now, and cradled it against him. "Edward."

itated. If he'd been up all night, maybe he was sleeping. She'd let herself in and be there when he awoke. He shouldn't be alone. She'd been so alone after Ivy died, and look how that had turned out—with her trapped in a soul-crushing striptease show. She turned the key in the lock and quietly twisted the knob so as not to wake him.

He wasn't asleep. From the shadow of the hallway she could see him sitting in a chair at the little maple wood puzzle table she'd picked out with him almost a year ago now. He stared out the window with his back to her. "Please just go."

Irene felt it like a backhand to her face. He hated her that much.

But then another voice answered from the direction of the kitchen. "Mr. Sharp said I'm to stay here with you until he finalizes—"

"I don't care what that *mamzer* says, I don't need a babysitter."

"*Mamzer* is a bit harsh, sir."

"You speak Yiddish?"

"Well, I—"

"Then get the hell out, you little *putz*."

Irene stepped into the room. "I'll stay with him."

Henry twisted around in his seat, and a young man with a suit that was a size too big stepped out in front of her. "How the heck did you get in here?"

She held up the key.

He shook his head. "Mr. Sharp says—"

She drilled him with a look so menacing that he took a step back. "You get out of here right now or I'll go straight to the papers. Louella Parsons would love to hear from me." She opened the door and moved into the room. He scurried out and thumped the door closed behind him.

And there was Henry, face pale, clothes disheveled, and was that . . .? Yes, a swipe of blood on his shirt. He gazed up at her, confused, and then his eyes started to leak. "Irene."

She strode quickly across the room and knelt in front of him, sliding her hands up his shoulders. "Henry, I'm so sorry." He collapsed into her arms and wept.

After a few moments, he sat up and reached for a handkerchief to wipe his eyes, the initials *EO* embroidered on one corner.

Henry folded and refolded the handkerchief. Irene didn't know what to do in the silence that had suddenly enveloped them. Should she apologize for their withered friendship, or was that absurdly beside the point now that someone so important to him had died?

She rose and went to the kitchen to give herself a moment to think and brought out glasses of water. She had half a mind to go downstairs to Dan's apartment and pilfer some of that soothing greenthread tea. She still had his key, too.

"How much do you know?" asked Henry, not meeting her gaze.

"Only that he was shot."

"It was Hazel."

~~"Hazel Hampton *shot* him? He was the only friend she had~~ left in the business."

"She was drunk at a party, and he took her back to his apartment till she sobered up. Some insomniac neighbor saw him put her in a cab just before two men showed up. She owed everyone money, and they were likely trying to get it out of him."

"Do they know who?"

"No, but they've got Hazel down at the station looking at mug shots." Henry closed his eyes. "I can't believe I'm saying these things, that I'm telling you all this like it's . . . real."

"It won't seem real for a long time. A small part of you will never, ever believe it."

He turned to look at her, finally, and she could see him remembering her own loss. She didn't need to remind him how well she understood the utter devastation. Besides she had something more important to say.

"I didn't know what to make of it—you and Edward. I . . . I thought I knew you."

"You do know me."

"Yes, I do. I just didn't . . . I'll admit I was shocked. I'd never known any . . ." She laughed awkwardly. "I'm from Ohio!"

"So was Edward."

"I'm so desperately sorry for reacting badly. I've wanted to tell you for months, but I didn't know how to bring it up. It was naive and stupid of me. And of course I know there are plenty of your kind in the business . . . I just didn't realize . . ."

"It's not like we're going to wear lapel pins with a big *H* on them," he muttered.

She smiled weakly. "That would come in handy at parties, though. Ignorant people like me wouldn't make assumptions."

"I'll bring it up at our next club meeting."

"There's a club?"

He cut his eyes at her. "No."

She gazed back at him. "I am truly sorry, Henry. Even more sorry than when I jumped off that train without asking you to come along. Imagine if you hadn't been brave and stubborn enough to come anyway. Where would any of us be now?"

His face softened from anger to sorrow. She reached across the table and took his hand, ran her thumb gently over his knuckles. It was nice to be able to make such a gesture, wordless and comforting, and not worry that it would be taken the wrong way. "I want to be your friend again," she whispered.

He nodded. "I've missed you."

◇ ◇ ◇

He was tired, but he was afraid to sleep.

"I could cuddle up behind you, like Millie does with me."

"I thought that bothered you."

"It did at first, just because I wasn't used to being touched by anyone. But now I miss it."

He went into his bedroom and lay down, and she took off her shoes and got in beside him. She fixed the blankets and smoothed his hair. He lay on his side facing away from her, and she pressed herself up against his back and slid an arm around his waist. "Is this okay?"

"Yes, it's nice."

"Good. It's better to keep touching people. Otherwise you lose the knack and then you need someone like Millie to come along and make you."

He began to cry again—she could feel his ribs shaking against hers—but after some minutes he was worn-out and dozed off.

◇ ◇ ◇

Carlton Sharp showed up around three that afternoon.

"I understand that you dispatched my assistant with talk of going to Louella Parsons at the *Examiner*. I hope for the sake of both your careers it was an idle threat."

Henry had showered and changed into fresh clothes, but exhausted and colorless, he still looked like he was on leave from a tuberculosis ward.

"It was," said Irene. "But that doesn't mean we're going to put up with your sending pimply-faced boys around to keep us in line."

"I'm not trying to keep you in line." He jabbed a finger in Henry's direction. "I'm trying to save his career!"

"The career of an up-and-coming star who already has plenty of fan mail pouring in. For all you know, he's the next Rudy Valentino or Douglas Fairbanks. Your interests are the studio's interests. My interest is Henry."

Sharp crossed his arms. "Good. Then you'll marry him."

Henry's gaze spun away from the window and toward Sharp. "Excuse me?" said Irene.

Sharp glared at Henry. "The insomniac neighbor who saw Oberhouser put Hazel in the cab, and the two men turn up after that? She's seen you coming and going at all hours these last several months. She's got some daffy idea that you're one of those two dope peddlers. It never occurred to her that you and Obie were just a couple of daisies.

"If you become a suspect, even if you can lie better than Lizzie Borden, all kinds of things will come out. They might come out anyway if the newspapers get wind of it. I'm working with the police—"

"What does that mean, 'working with the police'?" asked Irene.

"It means they come to me and I go to them. We work together."

"And you pay them."

"I provide incentive for them to call me first." He turned to Henry. "Which worked out, didn't it? You got all those sweet little notes you wrote and a couple of things to remember him by that his greedy relatives will never know about. Oh, yes, I've been dealing with them, too. A couple of sisters in Ohio who have no idea about his . . . proclivities."

Henry closed his eyes. Irene grabbed his hand under the table and squeezed.

"We need to marry you off before someone picks up the scent, or your career is over." He turned to Irene. "And yes, that's in the best interest of the studio *at the moment*. In the next moment it might not be, and then he's on his own. So, young lady, I suggest you consider very carefully any advice you may give in that regard." He stood up and buttoned his suit jacket. "And start shopping for a wedding gown."

44

◇ ◇ ◇

*Joan Crawford thought we should get married . . . I told
her, "That isn't how it works in Hollywood. They usually pair men
who like men and ladies who like ladies." Because if we both liked men,
where would we be as man and wife? She'd resent me, and that
would be the end of our beautiful friendship.*
William Haines, actor, interior designer

Gert was there by five. "I was way out on the back lot," she said, still panting from running up four flights of stairs when Henry answered the door. "I had no way to get to you!"

Henry could feel his eyes start to leak again, and he wondered if it would happen every time he saw someone he knew, someone who cared about him even a little bit. Because if this was going to happen over and over again, he wasn't sure he could take it.

A neighbor across the hall opened his door and peeked out. Henry pulled Gert in and closed his quickly. He didn't want to fall apart again. He'd been sobbing off and on all day, and he felt like an old handkerchief, soggy with tears and fraying around the edges.

Gert pulled him into a tight embrace, her former-acrobat's arms strong and sheltering even though he had a good eight inches on her. And he was crying all over again.

◇ ◇ ◇

He was in the middle of telling her about the neighbor thinking he might be one of the killers, when Irene returned with a sack of takeout food from The Cottonwood down the street.

"Oh," she said. "Hello, Gert."

Gert's lips went flat. "Hello, Irene."

Henry looked from one to the other. "Please," he said. "We're all friends now."

"We are?" said Gert skeptically. "Because there didn't seem to be much of that going around the last few months."

"We've sorted that out," said Irene.

"About time," muttered Gert.

"Not that it's any of your business."

Gert crossed her arms. "It's none of my business at all. It's completely between you and Henry, of course. But I can't help having an opinion about it."

"I'm not interested in your opinion, Gert—"

"Well, I'm going to tell it to you anyway, *Irene*, because you need to hear it. You grew up in a small town. So what. So did ninety percent of the people who now call this madhouse town home. You don't get to come here and live this life, in this business, and suddenly turn into one of those church ladies from East Buggy Whip, Oklahoma, with corsets so tight they cut off all blood flow to their small brains."

"Gert, for godsake—"

"I'm not done. He was your friend. He saved your bacon over and over. And you think you're on some high pedestal, so morally superior that you get to judge him—"

"I do *not* think I'm morally superior! Far from it! I just didn't know how . . . to . . ."

"Enough," said Henry.

"Didn't know how to what, Irene? Be a friend? Be a human being?"

Henry banged his hand on the table. "I'm begging you . . ." And he felt his eyes filling again.

Both heads swiveled toward him, fury at each other turning to contrition at the sight of his tears.

"You know how sorry I am, Henry," Irene murmured, and he nodded.

Shame staining her pale cheeks, Gert looked away. "I won't mention it again."

After a moment, Gert went into the kitchen to get plates and forks: Irene busied herself with unpacking the food. There was a knock at the door, and she went to answer it, ready to throw her shoulder against it in case it was a scoop-seeking reporter or a nosy neighbor.

She was also ready to play the fiancée if she had to, though she still wasn't sure how she felt about it. In the abyss of Millie's absence, the idea of having someone permanent to come home to every night sounded incredibly comforting. Even if he slept in another room and snuck around with men.

She opened the door only about six inches and peeked around it.

Dan stood in the hallway.

The briefest flurry of surprise crossed his face before he was able to iron it into some semblance of composure. "I just came to check on Henry and offer my condolences."

"You knew."

"About Edward and Henry? Yes. I assumed a lot of people did."

"Who is it?" called Gert.

"It's just me, Gert," he answered.

"Oh, Dan, how are you? Why are you barring him at the door, Irene?"

So much for "We're all friends now," thought Irene. Apparently not mentioning it again didn't preclude Gert from sneaking in a jab on other matters. She stepped back, and Dan followed her into the apartment. He said nothing, only walked over to Henry and rested a hand on his shoulder. Henry turned away toward the windows, and his shoulders began to shake. Dan waited quietly, never taking his hand off his friend. Then Henry put a napkin to his eyes, and Dan sat down.

"Cottonwood," he said nodding. "Mutton and blue corn dumplings. Who bought all this food?" He looked at Gert.

"Irene did. She must have been hungry."

Irene was tempted to shoot back some sharp comment, but Henry looked so ragged, and it didn't matter anyway. Let Gert be the one to lob snotty comments. She would abide by his wishes.

"I was thinking Henry might like the extras for lunch tomorrow, but I can go out and get more." She smiled. "Maybe I'm just practicing to be a good wife." She meant it as a joke, but Henry looked up quickly.

"You don't have to do that. He was just trying to scare you."

"Who's he?" said Dan, his fork stalled halfway between his plate and his mouth.

"Carlton Sharp," said Irene. "He thinks Henry needs to get married so his fans won't suspect him of being homosexual." She had only paused for a fraction of a second before she said the word. It was the first time she'd ever said it, and it felt a little strange on her tongue, almost like she was cursing in polite company. But it was a perfectly good word, she reminded herself, merely descriptive, not derogatory. At least it didn't have to be. Other words for such a thing were far worse.

Dan put his fork down. "You two are getting married?"

"No," said Henry.

"It wouldn't be a real marriage," said Irene. "It would just be to help Henry."

"I don't want to talk about this now!" said Henry, with more force than he'd managed all day. Then he was immediately penitent. "I'm sorry, I'm just . . . I'm not ready for this."

"No, I'm sorry," said Irene. "I shouldn't have said anything."

Henry pushed his chair back and stood up. "I'm just going to sit on the sofa for a bit."

Without a word, Gert followed and sat close beside him, threading her arm through his. Irene and Dan brought the remaining food back to the kitchen.

"He might need a little quiet right now," Dan said.

"I know," Irene muttered as she washed up the few dishes. "I feel bad enough already."

"That's not what I'm saying. He knows you're just trying to be a good friend. But Gert's here, so let's let them be."

Irene knew he was right. Henry didn't need an entourage; he needed one person to sit with, to get through the next hour, and the next after that. She dried her hands and went over to him. "I'm going to head home now," she said.

"You're leaving?"

"Yes, but I'll come back tomorrow. Gert and Dan will need to be on set, and I can just call in sick with a headache or something."

Henry turned to Dan. "You'll walk her home."

"'Course I will."

"It's just a few blocks," Irene protested.

But Dan was already heading out the door, and after Irene kissed Henry on the cheek and said a polite, if cool, goodbye to Gert, she followed.

The night air was chilly, even for October, and she would have liked a sweater. They walked in silence until she couldn't stand it anymore and blurted out, "How've you been?"

"Miserable."

She stopped and looked up at him. He slowed and turned back to face her.

"Why've you been miserable?"

"You know why," he said. "I'm still angry about that Navajo script, but . . . everything else about you, I miss."

She sighed. "I miss you, too. And I'm sorry about the script. I just wanted to tell a story about your people. Honestly, Dan, I imagined you playing the lead! But I guess I thought too highly of my ability to write something bankable that would also feel true. And I'll admit, I got caught up in thinking it could be a career-maker, and that I might even get to direct."

"I shouldn't have brought up the business with Millie."

"No you shouldn't have. It was too personal. I suppose that story felt personal to you, too, though."

"I thought I was . . . I was sure I'd settled all that. Being white and Navajo. Living here instead of on the reservation. It all got stirred up again."

"That's not what I intended—actually just the opposite. I thought it would make you happy if I could get the studio to tell that story, even a watered-down version of it."

"Are they making the picture?"

"Last I heard, no. Zane Grey is pushing back on some of the changes, and there's a lot of back and forth that doesn't seem to go anywhere. If it does get made, it won't be anytime soon."

He gazed at her for a long minute. Finally he asked, "Are we getting back together?"

She smiled. "Are you asking me?"

He put his warm hands on her chilly shoulders. "Are you saying yes?"

She stepped into the circle of his embrace. "I think I might be," she whispered.

"Good," he murmured into her hair. "Because I'm asking."

"And if that flicker ever gets made, we just won't see it."

"We'll go to a deserted island until the run is over."

"That sounds kind of nice," she said. "Maybe we should go anyway."

He tugged her in closer, burying her in his chest, the sweet warm scent of him enveloping her. "Irene Van Beck. The girl I couldn't forget."

"Dan Stars Lying Down Russell. I hope you never do."

◇ ◇ ◇

For the first time in three months, Irene had absolutely no interest in getting out of bed. The birds sang in the jacaranda tree behind The Hillview Apartments, and she could have lain there all day long, entwined with Dan.

He tickled his fingers along the small of her back. "How serious is this business about Henry getting married? Was Sharp just making idle threats?"

"I'm not sure. But we both know the studio pushes people into marriage, especially if they've been sleeping in the wrong beds. Eva told me they were gearing up to give *Fox Trot on the Congo* the full treatment, a huge national push, so they must think Henry is worth the effort."

"Hate to say it, but it'll probably be a huge hit, now that it's famous director Edward Oberhouser's last picture. Especially with the way he died."

"Except if there's some scandal involving Henry. That could kill it entirely. So if I had to bet money, I'd say Henry's getting married, unless he wants to get out of the flickers altogether."

They lay in silence for a few moments, and Irene wondered if Henry might actually want to get out. It would be excruciating to go on as if Edward's death meant nothing to him, which is exactly what would be required. But what could he do—go back to standup comedy? Laying bricks? He was fairly recognizable now, after *Husbands for Sale*. There was nowhere he could go and lead a normal life.

She would marry him if it would keep him from going down an endless road of misery. She'd been on that road after Ivy died, and she wouldn't wish it on anyone. Except maybe Wally Walters, that bastard. Or Chandler. Or Barney. She hoped they were all begging for change together in Tijuana.

"Please don't marry Henry."

She looked up at him. "What? Why not? It wouldn't be real, Dan. We could still be together."

"It'd have to look real, though, wouldn't it? Real enough that we'd have to sneak around. If you're the wife of a famous movie star, we couldn't so much as grab dinner at The Cottonwood without him being there as your official date."

"I guess you're right about that."

"Also . . ."

She waited, worried.

"I don't want you to be another man's wife."

45

◇ ◇ ◇

*Being a movie star, and this applies to all of them, means being
looked at from every possible direction. You are never
left at peace, you're just fair game.*
Greta Garbo, actress

enry knew he'd have to give a statement to the police. Carlton Sharp had warned him about that, but he thought it would be the next day, not at ten o'clock at night. Sharp came to the door and told him to put on his best suit and tie, and for godsake get his hair in order.

"We can't go in the morning?"

"We can if we want the entire city of Los Angeles to see you walk in, and for there to be pictures from every angle on the front page of every newspaper in the entire country just in time for the evening edition." He looked at Gert. "Miss Turner. I don't believe we've met. I'm Carlton Sharp, head of publicity. I'll have my driver take you home."

"Thanks, but I'll stay. I don't want Henry to face this alone."

He eyed Gert, and she eyed him right back. "You're his alibi," he said.

"Alibi? But I wasn't with him when it happened."

"Where were you?"

Gert looked at Henry, but Henry could barely think straight. "You were at the Studio Club, right?"

Sharp shook his head. "Unfortunate. We need someone whose whereabouts wouldn't have been known by others."

"Do I need an alibi?" said Henry wearily. "Can't I just say I was home in bed?"

"You can. How do you feel about a first-degree murder charge?"

"I wasn't at the Studio Club," said Gert. The two men turned to look at her. "I was out."

"Out where?"

She cut her eyes at Henry again, looking for help, but he could barely button his shirt properly.

Sharp drummed his fingers on his thigh. "Actually it doesn't matter where you were, so long as whoever you were with won't show up at the LAPD at any time in the future and say, 'No she wasn't with Henry Weston on the night of the murder, she was with me.'"

"Oh, he won't," said Gert. "Trust me on that score. He wouldn't go anywhere near a police station."

Sharp raised an eyebrow. "And no one else saw you? Not one single soul can place you with this ... whoever it was?"

"No. We're good at finding places to be alone."

"Aren't you all," muttered Sharp, "until you aren't, and then suddenly I don't have five minutes to so much as go to the john." He let out a long breath. "Okay, I'm going to ask you both questions, and we're going to come up with answers that match, and you're going to memorize them so thoroughly that by the time we get to the station, you'll think it's all true."

It was midnight by the time Sharp thought they were sufficiently prepared, and the streets were, in fact, almost empty. Sharp sat up front with his driver, and Henry sat in back with Gert.

"Henry," she murmured. "Listen to me. I know just saying Edward's name will make you want to lay down on the floor and weep." She took his hand. "But if you do that, they're going to put two and two together, and then they're going to jump to the conclusion that it was a crime of passion.

"He was a good friend, someone you admired and enjoyed working with. Also, hush hush, but you're having an affair with me. Those times you visited Edward late at night were when you and I were on the outs, and you needed the shoulder of a friend. If they get a whiff that any of that isn't true . . . well, it's not what Edward would want for you. You need to make him proud tonight. Use what he taught you, and give the performance of your life."

46

◇ ◇ ◇

He smiled and gurgled, and I smiled—and that was all. I didn't have any idea of adopting a baby when I went there, but something about him just made me pick him up—and then I couldn't bear to go away without him. So that very afternoon I cut through all the red tape and adopted him.

Barbara La Marr, writer, actress, on "meeting" her biological son at a Dallas orphanage

Millie was apoplectic about not going to the wedding. As if the stupid little backwater town of Las Vegas, Nevada, wasn't punishment enough! Not that she got to see much of it in the three and a half long, boring months she'd been here. Nurse Johnson, in whose rambling farmhouse she was living, had strict orders that unwed, pregnant starlets were not to be visible to anyone, lest they be recognized and revealed. The population of the few dusty streets they called a town wasn't even three thousand people, and there was only one movie theater, The Majestic. By the time *A Baby's Cry* made its way to this Podunk berg, Millie figured she'd be a grandmother. How she could be "revealed" was a mystery.

The Johnson property was a cattle ranch about five miles outside of town, and Nurse Johnson and her husband took in as many as three "studio girls" at a time. At the moment there was only one other girl, a well-known actress of the stage and screen, whose husband was a navy man—oh, how the movie magazines loved to print pictures of her with her husband in his starched dress whites! Unaccountably, he'd been on a ship for three months before and after the probable date of conception, so the great lady had suddenly developed a "lung condition" and been whisked away to the desert to improve her breathing.

I'm having trouble breathing, too, thought Millie, now eight and a half months pregnant, the baby pressing so hard in every direction she thought a foot might pop out of her mouth one of these days. *But at least I don't lock myself in my room with all the copies of* Photoplay *in the house and insist my dinner be brought to me.*

In fact, Millie's sole enjoyment was working in Nurse Johnson's herb and vegetable garden. She had already decided that when she bought her own house, which she planned to do when she returned to Hollywood to make room for the baby and a nursemaid, she'd have a little garden in the yard.

But even the garden couldn't distract her on December 16, when she knew the wedding was taking place without her.

I could come back in disguise! she'd written to Irene.

> *You'd have to shave your head, wear fake whiskers, and dress as a potbellied old man. And even then, you'd be taking chances. It's not worth it, Millie. It isn't even a real wedding.*

Millie had been writing letters to both Henry and Irene at least once a week since she'd come to this godforsaken outpost; they were generally short, "as nothing, absolutely *nothing*, ever happens here."

But when she learned about the terrible loss Henry had suffered—of having to keep such a loving relationship secret in the first place, and then to have that love snuffed out so violently—she knew a different kind of letter was in order.

Dear, dear Henry,

We go back to the dark ages, you and Irene and I, and the only way we got through was that we had each other. Well, you are having a very dark age right now, and I am sorry that I am not right there next to you where I should be.

You are so brave, Henry. You had the courage to accept love where you found it, even though it was in a place that some people don't understand. And it's still there, inside you. Real love changes us, makes us kinder, better, braver.

Your love, and Irene's, even made me smarter! You each taught me things and even loved me when I was foolish sometimes. You loved me into a wiser Millie. Thank goodness!

We will love you with all our might through this dark age you're in, Henry, because you are ours and you are so easy to love.

Holding you in the warmest,
brightest part of my heart always,
Millie

She'd thought a lot about Henry and Edward since then. She imagined it was the way she felt about Irene (except with sexual attraction), and the idea of it always made her teary. And now the studio was making him marry someone for whom he'd never feel any desire. It all seemed terribly wrong and unfair. Still, she wanted to go to the wedding. She felt she should be there for him, to be a loving face, a face that *knew* him, in the crowd of mere stargazers.

The engagement was announced a week after Edward's death, and the studio pushed up the premier of *Fox Trot on the Congo* to the day before the wedding. Irene had gone back to the cutting room to edit it herself so it would be ready in time. She said Carlton Sharp was earning his silver by whipping up a froth of publicity, putting pictures in all the movie mags of the happy couple spending time together before the ceremony. He'd even chartered a yacht to take them out to Catalina with a photographer to capture the love. Apparently Henry got seasick. *He says from now on he won't even float a boat in the bathtub*, Irene wrote. But the pictures were beautiful—Millie had seen them in *Photoplay* herself, before the other pregnant "studio girl" had gotten her claws into that and every other issue.

Irene said they'd spent a lot of time house hunting and considered Beverly Hills, which had become quite popular since Douglas Fairbanks and Mary Pickford had moved there in 1919. But they'd very quickly learned that the entire town fell under something called a "restrictive covenant": no Jews or colored people allowed. They ended up in Laurel Canyon. Henry said the place was special to him, and it was out of the way enough for them to just be themselves.

Just be themselves. Millie pondered this concept as she slid her trowel around a sage plant to transfer it to a pot and take it inside before the desert nights got too cold. In many ways Hollywood was uniquely a place where people could be themselves. But then there came a point when even Hollywood couldn't hide you, and you ended up having to do something drastic like marrying someone you would never kiss.

She felt the tightening in her belly and knelt down between the rows for a minute until it passed. This had been happening off and on for a week or so, and Nurse Johnson had been plainly unimpressed. "It's just false pains," she said. "You'll know when it's real. It's the difference between a clap of the hands and a clap of thunder."

For the last day or so, these pains had been more like a full house round of applause, and as she knelt there in the sandy soil in the middle of nowhere, it felt like thunder—far off but approaching.

Then she peed herself. So embarrassing. She'd gotten her drawers damp straggling to the bathroom half asleep more than once. By the third or fourth time in the course of a night, she sometimes found the decision of whether to haul herself to the privy or just soak her own bed a difficult one to make. But this was in the middle of the day, and she hadn't realized she even had to go.

Nurse Johnson came out to hang some washing. "How're those plants coming? Don't even bother with the thyme—it'll come back in the spring on its own." She peered at Millie an extra moment. "Did you tip the watering can on yourself?"

Millie shook her head.

Nurse Johnson heaved a great sigh that made the waddle under her chin quiver. "All right then. Go on in the house and get out of those clothes. I'll finish hanging these britches and be along directly."

◇　◇　◇

It was a long day and an even longer night. By dawn, Millie was sweating and calling for Irene.

"Hush that squawking!" said Nurse Johnson. "The hens won't be able to lay their eggs from fright."

Millie gritted her teeth. "Are you even a real nurse?"

"Of course I am."

"Where did you train?"

"At my mother's elbow."

"*Irene!*"

◇ ◇ ◇

It's an earthquake, Millie thought as her body shuddered and strained as if it might split in two. *A human earthquake.*

And then it was over—finally—only the trembling after-shocks rippling through her body.

She waited.

Please. Oh, please, God.

A quivering squawk, like the newborn lambs on the farm where she'd worked. Lifetimes ago now.

"Girl," said Nurse Johnson matter-of-factly.

"Give her to me!"

"I'm cleaning her up, so you'll have to wait until—"

"I don't want her cleaned up! I want her just as she is!" Millie thundered. "*Give me the baby!*"

Nurse Johnson plunked the tiny human, hastily wrapped in a piece of old bedsheet, into Millie's arms and harrumphed, "She's a mess."

But she wasn't. She was damp, yes, and ruddy from the journey—Millie was a bit damp herself. But this baby, with her tiny nose and waving arms and ears like the most delicate pink shells . . . this baby was perfect just as she was. Whoever she was, and whoever she might grow up to be.

47

◇ ◇ ◇

To me, love has always meant friendship.
Jean Harlow, actress

"I have the best news!" Irene sat at Henry's kitchen table. She'd taken to going over to the house in Laurel Canyon in the mornings, knowing how hard the first hour of the day could be when you woke and had to remember all over again that your life had shattered into a thousand shards of pain.

He was grateful to have someone to talk to who understood his grief, with whom he could be fully himself. Surprisingly, she found that she could be more open, too, revealing parts of herself that she'd kept carefully locked away. In those early struggling days when they'd first arrived in Hollywood, she'd grown to love him, but she hadn't realized how little they'd actually known each other.

He'd slept a lot after Edward's death and was just now getting back to work. *Fox Trot on the Congo* had been a solid hit, and the studio had decided to reprise it with *Charleston in China*—same basic story with the same stars, but set in Asia, of course.

At the moment he looked like a little boy, with his hair all sleep tousled and his pajamas creased and crooked. The kitchen was open and sunny, and the light set off hollows below his cheekbones that hadn't been there before the loss of Edward. She would have to mention it to Gert. Maybe they could plan some dinners together with lots of rich food.

He sipped at a cup of coffee. "Tell me the news."

"Millie had the baby!"

"What? Isn't this early?"

"A couple of weeks, yes, although you never can know for certain with these things."

"It went well?"

"I'll spare you the excruciating details. Suffice it to say, she's likely never to get herself into a similar situation."

Henry smirked at this.

"Yes, I know," said Irene. "It's Millie. Anything could happen."

"Boy or girl?"

"A squalling pink baby girl."

"Name?"

Irene had cried when she'd first read the letter yesterday. This morning she promised herself she was done shedding any tears over it, but her eyes went shiny all the same. "Ivy."

"Oh, Irene."

"Yes, well the poor thing's middle name is Sage, because that happens to be the plant Millie was digging up when the pains started. Imagine if she'd been pulling turnips!"

Henry let out a full belly laugh, a first since his terrible loss two months before.

"When does she bring little Ivy Sage home?" he asked, still smiling.

"Oh, not for a while. Apparently if you show up with the baby right away, it's far too obvious. She'll stay there and nurse for a month or two, get her shape back, and then come home. Carlton Sharp will cook up some story about Millie meeting the baby on location, and we'll get our little bundle of love in six months or so."

Gert came down the staircase, tying her robe around her waist and pushing blonde locks off her cheeks. She squeezed Henry's shoulder as she went by. "More coffee?"

"Yes, please."

"I'll take another splash," said Irene. "Thanks."

"How are you doing with house hunting?" Gert brought the pot over and freshened their cups.

Irene grinned. "I'm looking at one right up the street!"

"Gosh, that's jake! Room for Millie and the baby?"

"And a decent-size yard for the garden she keeps talking about."

"Have you told her yet?"

"No, I thought I'd save it all for when she gets home. She's had enough of learning big news from letters."

Irene and Dan had talked about getting a place together, which had precipitated a long conversation about the possibility of formally joining their lives, as well. Dan was in favor . . . but the more they talked about it, the more Irene realized she wasn't ready to be someone's wife and certainly not someone's mother. She had a growing career in a growing industry and she was only twenty-two. There would be time for all the rest someday. But not quite yet.

"Will Tip want coffee?" Henry asked. "I can perk another pot."

"Thanks, but he left hours ago. He's got a show in San Francisco, so he'll be back in a week." Gert took her coffee and headed back up to her room but turned at the bottom of the stairs.

"Irene, are you hurrying off?"

"No, I've got some time."

"Henry, why don't you get dressed and we can all go to the lot together."

"Yes, dear," he said as he stood and headed for his bedroom. She rolled her eyes at him and continued up the stairs.

Irene sipped her coffee and waited for her friends. It certainly was an unusual arrangement, Gert and Henry living together as husband and wife, while she carried on a love affair with another man (a dark-skinned one, no less) with Henry's full knowledge and approval. Irene hoped he would find love again, too, and she prepared herself to be as welcoming to his new love as she wished she'd been to Edward.

Her own circumstances were almost as unorthodox. She had a loving and devoted man, yet no interest in marriage. She was about to purchase her very own home and would soon be joined by the ever-impetuous Millie Martin and her "adopted" daughter.

Ivy Sage Martin. When she got older, how would they explain it all to her?

Friendship would be their only defense.

We were friends, they would say. *We would've done anything for one another.*

Author's Note

◇ ◇ ◇

Many months of research went into writing *City of Flickering Light*, and I wish I could have included even more of the fascinating information I learned in the process. Here's a little further detail on some of the people, places, films, and history behind the story.

The three main characters are completely fictional, although Millie sometimes channeled a bit of Jean Harlow's sensuality, humor, and preference for skimping on underwear. Some of the secondary characters, however, are loosely based on real people.

Edward Oberhauser was patterned after well-respected director William Desmond Taylor, who was shot in his apartment on February 1, 1922. At the time of his death, he'd been in a years-long relationship with art director George James Hopkins. His murder remains unsolved. It was at first speculated that his friend Mabel Normand, who had left shortly before the likely time of the murder, was involved. Normand was known to overindulge in alcohol and drugs, and Taylor was a good friend who wanted to help her. Starlet Mary Miles Minter was madly in love with Taylor, and her extremely protective mother was also a suspect. Finally, there was a deathbed confession of former actress Margaret Gibson. For more on this fascinating story, I recommend *Tinseltown: Murder, Morphine, and Madness at the Dawn of Hollywood* by William J. Mann

Hazel Hampton was inspired by Mabel Normand, a brilliant comedienne and star of more than two hundred films. She never got over the death of her dear friend William Desmond Taylor and died of tuberculosis in 1930 at the age of thirty-seven.

Eva Crown was based on Frances Marion, one of the most prolific, respected, and highest paid screenwriters of all time, who also acted in, directed, and produced many films. She won Academy Awards for best screenplay for *The Big House* and *The Champ* and was able to maintain her high standing in an extremely competitive industry for more than thirty years. *Without Lying Down: Frances Marion and the Powerful Women of Early Hollywood* by Cari Beauchamp is a wonderful, information-packed read.

Carlton Sharp was inspired by Howard Strickling, who began working for Metro Studios in 1919 and was head of publicity at Metro-Goldwyn-Mayer until 1969. He promoted and protected stars such as Clark Gable, Spencer Tracy, Greta Garbo, Jean Harlow, Joan Crawford, Mickey Rooney, and Judy Garland.

Herbert Vanderslice was *not* based on Cecil B. DeMille, though they shared a love of snappy dressing and splashy films with high production costs. DeMille was a far more talented director than Vanderslice could ever have hoped to be.

◇ ◇ ◇

As a rule, I tried to use buildings and locations from the time period that still exist today. A few of them opened a year or two after the novel takes place, but are so iconic I decided to include them.

The old Warner Brothers Studio, 5800 Sunset Boulevard, was

the inspiration for the Olympic Studio lot. It was built in 1919 and used by Warner Brothers for their main offices and central studio. In 1937, the studio consolidated its locations in Burbank, and the building was converted to a sports center with a bowling alley. Now called Sunset Bronson Studios, it has reverted to its original use as a film production facility.

Musso & Frank Grill, 6667 Hollywood Boulevard, opened in 1919. It boasts the first pay phone to be installed in Hollywood (the phone booth is still there), and was an upscale favorite of film folk. The food is unabashedly retro—and delicious.

Hollywood Athletic Club, 6525 Sunset Boulevard, was founded by Charlie Chaplin, Rudolph Valentino, and Cecil B. DeMille in 1924. It charged a $150 initiation fee and $10 for monthly dues. Membership included John Wayne, John Ford, Douglas Fairbanks Sr., Mary Pickford, Humphrey Bogart, Clark Gable, Jean Harlow, Mae West, and Joan Crawford.

The Iris Theatre, 6508 Hollywood Boulevard, was built in 1918 and opened with *Birth of a Nation*. Carol Burnett worked there as an usher in her teens. It has undergone several remodels and name changes, from the Fox Theatre in the 1960s (the sign remains) to the current Playhouse Nightclub.

The Egyptian Theatre, 6706 Hollywood Boulevard, opened in 1922 and was the site of the first ever movie premiere, *Robin Hood*, starring Douglas Fairbanks, on October 18, 1922. Its Egyptian theme reflected the world's fascination with the search for King Tut's tomb, which was discovered two weeks after the theater opened. Original plans called for a Hispanic design, but when the plans were changed, red tile for the roof had already been ordered. It was installed and remains today.

The HOLLYWOODLAND sign was built in 1923 by *Los Angeles Times* publisher Harry Chandler as an advertisement for his new real estate development. Costing $21,000 and lit with four thousand twenty-watt bulbs, it was intended to remain for only eighteen months but soon became iconic of the movie industry and was left in place. LAND was removed when it was refurbished in 1949 so that it no longer represented the housing development but the district.

Mulholland Drive opened on December 27, 1924. It follows a ridgeline of the Santa Monica Mountains, with panoramic views of Hollywood, Los Angeles, and beyond to the south, and the San Fernando Valley to the north. Construction facilitated the development of the canyons of the Hollywood hills, while also providing generations of car enthusiasts with opportunities to risk life, limb, and property speeding along it, including John Carradine, Gary Cooper, and, of course, James Dean.

The Alto Nido apartment building, 1851 N. Ivar Avenue, was made famous as the home of writer Joe Gillis (played by William Holden) in *Sunset Boulevard*.

The Hillview Apartments, 6533 Hollywood Boulevard, was built in 1918 by studio heads Jesse Lasky and Sam Goldwyn for people in the film industry because they were often discriminated against by local landlords. Movie star tenants included Clara Bow, Stan Laurel, Viola Dana, Barbara La Marr, and Mary Astor.

Laurel Canyon, where the main characters purchase homes at the end of the story and live in unorthodox arrangements, was famous in the 1960s for the similarly unconventional lifestyles of the rock and folk musicians who gravitated there. These include Joni Mitchell, Frank Zappa, Neil Young, Peter Tork of the Monkees, Cass Elliot of the Mamas and the Papas, and Glenn Frey of the Eagles.

◇ ◇ ◇

These buildings and locations were fun to visit and imagine the people who might have passed through. Unfortunately, some historic Hollywood buildings have been demolished.

The original Hollywood Studio Club, 6129 Carlos Avenue, was a pillared Colonial that served as the HSC's first home in 1916, with Marion Hunter as its director. Demand for lodging quickly grew, and in 1926 the YWCA opened newly built quarters at 1215 Lodi Place. All of the studios contributed to construction costs. Famous residents include Dorothy Malone, Barbara Eden, Donna Reed, Rita Moreno, and Marilyn Monroe, who posed for nude pictures to make money to pay her rent at the club. The Hollywood Studio Club ended its run in 1975, but the second building still stands and serves as a YWCA.

The Hollywood Hotel, 6811 Hollywood Boulevard, built in 1902, held legendary Thursday night dances that made it the place to see and be seen. Many film industry people stayed or lived there, including Louis B. Mayer, Irving Thalberg, Norma Shearer, and Ethel Barrymore. Rudolph Valentino lived in room 264 and reportedly met both of his wives, Jean Acker and Natacha Rambova, there. Deteriorating after its heyday, it was demolished in 1956.

The Ambassador Hotel, 3400 Wilshire Boulevard, opened in 1921, and its Cocoanut Grove nightclub quickly became synonymous with movie stars and glamour, inspiring similarly named venues across the country. It was often used as a filming location for upscale hotel scenes, such as Jean Harlow's *Bombshell*, *The Graduate*, and *Pretty Woman*. Around the time of Robert Kennedy's assassination there in 1968, the hotel went into decline and was demolished in 2005 to make way for the Robert F. Kennedy Community Schools. Mae Murray did live in one of the bungalows on the property for a time.

The Garden of Alla, 8152 Sunset Boulevard (which at the time was unpaved west of Fairfax Avenue), was purchased in 1918 by major film star Alla Nazimova. It immediately became known for its hedonistic parties, which included Nazimova's "sewing circles" of lesbian film stars. From then until its demolition in 1959, it attracted a who's who of film, literary, and music circles. Residents included F. Scott Fitzgerald, Sergei Rachmaninoff, Harpo Marx, Ava Gardner, Errol Flynn, Frank Sinatra, and Ronald Reagan.

◇ ◇ ◇

As much as possible I wanted to use actual films of the time, so I "borrowed" several.

The Queen of Sheba (1921) did star Betty Blythe and Fritz Leiber, but it was actually directed by J. Gordon Edwards from a scenario by Virginia Tracy. Miss Blythe was known to speak her mind, though it's not clear how salty her language may have been in private or how much, if any, she drank. I took a bit of literary license with that, and I apologize for any misrepresentation. The film was tremendously successful, in large part due to the scantiness of Miss Blythe's costumes, one of which involved only a string of pearls from the waist up. The completely topless scenes were shown only in Europe, but the American cut was hardly puritanical.

Beyond the Rocks (1922)—referred to as *Behind Her Socks* in the novel—was based on the novel by Elinor Glyn and starred Gloria Swanson and Rudolph Valentino, who were paid $12,500 and $1,000 a week, respectively. It was the only movie in which the two extremely popular stars worked together. Though there were scenes set in Africa and the Alps, the entire picture was filmed in California. It was thought to be one of the many lost silent films until a copy was found after the death of an anonymous Dutch collector in 2004.

The story *The Vanishing American* by Zane Grey was first published in serial form in the *Ladies' Home Journal* in 1922 to 1923. It was even more scathing with regard to the Bureau of Indian Affairs and white missionaries than the book, which was published in 1925. The movie premiered in 1925 and was much diluted in its presentation of white malfeasance. I was also disappointed to see that the main character, Nophaie, was played by white actor Richard Dix wearing a lot of reddish-brown greasepaint.

◇ ◇ ◇

The historical events and circumstances woven into the story are all factual. The songs used were all popular hits of the early 1920s. Product, price, retailer, and promotional text information was generally taken from actual advertisements in the *Hollywood Citizen* of the time.

Prohibition, the ban on the production, sale, and consumption of alcohol, was instituted as federal law in January 1920. It had far less of an impact on Hollywood than it did in most other areas of the country. There were countless speakeasies, or blind pigs as they were sometimes known, and most people of means had access to bootleggers.

Drugs like morphine, heroin, and cocaine were widely available in Hollywood, and their use by stars sometimes progressed to addiction. Studio doctors were known to give morphine to injured stars in order to get them working again. Thus when Wallace Reid was in a train crash on his way to film *The Valley of the Giants* in 1919 and suffered a head injury, he was injected with morphine to dull his headaches so he could work. Similarly, when Barbara La Marr sprained her ankle on the set of *Souls for Sale* in 1923, she was given morphine. Both became addicted, and their deaths were directly related.

When heroin was first developed by the Bayer Company in the 1890s, it was thought to be a nonaddictive derivative of morphine and was on every drugstore shelf, marketed simply as heroin. Cough syrup often contained the drug, as it suppresses breathing and consequently makes one cough less.

By 1914 the addictive nature of morphine, heroin, and cocaine had become clear, and federal law made it illegal to purchase without a doctor's prescription, making it harder but not impossible to obtain. It wasn't until 1924 that the Heroin Act made the drug completely illegal.

Roscoe "Fatty" Arbuckle was at the pinnacle of his career in 1921, rivaling Charlie Chaplin in popularity, reportedly making a million dollars a year. On September 5, he held a party in rooms at the St. Francis Hotel in San Francisco, which was attended by Virginia Rappe, a Hollywood hopeful. She suffered peritonitis from a ruptured bladder, likely brought on by a recent abortion, and died four days later. Her friend Maude Delmont, a known blackmailer, told authorities the cause was Arbuckle's great weight when he forced himself on Rappe. This was fueled by overeager District Attorney Matthew Brady and by yellow journalism, most notably at the behest of newspaper tycoon William Randolph Hearst. Two juries failed to convict Arbuckle, and the third exonerated him after one minute of deliberation, stating, "Acquittal is not enough for Roscoe Arbuckle. We feel that a great injustice has been done him." Nevertheless, his films were banned, his career ruined, and he died a broken man eleven years later at the age of forty-six.

The history of the Navajo or Diné people reaches back approximately one thousand years in the Four Corners area of present day Arizona, Utah, New Mexico, and Colorado. Nevertheless, in what was a "scorched-earth" campaign conducted by Colonel Kit Carson in 1863, the Navajo were forced to march some three hundred miles to Fort Sumner, New Mexico, during which many died. In 1868, a reservation for the Navajo was negotiated in their original homelands. It was far smaller than their original territory, and in return, they were forced to send their children to schools set up by the US Bureau of Indian Affairs, which would assimilate them to European American customs. Children were punished for speaking their native language or following traditional ways and were often used as forced manual labor. Greenthread tea, mentioned in the novel, is a traditional tea of the Navajo, and I must say that I've become a fan.

Taxi dancers, or dime-a-dance girls as they were often called, were employed to dance with men for pay. Patrons would buy tickets for ten cents apiece, entitling them to dance with the girl of their choice for one song. The girls were on commission, usually paid five cents for every ticket they turned in at the end of the night. These dance halls were closed to women who didn't work there and were not considered terribly reputable.

Unplanned pregnancy was a fairly common problem in the film industry. Studios strongly encouraged abortions, as it was the quickest way to get an actress back on the job, however, bearing the child and later adopting it was also an option. Barbara La Marr, a silent star known as "The Girl Who Is Too Beautiful," became pregnant in 1922. Upon birth, the child was taken to Dallas, Texas, where several months later, Barbara was to attend the opening of a car show. She staged a serendipitous trip to a local orphanage, where she pretended to see her son for the first time and spontaneously adopted him on the spot.

Max Factor, born Maksymilian Faktorowicz in 1877, immigrated to the United States from Poland in 1904 and soon headed for California to sell makeup and wigs to the burgeoning film industry. Greasepaint made for the stage was far too thick to look right on screen, and he was the first to develop makeup specifically designed for use by film actors and actresses. "Flexible greasepaint" was a revolution, and he went on to create many more products for the industry. He developed personalized makeup for major movie stars such as Gloria Swanson, Mary Pickford, Jean Harlow, Claudette Colbert, Bette Davis, and Joan Crawford, riding his bike to the studios to apply it personally in the early days. His company was instrumental in the proliferation of makeup for nonactresses, which was not generally considered respectable before the 1920s.

◇ ◇ ◇

For those interested in learning more about the silent movie era, *Hollywood*, a thirteen-part documentary by Kevin Brownlow and David Gill, is an entertaining and information-packed series, with silent film footage and interviews with former stars, such as Colleen Moore, Viola Dana, and Gloria Swanson.

Acknowledgments

◇ ◇ ◇

Heartfelt gratitude to the many people who helped me learn so much about the fabulous and gritty world of early silent filmmaking. At the Los Angeles Public Library, Eileen King in the Art, Music, Recreation, and Rare Books Department found countless resources for me and unearthed more books from deep in the stacks than I could ever have found myself. Then she sent me down to microfiche to read the newspapers of the day, which were full of the Fatty Arbuckle scandal, Hollywood gossip, movie premieres, and advertisements for everything from sock garters to automobiles "at prices never before seen on this planet!" My stint in LA was hosted by my dear friend Sandy Kiley, who joined me to tour the Hollywood Heritage Museum and "research" nostalgic dining at Musso & Frank.

The Flagstaff, Arizona, leg of the journey was graciously hosted by Kristen, Keiji, Tea, and Lucas Iwai. Brianna Fay was patient and kind enough to spend hours poking around the old train depot, Weatherford Hotel, and Orpheum Theatre with me. Mike McAllister, the Burlington Northern and Santa Fe Railway property manager, offered lots of interesting facts about the depot, and Bob McGill at the Orpheum gave me the nickel tour and let me peek around backstage.

Deepest appreciation to Paul Kuppinger, who is a whiz at finding photographic documentation and creates wonderful albums for me. His generosity with his time and research skills is such a gift.

After the research comes the writing and, as always, I'm enormously grateful to early readers Megan Lucier, Cathy McCue, Kristen Iwai, Brianna Fay, Tom Fay, Randy Susan Meyers, Kathy Crowley, Liz Moore, and Nichole Bernier. Without them I'd never find my way from that tangled first draft to something presentable.

My agent, Stephanie Abou, always seems to have the right advice at the right time, goes to bat in just the right way, and has the perfect blend of frank honesty and good humor. Editor Lauren McKenna digs deep to get the best out of every last character and story line, and this novel is far better for her dedication and editorial wisdom. I'm so grateful to have these two smart, savvy, hard-working women in my corner.

Special thanks, gratitude, and love to my husband, Tom Fay, who is, as the saying goes, the cat's pajamas.

Introduction

When Irene Van Beck jumps off a moving train to escape her harrowing life in burlesque, she sets in motion a series of life-changing events for herself and her friends Millie Martin and Henry Weiss. The unlikely trio has high hopes of making it big in Hollywood, but the road to stardom is arduous. The friends have only one another to turn to as they face brutality, poverty, and near hopelessness in an unfamiliar city. In the end, all three create lives that are rich in success and modern flair, but not before they learn invaluable lessons about love, loyalty, and self-acceptance.

Topics and Questions
for Discussion

1. Irene, Millie, and Henry each have their own particular shortcomings to grapple with over the course of the story. How do they compare to those of the Scarecrow, the Tin Man, and the Cowardly Lion in *The Wizard of Oz*? Are they able to overcome these difficulties in the end, and if so, how?

2. Each of the main characters has been separated from their families in some hostile or tragic manner. Though they don't know one another well at the beginning of the novel, Millie claims Henry with the words "you are ours" by its end. How were they able to create this unconventional "family" so quickly and securely? How do you think this bond will impact baby Ivy as she grows up?

3. When Millie is raped in Chapter 13, Irene ponders how she was raised to think that it only happens to "bad girls." Neither Millie nor Irene ever considers reporting it. Did

this aspect of 1920s Hollywood life surprise you, or was it expected? Do you think Millie and Irene handled the situation as best as their status allowed? What might you have done differently?

4. Were you surprised by Eva Crown's statement in Chapter 34 that "there are a lot of women directors," given that there are relatively few today? It's true that women did enjoy more power in the industry's early days than they currently do. Do you think there could ever have been a Hollywood #MeToo movement in the 1920s?

5. In Chapter 16, when Agnes offers Millie heroin, did this humanize Agnes for you or make you dislike her even more? Does her pain explain her behavior? Were you surprised by the easy availability of drugs?

6. The road to success is harrowing, yet even in the darkest moments of the story there are glimmers of humanity, such as when Eva Crown gives Irene the book on screenwriting. What are other examples of hope and generosity you find in the novel? In the end, does the portrayal of 1920s Hollywood feel optimistic? Do you think it's easier or harder to break into filmmaking today?

7. Henry's sexual orientation isn't revealed until halfway through the novel; in fact, he tries to hide it even from himself. Was he able to hide his sexuality from you, the reader, or did you guess early on that he might be gay? How does Henry eventually come to terms with being in love with another man?

8. Each chapter in *City of Flickering Light* features a quote from a famous silent film star, director, cameraman, or screenwriter. One of these is John Barrymore's: "Happiness often sneaks through a door you didn't know you left open." How does this quote serve as a theme for the novel as a whole? Which was your favorite quote and why?

9. Which character did you identify with the most? Which character did you *like* the most? Are they the same?

10. Which stars of today remind you of characters in the novel?

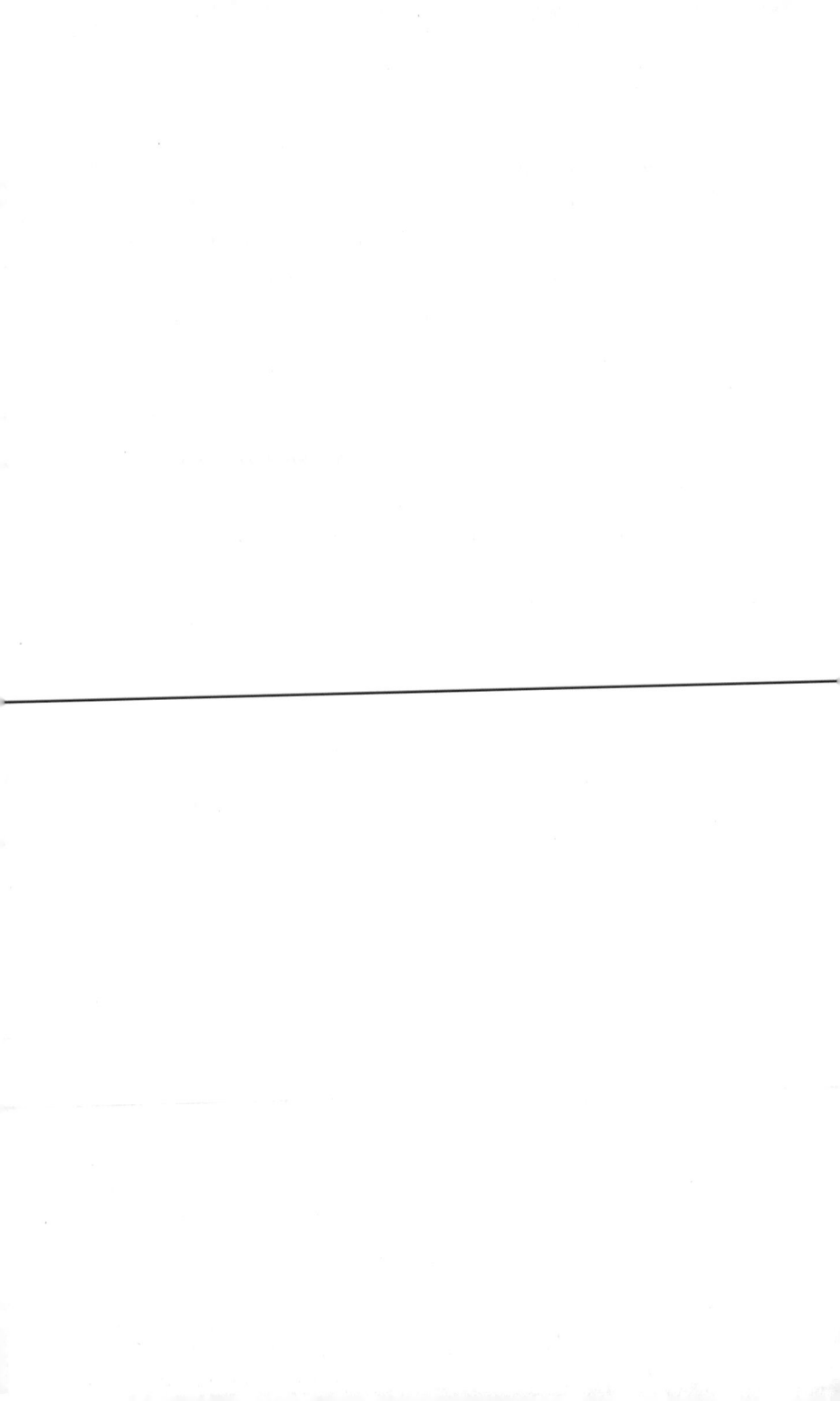

Enhance Your Book Club

1. Host a movie night with your book club and watch a silent film together. A few suggestions:

   Beyond the Rocks, starring Rudolph Valentino and Gloria Swanson

   Robin Hood, starring Douglas Fairbanks

   Stella Maris, starring Mary Pickford (written by her friend Frances Marion)

   The Kid, starring Charlie Chaplin

   Hell's Hinges, starring William S. Hart

   The Sheik, starring Rudolph Valentino (See what made women swoon!)

   Have each person make up a silent film star name for themselves. You could also watch the thirteen-part documentary *Hollywood* to learn more about this bygone era, but that will take multiple nights!

2. In Chapter 28, Dan offers Irene greenthread tea, a traditional Navajo beverage, to soothe her. The simplicity and kindness of this act, coupled with Dan's patience and quiet strength, contributes to Irene's falling in love with him. Purchase some greenthread tea for your book club (available online at various sites, including https://www.slowfoodusa.org/ark-item/greenthread-tea). Over tea, talk about a simple gesture or moment that made you feel loved.

3. Read *The Vanishing American* by Zane Grey, the popular novel that sparked the fight between Irene and Dan. Then watch the silent film version with Richard Dix. Does this help you better understand why Dan had such a strong reaction to Irene's script?

4. Talk about the novel with the author! Juliette Fay is happy to discuss the novel by Skype or other video format with groups of five or more, subject to availability. To schedule, contact her at www.juliettefay.com/for-book-groups/book-group-chat-request/.